John Strange Winter

Beautiful Jim, of the Blankshire Regiment

John Strange Winter

Beautiful Jim, of the Blankshire Regiment

ISBN/EAN: 9783337412302

Printed in Europe, USA, Canada, Australia, Japan

Cover: Foto ©Andreas Hilbeck / pixelio.de

More available books at **www.hansebooks.com**

BEAUTIFUL JIM,

Of the Blankshire Regiment.

BY

JOHN STRANGE WINTER,

AUTHOR OF

"BOOTLES' BABY," "ARMY SOCIETY," "GARRISON GOSSIP,"
"A SIEGE BABY," "MIGNON'S HUSBAND," "BOOTLES' CHILDREN,"
"MY POOR DICK," "A LITTLE FOOL,"
"BUTTONS," "MRS. BOB," ETC.

SEVENTH EDITION.

LONDON :
F. V. WHITE & CO.,
31, SOUTHAMPTON STREET, STRAND, W.C.
1891.

PRINTED BY
KELLY AND CO., GATE STREET, LINCOLN'S INN FIELDS, W.C.
AND KINGSTON-ON-THAMES.

CONTENTS.

Dedication.

—:o:—

TO

THE BEST HUSBAND IN THE WORLD
I Dedicate
BEAUTIFUL JIM.

THE BEST HUSBAND IN THE WORLD

BEAUTIFUL JIM.

CHAPTER I.

JIM AND JIM'S FRIEND.

NOBODY ever knew why he was called "Beautiful Jim," and yet nobody ever dreamt of calling him anything else. It was certainly not because Jim was a beauty and that his brother officers were anxious to impress the fact upon mankind in general. Oh, no; for Jim Beresford was a young man whose best friend could not have said that he was anything but downright ugly.

And yet it was such a pleasant phiz, clean-shaven and ill-assorted as to features, though the blue eyes had a merry twinkle in them which made you forget that they might have been larger with considerable advantage, and the white teeth disclosed every minute or two by the merrier smile quite made you forget also that the mouth was a good deal too wide for its owner to fairly sustain the name of Beautiful Jim.

Yet Beautiful Jim he was, Beautiful Jim he had been from the beginning of the army chapter, and

Beautiful Jim he was likely to remain until he came to the end of it; and, ugly as he was, the name suited him down to the very ground.

Everybody liked him, everybody; indeed in all my life I never heard of but one human being who did not give in sooner or later to the influence of Beautiful Jim's attractions, and that—but, there, I have a story to tell about him, and that person will come in in due time and season.

Of course he was Irish—Jim, that is—with all the happy-go-lucky, careless humour which is so often to be found amongst the Irish people, all their love of fun and fund of mother wit; and as a story-teller, why not another man in the regiment was in the same street with Beautiful Jim—no, not one.

"Sure," said he one day, after a five days' leave spent in town, "I have some cousins in London, real smart girls they are, too—went to see 'em on Sunday and found some other fellows there. One was Brooke, of the 101st D.Gs., the chap that had the good luck to be left at home on depôt when the 101st D.Gs. went to the Zulu business; the other— well, such a howling, haw-haw, stiff-collared beggar, that I thought he must be at least half a dozen cavalry swells rolled into one. But this chap (whom I afterwards found belonged to the Pill Brigade, and was attached to the 101st during the Zulu business), evidently thinking Brooke a hum-drum, quiet sort of chap, not up to much, don't you know, and half a duffer at that, and evidently not having the least idea that he had anything to do with the 101st, began a too-delightful account of how the 101st not only ran away on the smallest provocation, but even fired on their officers more times than once.

" Course, this chap had an eye to my two cousins, who are pretty and smart, and never cast so much as a look at either Brooke or myself. He yarned on, enlarging as he went, till some people mightn't have been very far out of it if they'd thought it was all a pack of lies together; and Brooke got more nervous and fidgetty every minute, his face getting glummer and glummer, and his looks darker and darker.

" At last he couldn't stand any more of it, but got up and seized the poker and began smashing the fire with it, while my cousins were trying to signal to the doctor chap to shut up. But no; on he went with a detailed account of how one night they had been alarmed by their own sentries, and— and then Brooke couldn't stand it any longer, but just burst out :—

" ' 'Pon my word, you're quite right. *I don't know what we could have been about to do it!* ' "

" And what then, Jim ? " one of his hearers asked.

" Why," returned Beautiful Jim, " my little cousin Nell—who's a devilish smart little girl, no mistake about it—found out very conveniently that the sun in the Park had been rather too much for her that morning, and that she felt awfully ill; would I mind opening the window and getting her a fan ?   So I opened the window a bit wider and got her a fan ; and then she began to abuse me and said I was such a dunce I always made her ill every time I came near her, and I'd got scent on my handkerchief ; said I knew the smell of scent always made her feel faint, and yet I would persist in using it ; said I should just have to go and fetch the doctor, and that their doctor lived in Harley street.

" ' Oh, no,' said I—for I never dreamt that the other fellow had been anything less than galloper to some heavy swell out there—' I'll do no such thing. I'll just trot round to the Horse Guards and get one of the army doctors that are always loafing about round there. They get plenty of pay for very little to do.'

" I saw Nell making the devil's own faces at me. ' What's the matter ? ' said I, not knowing what she was after.

" ' Beautiful Jim,' said she——

" ' Nell Marchmont,' said I, and then she tipped me a wink at the Zulu fellow, and I realised that I'd put my foot in it, as usual. 'Pon my word, I thought he was an awful swell of a cavalryman, nothing less. Well, and what's the news whilst I've been away ? "

" Nothing much," answered Owen, " but the Colonel's going home to-morrow, bless him."

" H'm—field-day first, of course."

" Oh, yes ; the usual thing. But Mrs. Barnes got another baby this morning, and the Colonel's going to stop a fortnight."

"Another—that's seventeen, ain't it? By Jove! I don't know how that long-suffering woman stands it. By-the-bye, have you seen anything of the Leslies?"

"Yes; they were at Mrs. Paget's tennis yesterday, some of them. Why?"

"Because I heard in town that the second one is going to be married, that's all."

"Ah; very likely. By-the-bye, Mrs. Seton has a tea on this afternoon—music and all that. I promised to look in. Will any of you chaps come?"

"I will," said Beautiful Jim promptly. He was always ready for feminine society, even though he had only just got back from a five days' leave spent amid the rush and hurry of the best part of the London season.

"Jim," said Owen, as they walked down towards the town together, "that cousin of yours is very pretty, isn't she?"

"Oh, very!" returned Jim, without a moment's hesitation.

"Did you go about with her a lot?"

"A goodish bit," said Jim vaguely, yet in a tone which conveyed to his comrade that he had spent the most of his leave in the company of Miss Nell Marchmont.

"And are you likely to—— "

"Oh, my dear chap, not a bit of it! Even if I were ass enough to go in for that kind of thing, Nell would just laugh in my face. Faith, no! Nell and

I have done the brother and sister dodge too long for either of us to have any ideas of that kind. But why do you want to know, old chap ?"

" I just did want to know, that's all," Owen replied lamely.

Beautiful Jim walked on for full five minutes in silence. " Have you ever seen her ?" he asked at last.

" Yes," returned the other shortly.

" H'm," muttered Jim, as if he began to see light at last ; then after another pause, and with a total change of tone, " Yes, she's a pretty little girl and a good little girl, and I'd break any fellow's neck who said a word against her ; but that's all. I never thought any further of her, and I'll stake my life that she never did of me."

And then they walked on in silence again, yet feeling different both of them ; Owen intensely relieved, for, although a handsome man and popular, he would not have cared to enter the lists against old Jim, who had been his special pal ever since they had been together in the regiment.

As for Beautiful Jim, he was greatly pleased at his discovery—pleased as Punch, as he told himself ; and yet he was so tickled by the idea of such a man as Owen being seriously anxious lest little Nell Marchmont should have been snapped up by somebody else—little Nell, whom only the other day he had caught sliding down the bannisters like the regular little tom-boy she was still at heart ; little Nell, whose lately-acquired airs and graces invariably gave him the most intense amusement—well, it was funny. But, then, as Beautiful Jim reminded himself, to a man with an ordinary insight into our poor weak human nature and blessed with a fair sense of humour, the doings and undoings of most people, and particularly those whom we know best, are funny, very funny.

And for old Owen to be " gone " on little Nell! " By Jove," laughed Jim to himself, " how I could make old Owen's hair stand on end if I liked." Aye, how many a bit of mischief he and Nell had been up to together—before she began to give herself airs and graces, of course. There was that time, for instance, when they had all been at Scarborough together, years and years before, when he and some other fellows—yes, he called them " fellows," though they were all little better than children at the time, and little Nell the youngest of the lot—had got themselves up in seedy garments one dark October night, and had gone round the streets upon the South Cliff singing, not only they, but also little Nell, huddled up in a huge shawl, with a bandage tied over one eye. How well he remembered it ! Her father and mother were dining out at a very smart house indeed, and this party of young ruffians had gone and sang outside the windows, and had reaped a goodly harvest, when Nell was supposed to be safe under the wing of the old nurse who had nursed her from a baby. Yes, but old nurse was easily bamboozled, and Nell was an adept at *that* process. " Jove, how she'll twist old Owen round her fingers by-and-bye," chuckled Jim to himself as he thought of it.

And then there was another expedition during that visit to the northern Queen of Watering-places, when Nell had aided and abetted him, together with Ted and Tom, her brothers, in getting himself up to go over to Bridlington Quay as one of the Scarborough bellringers. That was later, when they were just on the eve of returning home to town.

There were five of them altogether. Ted and Tom Marchmont, Viv Gervase, little Dickey Hunt and Beautiful Jim. And what sport they had! He well remembered it. How they went to house after house, asking in the humblest and most mealy-mouthed tones for contributions to the Scarborough bellringers. Young rogues and vagabonds that they were; the shillings and half-crowns seemed to pour upon them, until at one house a pompous old butler returned to ask a question: "The mistress would like to know *which* bellringers?"

Beautiful Jim had been spokesman at this house, and was perforce compelled to answer without hesitation.

"Mr. Balgarnie's," he said promptly, without taking time to think.

"Mr. Balgarnie's," repeated the pompous butler, and waddled in to carry the information to his mistress.

In a minute or two back he came. "Young man," he said with severity, "it ain't no go. *Mr. Balgarnie ain't got no bells.*"

After all these years, Beautiful Jim fairly chuckled as he thought of it. Not, all the same, that Nell had had much to do with that episode—nothing, in fact, beyond helping them to dress for the part. Still, how she had laughed over the story and enjoyed it!—and *now—now* she was all the world to a dear old sober-sides like Owen ; Owen, who couldn't see a joke for the life and soul of him ; Owen, who would have roundly and soundly lectured his chief or a prince of the blood-royal, if he thought their morals needed it ! Well, it *was* funny.

CHAPTER II.

AN INDISCRETION.

MRS. SETON was the wife of the senior major of the Blankshire Regiment. A pretty little woman who had been brought up in a gay London set, half society and half Bohemian. She was very much in love with her slow and stolid lord and master, and stood by him through many a dull and dreary time when her natural inclination would have prompted her to pack up her things and hie herself back to her mother's pleasant house in South Kensington.

"It is awful," she said to Beautiful Jim, one day when they were first at Blankhampton. "I never was in such a hole in my life. I went out with Tom this morning, just for the sake of walking along the streets with some one, and every one looked at me from under their eye-lashes as if they weren't sure whether it was quite proper to be seen with a man in uniform or not. And then this afternoon some people came and called, all women, of course. I asked one if the theatre here was pretty good, and she said she didn't know—in *her* position it didn't do to be seen in such places. I asked her when her day was, but she said she didn't have a day—if she was in the house she was always pleased to see her friends if they would take her as they found her; so I suppose if she happened to be in bed with an influenza cold she would receive in her bedroom. I only hope," the little woman went on, " that I may be lucky enough to call on that good lady when she is not in the house."

" Oh, go when you know she is out," suggested Jim, coolly.

" Trust me for that if I can," returned Mrs. Seton, nodding her head knowingly. " Still, I must confess, it puzzles me to think why she wanted to know me at all. She *never* goes to balls, they're like the theatres, ' they wouldn't do in *our* position '———"

" What is *our* position ? " inquired Jim with interest.

" I don't know at all; a very uncomfortable one I should think," Mrs. Seton replied.

However, the months had gone by, and the Blankshire Regiment had settled down very comfortably and had come, as other regiments had done before them, to look upon Blankhampton as an unusually desirable station.

But first and foremost in all schemes and plans for enjoyment was little Mrs. Seton, who loved the world dearly and paid herself in liberal coin of pleasure every day for sticking so faithfully to her gallant if stolid Tom, the Major. Nothing of a pleasuring kind could be organized without her, and mothers and daughters alike regarded her as an unmitigated blessing—a sort of social fairy-god-mother.

She had one of the very pleasantest houses in Blankhampton, and seemed never so happy as when it was full of people, unless indeed you took exception to such times as she made one of a crush else-where. She was a flirt of course, for she flirted with all the men, young and old alike, and with her Tom the hardest of all; but she monopolised none, and the girls knew that if any of them should get engaged to one of Mrs. Seton's men there would be no awkwardness on her part, but that the very heartiest congratulations would come from her.

"She's such a good little soul," said one Orford —after she had wished him joy of his engagement with Madge Trafford and had told him if he made Madge half as good a husband as her Tom made her she would be a happy woman — "some women are so nasty to a fellow when he wants to get married. But she's not that sort. By Jove, she told me the whole duty of husbands to-day, as if she'd been my sweetheart's mother and I hadn't at all the best of characters at the back of me.   I like the little woman, she's so genuine."   And a good many other men and women beside Marcus Orford had the same opinion of Major Seton's gay little wife, so that she was on the whole one of the most popular women in the garrison.

When the two men reached the house they found the party in full swing—Mrs. Seton herself standing in the hall with a merry crowd around her, music going on in the drawing-room, and in the rooms at the back of the house the clinking of ice-plates and of teacups.

As they presented themselves before her, Mrs. Seton began to scold them for their tardy arrival. "I was so afraid you were not coming.   What? You've only just got in from town!"

"Didn't know till twenty minutes ago that you had a party," Beautiful Jim broke in; "if I had known, Mrs. Seton, I should have come back by an earlier train; yes, I assure you I should.   How do you do, Mrs. Trafford?" bowing to little Mrs. Trafford as she passed on her way to the tea-room.   "I wanted you to talk to a girl who has been brought by Lady Margaret," said Mrs. Seton in an undertone.   "Miss Adair is not well—headache or something—and this girl has never stirred from Lady Margaret's side, and must be simply bored to death. Not "—with a gay laugh—" that I wish to cast reflections on Lady Margaret; only you know what a lot of kow-tow a dean's wife has to get through;

and really I could not introduce any men—there are
so few here to-day, somehow."

Beautiful Jim laughed. "I'll trot her round,
Mrs. Seton. Will you take me to her, or must I ask
Lady Margaret ? "

"Oh, I'll take you—— What a good boy you are,
Mr. Beresford ; one can always depend on you."

"Oh, I hope so. We all depend on you for a good
deal of our pleasure, Mrs. Seton," he said.

So Mrs. Seton struggled into the crowded drawing-room, and Beautiful Jim faithfully followed,
not a little to the disgust of more than one young
damsel who would fain have detained him beside her
But Jim was true to his trust, and followed closely
at his hostess's heels, and in time was formally
presented to Miss Earle.

"Pretty eyes," he said to himself as she returned
his bow.

"May I take you to have an ice or some tea ? " he
asked. Then he looked deprecatingly at Lady Margaret as if to say, "How can I take you both ? I've
been told off to this girl, and——"

But Lady Margaret saw and understood the look.
"Yes, take Miss Earle," she said kindly. "I have
promised to go with Major Seton for a cup of tea in
a few minutes ; but this poor thing has been sitting
by me all the time, and must be not only bored but
fainting."

Miss Earle, however, disclaimed any such feeling,
though she took Jim's arm with alacrity when he
suggested that they should go off and get something

to eat at once. "Do you know, Miss Earle," he said, " I'm so fearfully hungry I can hardly stand up at all. I haven't had anything to eat since I had breakfast at the club this morning."

"The club here ? " she asked.

" Oh, no ; the Army and Navy."

"Oh, in Town. You have come from Town to-day ? "

" Yes, I've had a few days' leave. Now, what will you have—tea, coffee, cup or ice ? Mrs. Seton's cup is excellent."

Miss Earle, however, chose an ice, and Jim put her on a comfortable sofa with a generously large coffee ice and a plate of wafers within reach, while for himself he provided a tumbler of cup and several sandwiches.

"You are staying in Blankhampton ? " he remarked when he had established himself beside her.

" Yes, at the Deanery."

" Ah, yes—very jolly. Have you been here long ? "

"Only two days."

" And this is your first introduction to Blankhampton society ? Well, it's not a bad place on the whole—can't say I should like to live in it myself altogether."

Miss Earle laughed. " No, it's so quiet after Town, isn't it ? "

" It is. And you live in Town ? "

" Yes, most of the year. My father likes it; he is very old, and it suits him better than our country place, which is too far north for him."

"I see. And what part of Town do you live in ?" he asked.

"Hans Place," she answered.

"How jolly. I have some cousins not very far from that. And you find Blankhampton a little slow—no wonder. But the 25th are going to have a picnic next week, and we are going to have a small afternoon dance, which won't be bad."

"I am sure not. And the 25th, they are the Cavalry ?"

"Yes—much greater swells than us, you know. We are very small potatoes."

"Oh, but I take great interest in your regiment," Miss Earle exclaimed ; "because my young brother has just been gazetted to it, and will join in September."

"Oh, really—you don't say so ! How charming. I shall make much of your young brother, Miss Earle."

"Yes ?" with a smile and bright upward look which made him say to himself that her eyes were out of the common pretty. "He is a nice boy, a little spoilt ; but then he is the only Earle left. We have gone on from father to son since Henry the Seventh's time, and now we have come almost to the last, for my father and he are the only Earles left."

"You forget yourself," interposed Beautiful Jim, to whom Miss Earle was a far more important person than all the fathers and sons of that house who had lived and died from Henry VII.'s time even until then.

"Ah, but I am only a woman, and the women don't

count," she said simply, and with evident belief in the assertion.

Beautiful Jim burst out laughing. " Faith," he exclaimed, "but the women count for a great deal more in some people's calculations than the men, I can assure you."

" Oh, perhaps," blushing at the implied compliment; " but not in a family tree, you know."

" No, perhaps not—and how old is your brother ? "

" Nineteen, and such a dear boy—so good-looking."

" *That* goes without saying," said Jim, looking at her.

Miss Earle suddenly became deeply interested in her ice-plate. " He is so glad to be going to the Blankshire Regiment. He has always had a fancy for it, ever since he was a child. Father wanted him to go into the cavalry, because so many of the Earles have been cavalry soldiers "—it was really wonderful how fast Miss Earle was talking—" but Stuart wouldn't ; he had set his heart on belonging to the Blankshire Regiment."

" I hope he'll like it when he gets there," Jim remarked—and surely never was a not-joined subaltern given so much importance before.

" Oh ; I think he will—of course I asked the Adairs all about the regiment, and they say all sort of pleasant things about you all. By-the-bye, Mr. Paunceforth, is the one whom you call ' Beautiful Jim ' here ? "

Beautiful Jim's blue eyes opened rather widely at this, for he gathered that she had not grasped his name at Mrs. Seton's introduction—but before he could recover himself sufficiently to disclose his identity, Miss Earle went on speaking.

"Aileen tells me he is too charming, and that the name suits him well in spite of his being so ugly."

"Well, he is an ugly-looking chap, not a doubt about *that*," said Jim, feeling the strongest inclination to laugh he had ever felt in his life, yet restrained by a sense that he must save the lady from the humiliation and shame of knowing what she had said.

"Is he here?" she persisted. "I should so like to see him."

"Well—er—I haven't seen him about," said Beautiful Jim, evasively.

"I suppose he is very popular, or he wouldn't have such a name," she went on, being determined to collect as much information for the benefit of young Stuart as possible.

"Yes, the fellows all like him pretty well, I fancy."

"And don't you?" she asked.

"Well, yes, Miss Earle. I—I—think old Jim's a —a—an uncommonly fine fellow myself—uncommonly—he and I are the best of friends. All the same, I don't know that his nick-name is any compliment either to his personal appearance or to his character. Most fancy-names in the Army are given in derision. It's only in fashionable novels that men are dubbed Venus or Adonis because they're so good-looking. Probably your young brother, if he's anything like you, will find himself called Jacko, or Snubby, or some hideous name or other, just to protest against his being better looking than the majority of the others."

" Oh, I see—oh ! there is Lady Margaret looking for me. I must go," in a regretful tone.

As she rose, he rose too. " You are staying some little time. I shall look in at the Deanery on Saturday, unless "—in a joking tone—" you send me a postcard and tell me not to come."

" Why should I do that ? " in surprise.

" Oh, well—you might, you know," laughing as they moved towards the door. " But if you don't do that, I shall come and look on at the tennis."

" And don't you play ? "

" Oh, yes, on occasion ; but sometimes one is better employed looking on."

He handed them into the carriage, which was waiting, and shut the door very carefully.

" I hope you will come in on Saturday," said Lady Margaret cordially.

" I shall be charmed," returned Jim, with a look at Miss Earle, a look which reminded her of the post-card suggestion, and made her wonder what he meant.

" Then good-bye. Good-bye ; " and then the carriage rolled away, leaving him standing bare-headed in the sunshine looking after it.

" He is such a nice fellow," said Lady Margaret, after a minute or so. " Always just the same, just as pleasant and charming one time as another. He is charming in spite of his ugliness."

" Oh ! Do you call him ugly ? " exclaimed Miss Earle, in surprise.

Lady Margaret laughed. " Well, I don't call him a beauty, certainly; but he is so nice in himself that you never notice his absence of good looks; all the same, it really is a shame of the others to give him such a name."

" What do they call him?" asked Miss Earle, wondering that while they were on the subject of nick-names, he had not told her his.

"I think I will have a shawl on—it is turning cold," said Lady Margaret. " Thanks, dear. What do they call him? Why—Beautiful Jim."

———

CHAPTER III.

A DEAR LITTLE WOMAN.

FOR a moment Nancy Earle felt as if she was going to choke. Then a mist came in front of her eyes, and carriage, coachman, footman, Lady Margaret and everything began to turn slowly round. Those few minutes seemed like hours, yet they could only have been minutes, and very few of them, for when she came to her right senses again, Lady Margaret was talking placidly on and Beautiful Jim was the subject of her conversation.

" . . . . . really a general favourite," she wound up, and Nancy filled in the blank as best she could, and made haste to reply.

"Yes, he seemed very pleasant and nice," she said, trying hard to steady her shaking voice, and succeeding very badly. " I am glad that Stuart will be in the same regiment with him ; he looks steady and reliable. I shouldn't have called him ugly, tho'," she ended, making a resolute stand in her own mind for her first impression of him.

They were not very long in reaching the Deanery, and Nancy was truly thankful for the shortness of the journey. She wanted to be alone to think over the awful thing which had happened—to think over what would be the best for her to do.

As in duty bound, she crept into Aileen's darkened room to inquire how the poor head was ; but, happily, Aileen was fast asleep, so Nancy crept softly out again, closing the door behind her and holding up a warning finger to Lady Margaret, who had come on the same errand.

" She is fast asleep," she whispered.

" Then it is all right," Lady Margaret whispered back. " When once Aileen falls asleep the headache is cured."

Then they parted—the lady of the house going to her own room ; the guest to hers. She turned the key in the lock, and sat down by the open window to think. The evening sunshine streamed down upon the great elms in the Deanery Close, the jackdaws flying about the tall towers of " The Parish " —(as they call the cathedral in Blankhampton)— called incessantly " Jâk, Jâk," the voices of some children playing on the sward below rose up to her, and a little further on there were two dogs snarling over a bone.

Generally Nancy Earle watched children and dogs and jackdaws with delight, but on that evening she took no heed of them at all. Her mind was fully taken up by trying to remember what she had said, and in trying to think what should she do?

It was but little use trying to lessen the enormity of her idiotic blunder, in trying to minimise the meaning of her words. They seemed to stand out before her in letters of fire—"Aileen tells me he is too charming, and that the name suits him well in spite of his being so ugly." Yes, that was what she had said—"*in spite of his being so ugly.*" What a fool she had been to say it! What a fool—and how ill-bred to say such a thing of one officer of a regiment to another! Why, supposing that his name really had been Paunceforth, and Beautiful Jim quite another person, still he might have been his best friend, in which case he would have resented it far worse than he had done for himself. Oh, fool, fool that she had been!

And what should she do now? What in the world should she, nay, *could* she do? For it was not only herself whom she had involved by her stupid and thoughtless blunder, but also her friend, Aileen Adair. Oh! what must she do for the best?

She did not find the question by any means an easy one to solve, and while she was trying to do so, she perhaps not unnaturally found herself thinking about "Beautiful Jim" himself. How well he had taken it, how pleasantly he had passed it off, and how delicately he had conveyed to her that if she did not like to meet him afterwards she could just send him a post-card to say he was not to come to the tennis party on the following Saturday. What a fine fellow he was in every way, and how fervently did she wish that an unlucky fate had never led her into making those unfortunate remarks. However, dinner-time came and still she had not solved the problem of getting over the difficulty of meeting him again.

"I must," she said, when she found herself back in her room for the night, " I must do something— yet what ? "

At last, however, she decided that it would be best to write to him—and—and say—well, to be accurate, she did not know exactly what. But she thought she would do it before she slept, or tried to sleep. So she got out her writing-case and began to write—which was quite easy at first, for she got as far as " Blankhampton Deanery, July 5th.— My dear Mr. Beresford," without any difficulty whatever. But after that she came to a standstill and did not know what to say next. What could she say ? She tried at least a dozen sentences, but somehow none of them either looked right or graceful—and she wanted her letter to be both.

At last, however, she completed a letter which she thought would do. It ran thus :—

"My dear Mr. Beresford,—I feel I must write you a line to say how sorry I am for the stupid mis-

take I made to-day. If it was not that, by my
thoughtlessness, I have involved Miss Adair in my
folly, I should just go home by the earliest train
to-morrow. But I can't go away and leave her to
bear the brunt of my utter foolishness; so I can only
ask you to forgive me, and to try to forget that I
ever said what I did. I am so sorry. I can't say
more.—Your very apologetic,

" NANCY EARLE."

Miss Earle read this effusion over, and thought it
would do as well as anything she would be able to
concoct; then, woman-like, she added a postscript:
and, woman-like, the postscript contained the whole
salt and savour of the letter.

" P.S.—After all, it is pretty good proof that I
didn't see much amiss with your looks.

" N. E."

On reading this production over, Miss Earle
thought it would do very well and was wonderfully
comforted by the conclusion. Then she went to bed,
and after lying awake for a little time thinking it
all over—and particularly over his looks and general
air—she fell asleep and slept, as young things do,
until the morning sunshine was streaming through
various chinks and crevices into the room.

When she had read the letter again and satisfied
herself that it would do, she went downstairs, and
cautiously opening the door which led into the
Close, slipped out of the house and went quickly

along the road to where a post-box was let into the wall only a few doors away; into this she popped her letter and fled back, feeling very guilty and scared, more as if she had been robbing the box instead of adding to its contents.

Fortunately not a soul saw her, and she was able to put her sailor hat, which she always wore in the garden, in its customary place in the hall before any of the family came down to breakfast.

Meantime a postman had come along with a bag and had cleared the box, so that it was already one stage further on its way towards its final destination.

In due time it was sorted out from among its fellows and tossed on to the heap for the infantry barracks. And before it had waited very long the post-corporal made his appearance and, after turning the heap over again, tumbled it into a bag and carried it off on another stage.

So in time it fell into the hands of its owner— "J. Beresford, Esq., Infantry Barracks, Blank-hampton "—and Beautiful Jim opened it.

He read it with surprise—surprise so intense, that several of the fellows, who had been loitering about on the look-out for the post-corporal, noticed it.

" Hello, old chap, that letter seems to be a sort of surprise to you," one laughed. " Is it an offer? What's the bid for Beautiful Jim ?"

"Oh, get out," returned Jim, folding the letter up and replacing it in its envelope.

" Yes, get out, of course; but is it an offer ? " Parsons persisted.

"An offer? *No!* It's from my mother," returned Jim, promptly, and in a disgusted tone.

He made his escape to his own quarters in peace. But then, with the door safely locked, he pulled out the letter again and read it once more.

"After all," he read, smiling, "it is pretty good proof that I didn't see much amiss with your looks." And then he folded the letter up again, and put it safely away in the most secret recess of his dispatch drawer.

"That's a dear little woman," he said, as he turned the key of the door. "I shall look in on Saturday."

———

CHAPTER IV.

THE PROUD AND VICIOUS FEW.

LIKE many other cathedrals, that of Blankhampton —familiarly called "the Parish" by the inhabitants of the town—stood in an open space.

It was open all round, so far as buildings were concerned, but only on three sides for vehicular traffic, except such as had the Deanery or the Residence for its distination. The three sides which were entirely open to the public had the ordinary appearance of a cathedral close, but the fourth one had a very different aspect. For you passed through wide and handsome gates, which were closed every evening at nine o'clock, and found yourself in a miniature park, with a broad and well-kept drive, and a footpath which was much used by foot-passengers as a short cut to the other side of the Parish.

In this little park the Deanery and Residence stood, and there on broiling summer and chill autumn days the children from the adjacent poverty-stricken slums came to play, and shared equally in the delight of green lawns, shade of huge elms, jingle of silver bells and the cawing of harsh-throated jackdaws, with their brothers and sisters of a higher class who had as much and more to make life lovely in the gardens of their own houses.

To these little atoms of humanity a greater boon could not have been given. The place was so cool, so green and lovely to the eye. There were no dangerous ponds or tempting flower-beds to get little folks into trouble, but they could play and roll in the grass from morn till night, and forget for a time the terrible slums in which they lived.

On the whole it could not have been particularly pleasant for the occupants of the Deanery and Residence to have these youngsters continually in front of their windows, the windows of their principal rooms too; and yet they were never driven away. They were left, no matter what annoyance they might have caused, to the un-disputed possession of this oasis in the desert of their unlovely lives.

Now it happened that at the Deanery and Resi-dence there were good-sized gardens running right up to the old city wall, which, in truth, formed their boundary.

Some forty years before, the houses used by the Dean and Canons had been on the other side of the Close; but the then Dean had succeeded in getting larger and finer houses built, where had been but shabby fields and market gardens, and had laid out the Close Gardens on the site of the Parish stone-yard, whose ugly sheds and untidy litter had existed right under the shadow of the grand old Cathedral.

Partly out of consideration for the great improvement the new mansions would be to that part of the city, and partly because no value was attached to the relics of a by-gone age, the Corporation of that day had executed to the Dean and Chapter a forty years' lease of the narrow strip of land on which the old walls stood, at a merely nominal rent, to be used as a terrace overlooking the gardens of their houses. Several other occupants of houses looking on the Close, whose gardens ran right up to the slope on which the walls stood, followed their example and secured the same permission, with the result that a very charming and picturesque terrace ran at the end of each of their gardens.

And forty years had come and gone. There had been an understanding that there would be no difficulty about renewing the lease of ground which could not be sold; that as the Corporation could not sell the ground on which the city wall stood, the slope should practically be sold by the easy renewal of the lease. Aye! But the old city of Blankhampton had changed considerably during forty years, and in the Corporation, which had once been respectable enough to keep in the letter a bargain which had only been made in the spirit, there was now a new faction—a faction which seemed to pride itself upon tearing down rather than building up all that seemed to make the old city attractive and somewhat unlike other places—a faction which cried out in righteous indignation that the beauty and seclusion of the Deanery Terrace should be enjoyed only by the few, and demanded vociferously that the right of way along this path should be given to the public and enjoyed by the many.

It was a faction which insisted on its Mayor going in State to any Nonconformist conventicle to which he might happen to belong, rather than following the custom which had lasted from time immemorial of State officers attending a State service in the State Church.

And yet, when the reigning Mayor happened to belong to the Roman Catholic faith and, not altogether unnaturally, ventured to think he might follow the same course, such an outcry was raised by this faction that you might have believed these saintly gentlemen fancied that the sacred sword and mace were in actual danger of being melted down, perhaps into coin which would help to swell the pockets of the Holy Father, or for conversion into censers or other vessels used in the Roman Catholic ritual such as made them shudder to think of.

To the mind of an outsider—such as this humble chronicler of Blankhampton history—a considerable amount of wonder and surprise presented itself that gentlemen with so holy a horror of the wily ways of this child of Rome, whose iniquities were so pronounced that he would not have hesitated to carry the sword and mace and all the paraphernalia of civic state and dignity into the dangerous and polluted atmosphere of a Romish Church, could yet easily bring themselves to break his bread and to drink his wine—in short, to partake eagerly of the hospitalities dispensed during that year in Blankhampton Mansion House, and paid for, not out of a civic allowance, as is the case in London (where if the amount accorded to the Lord Mayor is not sufficient to cover all expenditure, it is at least enough to satisfy the consciences of those who would not partake of the private hospitality of the chief magistrate of the city), but out of the private pocket of a perfidious Romanist.

Oh! Blankhampton—Blankhampton—the morals of thy citizens are as crooked as thy quaint and picturesque old streets, which have gone askew ever since the days of Tudor Henrys and Jacobite Stuarts. But to be better than our neighbours is the way of this world; and those who cried out loudest at the threatened pollution of the paraphernalia of civil state, were loudest of all in their utter and complete condemnation of the narrow-mindedness of John, Lord Bishop of the Diocese, whose principles would not allow him to pay the respect even of an afternoon visit to the Queen's representative in his cathedral city, for no other reason than that he was trying to win Heaven by a road different to his own!

"The faction" was exceedingly angry at the episcopal slight to their townsman; they cited his virtues, which were many; they spoke of him as a good son, a good husband, a good friend, an exemplary citizen, kind, generous, and eminently trustworthy—all this and more; and the faction cried shame upon the Lord Bishop for shutting himself up in his palace and ignoring the virtues of a man who was as good as, if not a great deal better than, himself.

But surely, you will say, these noble and generous sentiments did not come from the faction who had cried out so loudly at the prospect of their Chief doing homage to his Almighty Maker in his accustomed place! Oh, yes; but then you must remember their condemnation of the Lord Bishop came in neatly and conveniently between the first Sunday in December, when the Mayor usually attends "the Parish" in State for the first time, and the beginning of the year, when the banquets are given! Circumstances, you see, alter cases—and time affects both.

About this time, this turbulent faction of the Blankhampton Corporation were agitating to get the terrace, which ran under the city wall at the back of the Deanery and Residence, thrown open to the public.

Their remarks upon the subject in the solemn

council chamber of the beautiful old Guildhall were replete—as the advertisements say—with elegance and wit. They told how this lovely walk, shadowed by the ancient walls of their famous city—yes, all Blankhampton folk spoke of the place as famous; indeed, to do so had become quite a religious habit with them—had been for forty years past sacred to the aprons of idle and overpaid dignitaries of the bloated and arrogant State Church; but now, *now*, aprons of another sort would flourish there—the honest working-man would wend his way to and fro, at morning and at eventide, to enjoy the pleasures and innocent delights of a scene which was his birthright; for forty years past the proud and vicious few had fattened in the beauty of that secluded pathway, where *now* the virtuous and honest multitude would revel in its quiet joys.

Such was the attitude of the most vigorous faction in the Blankhampton Corporation. Theirs was a noble and generous crusade, a struggle for the rights of the poor against the unscrupulous, overbearing, grasping greed of the rich; indeed, to hear them gibing and sneering among themselves at the unreasonableness of the Dean and Chapter, you might have believed that in truth the poor of forty years before had clubbed together to lay out that terrace walk, and that the Dean and Canons had wrested it from them by main force! You might have believed that gold and ruby mines lay under the site on which the city wall stood; you might have believed anything—except that grass and gravel,

and ivy and creepers had been put there at the cost
of the dwellers in those houses and by the exercise
of their taste ; or that the use of the ground had been
granted out of consideration for improvements made
in that part, the most conspicuous of the whole city!

It was true that on the other side of the city wall
ran a similar embankment, which, as was mildly
suggested in various quarters, might at a very
trifling cost have been levelled and made into a
pleasant public path. It overlooked only a rope-
walk and a public road, and would, without doubt,
greatly have improved that part of the city by
giving an air of cultivation and care to what was
then merely a piece of waste land, used only now
and again by drovers for sheep and cattle brought
into the city for the fortnightly fair. Why not
then, it was suggested, give each set of aprons a
pathway of their own, leaving the occupants of
Deanery, Residence, and Cathedral Close in the
enjoyment of a repose which they had created
themselves ?

But this suggestion was scorned by the faction
as a stone might be flouted by one who had asked
for bread and felt that he deserved it. What!
Submit to a public walk on the *outer* side of their
own city walls, and feel that the bloated dignitaries
of the already too-arrogant State Church were pacing
up and down on the inner side of it in all their
pride, and in all their ostentatious display of proud
exclusiveness! Never! said the faction—Never!
And besides these considerations of *principle*—the

faction was great on principle—be the outer walls ever so pleasant, the honest multitude would not be able from that side to study the home life and ways and manners of the proud and vicious few.

CHAPTER V.

THE DEANERY TENNIS PARTY.

HOWEVER, as yet the old terrace was still in the possession of the vicious few; and about five o'clock on Saturday afternoon the Deanery tennis was in full swing.

The handsome Dean, looking as good as he was high—and he was not a small man—stood chatting with a couple of parsons, and Lady Margaret, fresh and buxom, sat under a tree with Mrs. Trafford, who, by-the-bye, was thinking of leaving Blankhampton, and had, indeed, been thinking of it for some time.

The two ladies were discussing the eccentricities of a certain lady of the neighbourhood, who, having suffered the pangs of an unrequited and undesired attachment to the late Dean, had, to the amusement of the whole town and the unutterable disgust of the present holder of that dignified office, transferred her blighted affections to him.

"You knew her before?" Lady Margaret was saying.

"Oh, dear, yes. Why, Lady Margaret, *every-*

body knew her—everybody. I assure you she was the very bane of Lady Emily's existence. You can have no idea how she persecuted them both ; and, indeed, if the Dean had not been the perfect angel of forbearance that he was, Mrs. Jonville would have found herself locked up in a lunatic asylum long ago. People used to wonder how he bore it, for she used to go to every service at the Parish, always sitting in a seat where she could command a good view of the dear patient Dean. And oh, dear, *what* a contrast they were ; he so tall and fair and aristocratic—she just a mad gipsy of a woman. She is a lady, of course—she was a Ponsonby, you know—and had known him as a boy. She used to tell everyone who would listen, that Lady Emily, 'the horrid jealous old cat,' had got him away from her with the help of her enormous fortune, and that he would come back to her after all. Oh, without a doubt, Mrs. Jonville was a person only to be excused because she was a little wrong in her head."

" A good deal wrong, I should think," said Lady Margaret, in her blunt out-spoken way.

Mrs. Trafford looked round, that she might find some other subject of conversation, having for the time exhausted the passages between Mrs. Jonville and the late Dean—about which she, having not been much longer in Blankhampton than Lady Margaret herself, knew less than most people.

"Who is that girl standing near your daughter ? " she asked.

"That is Miss Earle; an old friend of Aileen's," Lady Margaret replied.

"Ah, yes.   Is she not very pretty?"

"Very pretty," said Lady Margaret; "and a remarkably nice girl in every way.   By-the-bye, her young brother, Stuart, is just gazetted to the Blankshire Regiment."

From that they passed on to other topics of conversation, the Blankshire Regiment among others; and presently two of its officers came from the house towards them.   Beautiful Jim was one.

"Are you not going to play, Mr. Beresford?" Lady Margaret asked.

"Not to-day, Lady Margaret, thanks.   I will look on and make myself useful," he answered.

"Very well.   Will you have some tea? or there is some cup on that table."

"Many thanks.   I will help myself to cup presently," he said; and then some fresh arrivals came to take Lady Margaret's attention, and he was able to stroll away towards Nancy Earle's chair.

"Good afternoon, Miss Earle," he began.   "Not playing to-day?"

"I do not often play," she answered, turning a fine scarlet from chin to brow.   "There seems no time for tennis in Town—or, at least, I do not find that there is."

"Yes; and during the time when you *can* play tennis in Town, there is always such a rush of other things to do."

" Yes, just so ; and however much they bore you, you have to do them all the same," replied Miss Earle, keeping her attention well fixed on the tennis-players.

For a few minutes this highly uncomfortable and unsatisfactory state of stilted stiffness continued. Then Beautiful Jim played a bold stroke that they might get out of it and at the same time into a less prominent position.

" Don't you think, Miss Earle," he said, in a semi-reflective tone, " that we should get a much more comprehensive view of the play from the terrace ? "

Miss Earle looked round at the terrace and admitted that it wouldn't be half bad up there. So they abandoned the chairs under the big tree and betook themselves to the terrace, whence they could command a good view of the tennis-courts, and consequently of players and play.

There were some basket-work Hurlingham chairs on the terrace, and Miss Earle settled herself into one of them with a desperate kind of feeling that she would have to hear what Beautiful Jim should choose to say about the letter she had sent him, and that the sooner he began, the sooner it would be over. After all, this Beautiful Jim was a gentleman, and had before shown himself to be a man of very delicate care for the feelings of others. So there was really but little to be afraid of, certainly he would say nothing disagreeable ; and yet, as she settled herself in the Hurlingham, she could not help wishing devoutly that it was **at** that moment big enough to bury her.

But Beautiful Jim seemed in no hurry to begin discussing the mistake of the previous Tuesday. He talked a good deal, far more than she did; but he did not mention that subject, nor, in fact, did he **even** seem to be thinking about it. He told her a good deal about the regiment, and a good deal about his cousins and his five days in Town; and he contrived, too, to tell her a good deal about himself; but he never in any way approached the subject of her letter, or her unfortunate slip. At last, it would be difficult to say exactly how, Miss Earle gathered that Beautiful Jim had not the very smallest intention of mentioning the letter or her mistake at all. Somehow, the knowledge seemed to make her grow hot and cold in an instant, and she shrank into herself in something like horror that she had not sooner realised the delicacy and generosity of this man's nature.

Jim Beresford himself seemed happy enough.

"By that same token," he was saying, "I once did an all-night deck passage myself. Faith, it was the most awful night I ever passed! Nothing I ever saw in the Soudan was a patch upon it. It was when I was a lad at Woolwich, and home for long leave, that my young brother and I and another fellow went off to Scotland for a trip. We hadn't much money, for my governor hadn't come into his property then. So Neil and I had to do it pretty much on the cheap, don't you know?

Well, it did not much matter, for we were young
and strong, with awfully healthy appetites, and
roughing it a bit did not hurt us. But, of course,
we spent more money than we ought, and says I
to Neil one morning "—at once dropping into the
true Irishman's way of telling a yarn—" says I,
'We must just pack up our traps and be off, for we
have but enough to get ourselves a third-class
passage home by way of Glasgow and Belfast.'

"So home we started from Glasgow by the steamer
Lama—a fine big boat she was. But the crew on
board of her—I well remember there were about a
hundred and fifty harvestmen, all Irish—came on
board at Greenock, most of them rather drunk, and
the row they made—well, it was just something too
awful! It got very late and it got very cold. So
we went down and tried the cabins, first one and
then the other; but we couldn't stand them, couldn't
at any price; so we left the ghastly crush of fighting
men and crying sea-sick women in the full enjoyment of them, and went up on deck again, where the
cold was the worst and the air was pure enough not
to insult our lungs. Ah! well I remember it, that
it wasn't all as smooth as honey up on deck. For
there were two Irish-Americans, awful fellows, on
board. A big and a little one, both very drunk, and
both very quarrelsome. The big one was bragging
about his bowie-knife, and threatening to six-shoot
any one who presumed to interfere with him; and
after a good deal of this kind of swagger, up stepped
a strapping young Irish harvester, just drunk enough

to be valiant, and challenged him to fight at once. And a right down good drubbing he gave him—I never saw a fellow better handled in my life. 'Pon my word, 'twas so neat, that the little Irish-American stepped out of the ring and set himself to hamper the young harvester by the two-to-one process. However, another harvester stepped out of the ring to settle with him, and the fight went gaily with two couples instead of one.

"And at last the big Irish-American got a good deal the worst of it, and the young harvester took the opportunity of slipping out of the ring altogether, and took up his place just behind us, where he stood quietly peering over my shoulder, laughing at the rage of his adversary, who was too drunk to know him again."

"And did he find him?" asked Miss Earle with breathless interest.

"Not he, he was as drunk as a lord. But by-and-bye he started on again at another harvester, bowie-knife, six-shooter and all; and just as he was making for him there stepped up a little American, who just caught him a scientific crack on his head, which knocked him over as senseless as a log, and that was the end of him."

"But you don't mean to say that he was killed?" Nancy said.

"No, I don't suppose he was killed," returned Beautiful Jim; "but we heard no more of him for that night. They just dragged him downstairs and shoved him under a bench, and he was no more

trouble to anybody so far as any of us saw. And by
that same token "—Beautiful Jim went on with keen
enjoyment of the recollection—" that was one of the
beautifulest cracks I ever saw—quite scientific; for
it wasn't hard nor heavy—it was just neat, don't you
know. And then there was the little Irish-American.
He, after snarling and quarreling half the night, got
kicked out of the cabin and came up on deck, where
we, who couldn't stand the atmosphere downstairs,
were trying in vain to get a little warmth and comfort by huddling together round the funnel. And
it was cold—oh! how cold it was, with a strong hail-
storm beating on us, and the waves washing over the
bows of the boat every minute! I don't believe any
of us had ever been so miserable, forlorn, or thoroughly wretched in all our lives before. I know I
have never felt quite like that since.

"Well, this little chap came up to the group,
peering into every face as well as he could for the
lurching of the vessel and the unsteadiness of his
own standing. At last, however, he stopped opposite to me.

"' Come an' 'ave a drink,' he said.

"Well, I didn't dare refuse, for I was only a
youngster, and didn't see the force of letting him
use his bowie-knife or his six-shooter for my benefit.
So I looked up and said—' Have a drink—oh—er—
where is it to be got?'

"' Steward has it,' he answered with an uncertain
kind of wink. ' Steward says I'm drunk—won't
serve me. You go and get the whisky—(steward

can't say *you're* drunk)—an' we'll drink it together.'

" I didn't dare refuse, so I got up; but in trying
to follow me the little American happened to fall
foul of a Scotchwoman with a very large family of
children under her garments, like chickens under a
hen's wing. Of course she went for him tooth-and-
nail, and soundly belaboured him, and I took the
opportunity of just slipping round the other side of
the funnel and sitting down in the same place as I
had been before. And then, when he had gathered
himself up and apparently been all round the ship
in pursuit of me, he came back, trying to peer into
our faces so as to identify me again, and take me
along for 'the drink.' However, happily he was too
drunk or too sleepy or something to be sure of me,
and the old Scotch lady stood my friend and warned
him against getting too near to her; so, at last, he
seemed to get sleepy all at once, and he just rolled
himself under a hand-barrow or a hand-truck and
went off to sleep. I believe," said Beautiful Jim
solemnly, " that if we had known he was dying we
were all too ill and frozen and miserable ourselves to
have moved so much as a finger to help him. Not,
all the same, that he seemed in the smallest danger,
for he slept serenely on, and snored away as happily
as possible.

" However, when morning came and we found
ourselves alongside of the quay, some of the
ship's people came along and fished him out;
and if you'll believe me, Miss Earle, he was so

petrified he couldn't stand—couldn't move hand
or foot."

"But alive ?" she asked.

"Alive? Oh, yes. And they stuck him up with
his back against the funnel to get melted; and presently I heard him say to himself, in a sleepy sort of
tone:

"'An'bedad, I've got an ah-ful crick in me neck.'"

"And how did you get on after ?"

"Oh, as fine as possible—and when we got to
Dublin we found only first and second class in the
train ; but they took us second class, and said never
a word, and we got home and thought no more about
it; but, by that same token, it was an awful night,
the worst I've spent in all my life."

It would not be easy to say how deeply interested
Miss Earle was, so much so, in fact, that she forgot
all about the letter and the unfortunate slip.

"That's a very fine story," she said, with a flatter-
ing air of appreciation, as she lay at ease in the big
chair and idly watched the tennis-players on the
lawn before.

"Ah! I little thought I should ever have the
heart to make a story out of my misery," said he
with a laugh; "but oh! Miss Earle, I'm afraid
you're frightfully thirsty and hungry. I have kept
you an unconscionable time listening to all my old
yarns. Do come and have some ice, or cup, or something."

Miss Earle said at once that she should like a cup
of tea, so they sauntered down to the tea-table, and

he ministered to her needs. So their pleasant chat
came to an end. Others joined them as they ate
their strawberries, and Miss Earle was peremptorily
ordered to complete a set of tennis-players ; and in
vain did she try to get out of it.

"My dear, you must play," said the Dean's
beautiful daughter with kind insistance. "I know
you are sweet and good, and will give up for anybody ; but I have made up this set for you, and
am determined you shall not be done out of it."

"Well, let me finish my tea," Nancy entreated ;
and Beautiful Jim thought, though he hardly knew
why, that she would much rather have stayed
where she was, and, of course, have talked to
him.

However, she had to go, and Beautiful Jim, left
to himself, finished a very substantial repast, and
looked round for some one to talk to. Mrs. Trafford
was still sitting where she had been when he entered
the garden, but she was alone now, Lady Margaret
having moved away to speak to other guests. He
made his way to her at once.

"Mrs. Trafford, wouldn't you like to have a turn
round the garden ?" he asked.

"I would much rather have a cup of tea," she
replied, laughing.

Jim gave her his arm at once, and very quickly
settled her in a comfortable chair, with some claret-
cup and a plate of strawberries. Then he pulled
another chair near to it for himself, and prepared to
have a good time and enjoy it.

"What is the news, Mrs. Trafford?" he asked—
everybody went to Mrs. Trafford for the latest news
in Blankhampton.

"Well," she said, as she dipped a strawberry into
the little pile of sugar upon her plate, "the Corporation are going to take the terrace away from all these
houses.   I think that's latest of all."

"Awful shame," murmured Beautiful Jim, to
whom Blankhampton Deanery was merely a pleasant
but passing oasis in life's desert, and not a permanent
Mecca, as it was to the Parish set.

"And the Dean *says* if they do he'll lock up the
Deanery Close and make a private garden of that!
But they know well enough that he will never have
the heart to shut the children out just to spite the
Corporation."

"Well, it would be rough on the little beggars,"
said he.   "No, I shouldn't think the Dean would be
the sort to do that."

"Not he; it isn't in him, and the Corporation
people know it—and act upon it.   Still it will be a
great shame if they contrive to destroy the privacy
of all these gardens, for nothing is so unpleasant as
being overlooked in that way.   Of course you know
that Miss Antrobus is going to be married?" she
said, with a quick change of tone.

Beautiful Jim edged a step nearer.

"No; indeed I did not.   And who is the
man?"

"An old admirer; a man who has been in love
with her for years—for YEARS!" answered Mrs.

Trafford, unconsciously slipping into Mrs. Hugh Antrobus's grand and inflated style of speaking.*

" I told Mrs. Antrobus that I hoped she would be very happy, for happiness in marriage is such an important consideration. And she said :— ' Oh! de-ar, yes. Mr. Mandarin is *quite* the right husband for Polly. His de-VO-tion has been marvellous, and he has loaded her—simply *loaded* her—with valuable presents.' "

" Mandarin! What a queer name," said Beautiful Jim, who was deeply interested in the fortunes of the fair Polly.

" I believe," said Mrs. Trafford, looking down demurely as she toyed with her fork and plate, " that Mr. Mandarin's—er—father and—er—mother were —er—not *exactly* of the same race."

" Yes ? " said Jim, eagerly.

" His mother was a German Jewess, who—well, went out in some capacity to Shanghai and—and married a rich merchant of some repute in that city ; and—er—the fact is, Mr. Beresford, when you have seen him—as I have—I don't suppose you will be at all surprised at his bearing such a peculiar name : it suits him very well," Mrs. Trafford ended, putting down her cup with a very quiet and innocent air.

Beautiful Jim, by that time, was simply convulsed with laughter.

" Mrs. Trafford," he exclaimed, " you don't mean that the fair Polly is going to marry a China-man ! Good God! It's worse than marrying a nigger ! "

* See " Army Society " and " Garrison Gossip."

"The late Mrs. Mandarin," Mrs. Trafford reminded him, "was a German Jewess."

"Heavens! What a combination. And what is the result like?"

"He is certainly not much to look at," replied Mrs. Trafford rather drily. "However, he seems to be very rich, and Mrs. Antrobus is amply satisfied—amply. So I suppose it is all right."

"And the fair Polly?" Beautiful Jim asked.

"She was not gushing about it," she answered; "but she smiled, and thanked me very prettily, when I wished her joy."

Nor was Beautiful Jim the only person to whom Mrs. Trafford imparted her information that afternoon. It happened that she was particularly well up in all the details of the affair—so far as Mrs. Antrobus was able to impart them—for only that afternoon she had had occasion to go to her dressmaker's (that person, by-the-bye, lived a little way past the River House), and as she owed Mrs. Antrobus three calls, and a great deal of oily flattery and such-like attention as was dear to the little widow's patronising soul, she determined, for a two-fold, nay, a three-fold reason, to call on that stout and friendly lady. First, because her way that day led her actually past the door; secondly, because the fact that she was due at the Deanery tennis-party would enable her to cut her visit very short indeed, if she wished to do so, and found Mrs. Antrobus at home; and thirdly, because the mere fact that she must so hurry away would in itself help to keep Mrs. Antrobus's effusive friendliness within reasonable bounds. A clever, far-seeing little woman, Mrs. Trafford—a very clever woman.

But, as it happened, she felt no desire whatever to cut her visit short, and so interested was she in the news at, and the general atmosphere of the River House, that she almost forgot the Deanery party altogether. For when she inquired for Mrs. Antrobus the maid told her that she was at home, and invited her to enter, which she did. And as she followed her along the spacious hall—so much larger and handsomer than her own—she met Miss Baby, the youngest child of the house, now fast growing into a long-legged gawky girl, more like a hen as to gait than anything else, and giving no promise whatever in any way of blooming by-and-bye into the beauty of her sisters.

"How do you do, dear?" said little Mrs. Trafford graciously.

"Quite well, thank you," returned Baby.

Mrs. Trafford could not help thinking how very blank and childish the face was—for that long-legged gawky girl, that is.

"I'm going upstairs with Papa," said Baby, importantly—and by-the-bye, she had quite caught her mother's inflated voice, which contrasted oddly with her little vacant face—"he is going into the STRONG-room. He is going to get out the PLATE!"

"Ah, you will like that," murmured Mrs. Trafford, passing on, and thinking that they had evidently some entertainment on for that night, wondering, too, a little how it was that she had not been asked to take part in it—for the family at the River House were in general exceedingly anxious to secure her presence at their dinner-parties, far more so than she was to shed the rays of her patronage upon them.

But the little mystery was soon solved, for she had not found herself a chair before she perceived from Mrs. Antrobus's manner that something of unusual importance was in the air.

That, of course, was so; for, with the Antrobuses, a visit to the strong-room meant an occasion of the greatest importance. Indeed, as a strong-room, the receptacle for plate and valuables at the River House was all that could be desired. It was roomy and fire-proof, and was concealed from curious and prying eyes by being secreted at the back of an ordinary cupboard. It would have held, and with room to spare, an ample supply of plate for a much larger family than could be accommodated in the River House—so that the Antrobuses set of *entrée* dishes, with the extra forks and spoons, looked rather forlorn, reposing meekly in one corner thereof.

Of course, being of the same metal as Mrs. Herrick Brentham's tea and coffee service, they might very safely have remained in the excellent and commodious butler's pantry below; but what was the good of having a strong-room if you did not use it, and what would have been the good of locking the door at all if you did not do so with fitting solemnity and importance?

They say time levels all things. It is true. Once upon a time Hugh Antrobus had been used to be attended at the ceremony of getting out "The PLATE" by quite a train of admiring observers, Polly—To-To—Baby—a maid or two—and, on occasion, Mrs. Antrobus herself. Now, alas! only Baby was there to remind him of the value which had once been set on the family *entrée* dishes. For Polly was in the drawing-room with her mother, listening to the praises of Mr. Mandarin, of Thelston House, Liverpool, and of ——, Shanghai.

CHAPTER VI.

——AND OF SHANGHAI.

IT must be owned that the news of Polly Antrobus's engagement not only spread like wildfire throughout her native city of Blankhampton, but it also created a great sensation wherever it penetrated.

She was so pretty, so gentle and dreamy, and she had been so singularly unfortunate in her previous love affairs. Men had gone for her, aye, and had gone desperately hard too—men of high degree, with everything to recommend them.

First, she had been engaged to the Honourable Eliot Cardella; but she had given him up that she might fly at higher game in the form of his elder brother. But after all, Lord Cardella had not laid himself and his title at her feet, though he had eventually bestowed them upon a far less worthy person.

Then there had been an unfortunate affair with one, Sinclair was his name if I mistake not, who did not happen to mention, when his regiment marched into Blankhampton, that his little wife had gone abroad for the winter. Of course it was very pleasant for a man deprived of his wife for the time to be philandering after one of the prettiest girls in the town; but it was a little unfortunate that Mrs. Antrobus announced the engagement in a semi-official manner, when there was all the time that insurmountable obstacle in the background.

And then there was Lord Charterhouse—the "Mr. Winks" of the Black Horse—who had gone for Polly too—gone, aye, that was so indeed, gone over head and ears, past and beyond all sense of honour, and yet he had taken himself away from Blankhampton without a word of warning, and had married his cousin, Lady Nell Temple, after all.

Assuredly the love affairs of the delightful Polly had not so far been taken at that flood which leads to matrimonial fame and fortune, and from one cause or another the good people of Blankhampton took a sort of proprietary interest therein; they wanted to see the end of Polly.

Was this indeed to be the end of all her dreams and hopes and wishes? Was this to be the end of her great expectations?

It was hard, very hard. Three times she had deemed herself within an ace of being "My Lady" for the rest of her life; three times had gay and gallant men of noble birth laid themselves down at her feet and—apparently—worshipped her! And this was to be the end!

She had borne with dignity and a certain suspicion of contempt the airs of her younger sister To-To, who had married a well-to-do but briefless barrister of humble origin some time before, and she had made up her mind that when she should be Lady Charterhouse, To-To's husband, Mr. Herrick Brentham, should have but little intercourse with her or hers. But, alas, alas, Lord Charterhouse had failed her, and had effectually cut off for ever Mr. Herrick Brentham's chance of being on his visiting list—for the Lady Charterhouse of to-day would as soon have thought of asking her husband's troopers to dinner as of asking him.

There had been a certain awkwardness in the minds of both Lord Charterhouse and the Antrobus family as to the best course to pursue when the noble bride and groom returned from their honeymoon to take up their quarters at the Golden Swan. More than once "Mr. Winks" had hinted to his wife that he was sick and tired of the Service, and would be best pleased if he turned his back upon it. More than once he really thought he should send in his papers.

But Lady Charterhouse was the same breezy, strong-willed girl that she had been as Lady Nell

4—2

Temple, and but little heed did she give to her lord
and master's hints and deprecating efforts to get out
of going back to Blankhampton. She had always
had a strong fancy for trying what life in the Service
was like, and she had no idea of being, as she put it,
" completely done out of it because Charterhouse
chooses to have a fit of laziness."

Thus she carried the day, and they went to
Blankhampton at the expiration of his leave, and
took up their quarters at the Golden Swan.

It was very awkward for " Mr. Winks." He knew
that he had behaved shamefully badly to Polly from
first to last. He told himself—now that he was
safely married to some one else—that fond as he
was of Nell, and convenient as his marriage had been
for family reasons, Polly was the one woman in the
world who would have suited him personally down
to the ground; he told himself that he had been a
scoundrel, for he had made Polly fond of him. And
so—from some sense of shame, or some feeling of
delicacy—he never said a single word about her to
his wife; but when he found that his feeble efforts
to get out of the difficulty of meeting her by leaving
the Service had proved unavailing, he went back to
Blankhampton and let matters take their own course.

On the other hand, Mrs. Antrobus simply did not
know what to do. She never for one moment
suspected that Lord Charterhouse had scrupulously
avoided mentioning the name of Antrobus to his
wife, and she felt that it was incumbent upon her
to call upon Lady Charterhouse as soon as possible

after her arrival in Blankhampton; but unfortunately Polly, with that desperate courage which even a sheep will show on certain occasions, absolutely and without any circumlocution whatever, refused to go with her.

"But, Polly, we have been so intimate," she expostulated; "and what *will* it look like? What will people think?"

"I don't care what people think, Mother," Polly replied; "it can be nobody's business but ours whether we choose to go or not. Anyway, I am not going."

"But, Polly, dear—" Mrs. Antrobus began, when Polly interrupted.

"I will not go, Mother. Pray say no more about it."

"But it will look so odd," Mrs. Antrobus persisted. "We were so intimate."

"Well, Mother, I don't wish to prevent you and my father from calling on Lady Charterhouse if you wish; only *don't* ask me to go. I *could* not do it. It would be *most* painful to me."

"You shouldn't have refused *him*, then, my dear," remarked Mrs. Antrobus airily—for with her it was a constant habit always to make the best of things, *always* to wear a mask if she wore one at all; and in this instance, as in many another, she spoke of Lord Charterhouse to Polly just as she insinuated certain things concerning him to the world.

It is a wise and brave habit, though to be sure it

is neither lovable nor true, and Polly turned her
soft and pretty eyes upon her with such an agony
of reproach in their blue depths, that her mother's
mind went straightway back to a day, many months
before, when Mrs. Trafford had told her of Lord
Charterhouse's engagement to his cousin, when she,
believing that he was in love with Polly, and that
Polly would win him in the end, had kept the
knowledge to herself, and had left Polly in the firm
belief that his attentions to her pointed to but one
end—the end which would take her to the altar in
all the shimmer of satin and pearls, and make her
" My Lady " for ever.

Mrs. Antrobus was possessed of that very useful
and convenient kind of heart which takes a good
deal of touching, but that one reproachful look of
Polly's went straight to it and pierced it through;
for she remembered that if she had been open and
honest with her favourite daughter, she would
probably have been spared all the pain and humiliation which the affair with Lord Charterhouse had
caused her.

" I wish you would not say that I refused him,
Mother," she said, with some dignity; and then she
very softly went out of the room and walked upstairs to her bedchamber, where Mrs. Antrobus did
not just then dare to follow her.

So Mrs. Antrobus was in a measure obliged to let
the matter of calling or not calling upon Lady Charterhouse fall to the ground. She did not wish to go
in such a way as to give her any other impression

than that Polly had at some time or other refused her husband; she did not like to go without Polly, for that would have been pointed, and, moreover, the name of " Miss Mary Antrobus " had its place upon her visiting-card, immediately below her own.

So, though she thought it over and over, looked at it from this point and that, studied it in every light, and twisted and twined the circumstances of the case in every possible direction, Mrs. Antrobus finally came to the conclusion that she had better leave the call unmade, and take her cue from the way in which Lord Charterhouse should see fit to behave when they happened to meet—which, in so limited a circle as Blankhampton society, they were sooner or later sure to do.

However, before a meeting came about, the good people of Blankhampton were almost struck dumb with astonishment by the announcement of Polly Antrobus's engagement and approaching marriage to Mr. Mandarin, of Thelston House, Liverpool, and of Shanghai.

CHAPTER VII.

THE AGONY OF MR. WINKS.

AT the time of To-To Antrobus's marriage to Herrick Brentham, Blankhampton society had been pretty well kept agog by the various reports which emanated from the River House concerning the great event. Such a wonderful marriage had never before taken place within the memory of man, and the stream of grand ideas which was let loose on the world in general by each and every member of the Antrobus family, had been really so gorgeous, so grand, so out of the common, that people began to think there was something in this talk of Russian bridal tours, Continental travel, Mediterranean yachting, Town-houses, saddle-horses, riding-habits, and the like.

But all their grand expectations had resolved themselves into a trip to London to see the panto-mimes, and a joint-stock wedding present from the Brentham family of a plated tea and coffee service! So now it was no longer the custom of the Antro-buses to speak of Mrs. Herrick Brentham as a young lady who had made a great marriage. Mrs. An-trobus, on the contrary, invariably spoke of her with a tender and gentle pity. " To-To married so *very* young, poor child—and *quite* a LOVE-match ! "

The Herrick Brenthams, after spending some months under the ancestral roof of the Brentham family (where To-To had the pleasure of studying the character of her father-in-law, " a delightful old gentleman who is a little—*odd*," as her mother ex-pressed the state of mind which necessitated a per-sonal attendant of special training), had by this time set up a house of their own in London-town. There were people in Blankhampton, Mrs. Trafford among them, who fairly revelled in Mrs. Antrobus's oily descriptions of it.

" Quite a SMALL house," she explained—as if to

be small was the highest order of merit among London bricks and mortar—"but in the *best* neighbourhood, for Herrick was most particular about that; he declared that nothing should induce him to bury his beautiful little To-To in any out-of-the-way part." As a matter of fact, the house was at Notting Hill Gate; but that is a mere detail, and to anyone living as far away from Town as Blankhampton is from London, one district is not so very much unlike another, and there is not very much difference between Bayswater and Sloane Street—it is all London.

Since Polly's engagement to Mr. Mandarin, of Liverpool and Shanghai, To-To and her spouse had shrunk into very small potatoes indeed. Of a truth there never was so much money gathered into one heap before as that which constituted Mr. Mandarin's fortune—that is, if you in any way went by what Mrs. Antrobus had to say about it. And not only was Thelston House the most exquisite museum of art-treasures ever gathered together in any private house before, but Polly would have menservants and maid-servants as boots and shoes are bought for the outfit or trousseau of a royal princess —by the gross; she would have carriages and horses as other people have cups and saucers, and Thelston House was so well furnished with silver plate of every kind and shape, that Polly requested her friends in general to be kind enough to make their wedding presents personal and in the shape of jewellery.

And she was to have a house in Town, to be near To-To in the Season, which some people who knew the sisters well thought slightly unnecessary—judging by the display of affection between them, that is to say.

And then people began to ask, just as Beautiful Jim had done of Mrs. Trafford, what Mr. Mandarin was like? Mrs. Antrobus skilfully fenced the question.

"Oh, a *perfect* gentleman in every way, and de—VO—ted to Polly. *Not* tall"—as if for a man to be tall was as great a disadvantage as for a London house to be big—"but *very* ATHletic—quite an ATHLETE, in fa—ct. Out every morning by six o'clock for a swim, winter and summer; then has a few miles' run on his bicycle before breakfast. He hunts and shoots and belongs to the *Yeomanry* ——" and really then Mrs. Antrobus was obliged to stop short, and look at her hearer as if to say—"What more would you have?"

It is surprising how accession to or contact with great wealth smooths our path. For many weeks Mrs. Antrobus had been in a complete quandary about Lord Charterhouse, not knowing whether it would be best to call upon his bride or leave it alone; yet one afternoon when she was calling upon Mrs. Trafford and the Charterhouses were announced, Mrs. Antrobus was more than equal to the occasion—which was certainly just as well, for little Mr. Winks turned as white as chalk, and his knees fairly knocked together as if he had met with his death-blow.

Polly was not there. Mrs. Antrobus sat in a fat mass upon a sofa, like a queen upon a throne, and received Lord Charterhouse's deprecating greeting with the blandest and most charitable smile in the world.

"Oh! *How* do you do, Lord Charterhouse?" she began. "I am so charmed to see you. Pray introduce me to your wife."

And then she apologised for not having called upon Lady Charterhouse long before.

"The fa—ct is," she explained, to Mrs. Trafford's intense amusement, "I have been to stay with my daughter who lives in Town. Poor child, she is *very* young, and I have to go and look after her now and then."

"I hope she is well," said Mrs. Trafford politely, while "Mr. Winks" gave a murmur, which he meant for an inquiry after the Antrobus family in general.

"Oh, *quite* well, thanks. Very much delighted at her sister's engagement, of course," returned she, more blandly still.

"Oh!—is Miss Antrobus—" began Lord Charterhouse, then stopped short and sat staring at the stout lady on the sofa with all his soul in his eyes.

"Yes; Polly is going to be married immediately," replied Mrs. Antrobus complacently, as if the match was entirely of her making and she had a right to be proud of it.

"Indeed! No—I—I—had not heard of it," returned the wretched Mr. Winks with a stammer which would have betrayed him to his wife had not she just at that moment been talking to Mrs. Trafford, who, by-the-bye, contrived to keep one eye and one ear open, so that nothing passing between Mr. Winks and Mrs. Antrobus might escape her.

" Really ? That is surprising," returned Mrs. Antrobus in quite a patronising air of indulgence for his ignorance. " I thought *every* one knew it."

In truth it was not at all surprising that he had not heard of it, for he had been on the sick-list for ten days past, owing to a kick from a horse, and this was the first time he had been out. True, several officers of his own and of the Blankshire Regiment had been to see him since he had been laid by, but not one of them had quite liked to mention Polly Antrobus in Lady Charterhouse's presence, or as they already called her among themselves, " Mrs. Winks."

" No ; I had not heard. I have been laid up. I —I—got kicked by a horse the other day. And Miss Antrobus is going to be married ? I hope she will be very happy."

He looked at the stout and complacent old lady with a wistfulness which would have touched the heart of any woman less taken up with her own worldly importance. Mrs. Trafford saw it, and pitied the little lord profoundly ; but Mrs. Antrobus perceived nothing, and babbled blandly on.

" Oh, yes—yes—it is *quite* an IDEAL marriage in every way."

Little Mr. Winks fairly writhed. If he could

only have got away ; but as they had just come in
he could not in decency signal to his wife that he
wanted to be moving on. Even had they come
before Mrs. Antrobus, he did not know that sig-
nalling to Nell would have the very smallest effect.
He had tried it several times, but without success,
for Nell, with her gay, bright, breezy manner, and
her outspoken unconventional spirit, had either not
noticed his signals of distress, or had said :—

"What is it, Charterhouse? Aren't you well?"

However, happily before he had been on the rack
much longer, the door opened and Mrs. Marcus
Orford, followed by Lady Staunton, entered.

Mrs. Trafford jumped up and ran to meet them.

" My dear children ! " embracing her little
daughter and her tall niece with much warmth.
"Are you alone?" she asked, glancing towards the
door.

"Yes, dear Auntie," answered Madge Orford,
somewhat forlornly," we are alone. It is a general's
field-day again."

"I thought it was a field-day yesterday," exclaimed Mrs. Trafford in sympathetic accents.

"No, dear," returned her daughter; "that was a
commanding officer's field-day, and Monday was an
adjutant's; and to-morrow they are both on court-
martial. *Isn't* it rough luck?"

Mrs. Trafford laughed indulgently. As Lady
Staunton, she overlooked, or even admired, what she
would have reproved in Laura Trafford.

"It is too bad. Really," turning to Lord Char-

terhouse with a smile, " I had no idea that soldier-
ing was such hard work. These poor children
hardly seem to see their husbands at all."

" Awfully rough on the husbands," murmured Mr.
Winks, feeling quite grateful for the accident which
had gained him a little rest from all this work.

"I quite thought before I was married," Lady
Staunton exclaimed, " that the officers had nothing
whatever to do but make themselves smart and
come down the town and play tennis and so on with
us ; but now it's all very different ; nothing but
work, work, from Sunday morning till Saturday
night. It's all the General, of course, and I only
hope when we get away from Blankhampton, that
we may have the good luck to get into Sir Andrew's
command. He was something like a general, and
had some idea that his officers were made of flesh
and blood."

" And I'm sure," put in Mrs. Trafford, " that his
speech about turning our ' swords into ploughshares
and our spears into pruning hooks ' was quite too
lovely for anything."

" And these people have never given a dinner party
since they've been here," added Lady Staunton in
a disgusted tone. Meantime Mrs. Antrobus had
changed her seat, and to Mr. Winks's horror and
dismay had established herself on the very sofa upon
which Lady Charterhouse was sitting.

He watched the two in an agony of dread, no
less, for he knew Mrs. Antrobus and he knew Nell,
and was desperately afraid of them both. In a way

afraid of them apart—and together! well, then his fear amounted to agony—to agony.

He wondered what they were saying. If he had only pluck enough to go across and join them! But he hadn't; and, moreover, he was surrounded by Mrs. Trafford and her daughter and niece, and could hardly have moved, whatever his pluck had been. If he could only have heard what they were saying; but Mrs. Antrobus took care he did not do that, and Mrs. Trafford's sharp, metallic voice was ringing in his ears, so that he could distinguish nothing else.

But he could see; and he saw that his wife and Mrs. Antrobus were sitting very close together, with their hats or bonnets, or whatever they were, almost touching one another, and he guessed by the oily smile on Mrs. Antrobus's fat face and the satisfied nodding of her head and the outspreading of her broad fingers, that she was fully set going on the subject of Polly's engagement! And oh! what a sigh he gave when his thoughts got thus far—a sigh so big and full of regret that Madge Orford and Lady Staunton looked at one another with significantly raised eyebrows, and Mrs. Trafford said, in her most tender and sympathetic manner, " Is your knee *very* painful, Lord Charterhouse ? "

" Not the least in the world now," he returned promptly, waking out of his reflections with a start —then suddenly remembered that he had given a tremendous sigh, and made haste to retrieve his mistake. " It's really better, you know, Mrs. Trafford," he said gratefully, and beginning to nurse the injured limb very gingerly; " only I get the cramp in it every now and again, a touch of rheumatism, I shouldn't wonder; rheumatism does seem to get into sprains, doesn't it?   Anyway, it's a horrid nuisance, for being easy at times I forget to move it about as I ought to do."

Very cleverly fenced, but the explanation did not take in any one of the three women who were watching him—the three who heard the sigh; not in the very least.

Still Mrs. Antrobus and Lady Charterhouse chatted confidentially on, the young lady's attention becoming more and more interested, and the old lady's nods getting more and more pronounced. And at last, with a look at the girls, Mrs. Trafford rose and went to join them.

"——an exquisite string of pearls worth three hundred pounds," was what Mrs. Antrobus was saying.

" And what lucky woman possesses those? " asked Mrs. Trafford in her most winning tones.

" I was telling Lady Charterhouse about Mr. Mandarin's *last* present to Polly," Mrs. Antrobus replied.

" What a lucky girl! " cried Lady Charterhouse, in her loud hearty voice. "And Mrs. Antrobus tells me she is so pretty."

" Pretty is not the word," answered Mrs. Trafford, who had grown much more generous about other women's daughters than she had once been. " Pretty is not the word with which to describe Miss

Antrobus. She is lovely, quite the loveliest girl in Blankhampton."

"And the girls seem to me remarkably pretty here," put in Lady Charterhouse, who was also so situated she could afford to be lavish in her praises.

"Yes, there are pretty girls here," Mrs. Antrobus admitted with unusual modesty.

And at this point Mr. Winks's knee took a bad turn and became much worse, so that he got up suddenly and declared his "cramp" was so bad he must go home at once, in the face of which Lady Charterhouse had no choice but to say good-bye.

"What was that old woman saying to you?" he demanded somewhat roughly of her as they reached their carriage.

"That old woman!" she echoed. "Why, Charterhouse, I understood that they were quite the— well, great friends of yours."

"Oh! I knew them; but what was she saying?"

"Telling me about her pretty daughter's engagement, that was all. Is she pretty?"

Mr. Winks's heart grew sick within him at the question.

"Yes, she's pretty," he said shortly.

CHAPTER VIII.

A SWISS FAIR.

MISS EARLE was still a visitor at the Deanery, and was to remain yet another week in order that she might take part in a great bazaar, for which the ladies of every age and grade in the neighbourhood had been working for many a month past.

She had enjoyed her visit far more than she usually enjoyed visits of any kind, and in spite of the season of real hard grinding work under which every officer and man in the garrison was then groaning, she had seen a good deal of that lieutenant of the Blankshire Regiment who, in common, went by the name of Beautiful Jim. The more she saw of him the better she liked him, while Beautiful Jim was on his part, as he graphically put it, " So dead broke in the way of spoons that he could not possibly be any brokier."

This bazaar was to be an unusually smart affair. It was in aid of the funds of the City Hospital, and, as the Dean was the President of its Committee, was to be held in the grounds at the back of the Deanery and Residence. These were both large and spacious gardens, divided only by a park railing and a wicket-gate.

Then not only was there to be a bazaar, but also a Maske of Flowers and a Pastoral Play. The bazaar, in the guise of a Swiss Fair, was to be held in one garden, and the maske and pastoral was to be given in the other.

And it was really wonderful how this Deanery garden had been transformed; more than twenty châlets had sprung into existence in various parts of it, a row with open fronts being the bazaar proper, and others scattered here and there for such purposes as fortune-telling, refreshments, flowers, art-gallery, and a café-chantant, where almost all the amateur singers in Blankhampton were to hold forth as sirens, who would charm shillings and half-crowns out of the pockets of all comers for the benefit of those who were poor and sick in the community.

There was a fish-pond without any water, and an Alpine dairy where the sweetest and freshest of milk was dispensed (for a consideration) by the sweetest and prettiest of dairy-maids; and there was a very smart little shop with the sign of the red glove, next door to one in which pipes and sticks of every size and shape and price might be bought.

The whole thing was wonderfully well managed. Each châlet had its double set of ladies, one a permanent saleswoman, whose name hung over the door; the rest bright, and, as far as was possible, beauteous young damsels, who divided their labours between acting as assistant shopwomen to their head for the time being and taking part in the maske or pastoral in the adjoining garden.

The three principal châlets were those held in the names of the Dean's wife, the member's wife and sister, and the Mayoress. Other châlets there were, of course, and in goodly number, but these three stood at the head of the street and the others straggled away from it in the direction of the Residence garden and the fish-pond; among these, as you strolled along the street, you might read the names for yourself. There was Mrs. Leslie presiding over a shopful of tastefully set-out wares of fancy needlework and bric-à-brac, the needlework, so far as was the work of her five bright and popular pretty daughters, who were arrayed in the smartest of Swiss peasant costumes, being mostly of a kind suitable for masculine buyers, those things which were not distinctly masculine being of the neutral order, such as were suitable for the decoration of officers' quarters.

It was not yet the hour for the bazaar to be thrown open to the public, and the Leslie girls, after settling their own stall to their satisfaction, went off in two and three to see the effect of the others.

"Let us go and see how Lady Margaret's stall looks," suggested Sarah Leslie to her sisters as they went up the narrow street.

But before they could reach their goal they were stopped by the sister of the member for the city, who was standing outside her stall contemplating the effect thereof. This was Miss Gervase, perhaps the most energetic and charitable, and certainly not the least popular woman, for many a mile round Blankhampton. She was very tall and wonderfully fair, with crinkled golden hair, bunched up at the back of her head into a sort of cloud of glory; her eyes were blue, bright forget-me-not blue, and she had lovely hands.

"My dears," she said, in a brisk, fresh, bustling voice, the voice of a woman who could get through twice as much work as most of her kind, "my dears, *how* do you think my stall looks?"

"Oh! awfully well, Miss Gervase," Sarah Leslie replied heartily. Everything these girls did was hearty, and they were like a sea-breeze on a bright summer's morning for freshness.

"I got my picture done in time, you see. Oh! my dears, I worked like a slave to finish it; and there's my embroidered screen at the back. Like it? Yes. *I* think those water-lilies on it are pretty good; anyway they took me three months to work. And then I've got all that old china in the corner, and a case of curios, which, by-the-bye, Jack has bought already."

"Dear Miss Gervase, it puts us all in the shade completely," struck in Violet Leslie cheerily; "and so it ought, for you've worked harder than anyone, and the whole thing is your doing from beginning to end."

"I'm glad you like it," Miss Gervase said, looking at her stall once more. "I was to have had some things from India—little Mrs. Robert Cranston is sending them—of course they may come any time, but they are not here yet, so I had to fill the corner up as best I could. That pile of my books came in very useful."

"Is that the book you wrote yourself?" Norah Leslie asked.

"Yes," handing her a copy to look at.

"'The Chatelaine of Carisford,'" read the girl, "'price three and six.' Oh! I'd like a copy of that, I think," and forthwith she took out her purse and paid the money.

"We must be going on or we shall not see the other stalls before Lord Mallinbro' comes," said Sarah.

So they left Miss Gervase and walked on, two of the girls peeping into the pretty little green and gold volume, which was of the smallest dimensions.

"H'm—you heard her say that she wrote it herself, didn't you, Violet?" remarked Winnie, "and don't you remember that Mr. Chesson declared that he wrote it? 'I wrote the book,' he said, 'and she put Mabel Gervase on the title-page; a very fair division of labour.'"

"Nasty little wretch," struck in Sarah from behind them. "I don't believe he wrote a word of it. He just says so to seem important."

"Talk of the——h'm!" quoted Norah. "There he is, with his little pink cheeks and his little snub nose, doing the civil to Lady Margaret. Ah! she is soon tired of him," she added with a laugh, as the Dean's wife went into her châlet and shut the door behind her.

"How do—you do—ladies?" inquired the little clergyman who was the object of their amusement, hurrying up to them and speaking in odd, disjointed staccato accents. "We have a—grand display to-day, have we not?"

"Ah! how do you do, Mr. Chesson? We have been buying already," said Sarah Leslie. "We have gone in for a copy of your book."

"My—book? Oh! pray do not tease me about that. I was very glad to give our dear Miss

Gervase a lit—tle help with it; so you must not call it *my* book—it is not kind to her—it is not real—ly."

The Leslie girls laughed and passed on, huge contempt in every one of their honest hearts; then they came to Lady Margaret's châlet, where the Dean's lovely daughter and her friend Miss Earle were just putting the finishing touches to their display of fancy goods, with the aid of several other girls, all dressed alike as Swiss peasants.

They stayed there a good while laughing and chattering like a flock of birds, and presently Sarah Leslie noticed that Aileen's visitor kept looking towards the house.

"Are you looking out for somebody, Miss Earle?" she asked with frank curiosity.

Nancy Earle smiled.

"Yes; Lady Margaret has asked my young brother to come and stay for the bazaar; and he, you know, is just gazetted to the Blankshire Regiment, and so delighted at the chance of coming and seeing his brother officers. He is very young, you know, and it is almost impossible for me to think of him as an officer yet."

"Dear child," laughed Sarah Leslie kindly, "we are rather fond of griffs; you must hand him over to us and we will help to complete his education."

"How kind of you," cried Miss Earle impulsively. "He is really a delightful boy, though he looks what he is, awfully young. I hope he'll get on all right with the regiment."

"Well, he is sure to have rather a rough time at first," returned Sarah, "it's part of the system. I don't think though that they carry their system to quite such lengths in the line as they do in the cavalry. You must try and interest some of the others in him a little."

"Mr. Beresford said——"

"Oh! if Beautiful Jim is going to take him up he will be safe enough," broke in Sarah, whose admiration for Beautiful Jim was very great. "Oh! I say, there is Mrs. Antrobus and the fair Polly. I suppose the bridegroom elect will be in attendance to-day."

Nancy Earle craned her neck so as to look at Polly, who was to help at one of the stalls, and wore the Swiss dress, in which she looked lovely.

"I have never seen her before," she said, "though I have heard such a lot about her—Lady Margaret doesn't know them. How lovely she is, and how the costume becomes her; but "—with a flash of that quick humour which had made her so infinitely attractive to Beautiful Jim—"it's just as well her mother did not attempt to wear it; people would have taken her for one of the Alps!"

"Yes, there is plenty of her, that's true," laughed Sarah Leslie; "but her daughter is awfully pretty —quite the prettiest girl in Blankhampton. Lord Charterhouse was fearfully in love with her, in fact he was her shadow from the time the Black Horse came here until he went away and got married to his cousin without saying a word to a soul. I fancy," she said reflectively, " that he would rather have married her "—looking in the direction which Polly and her mother had taken—" only he couldn't get off his engagement to his cousin."

" Oh! here is Stuart," cried Nancy, gladly.

Sarah Leslie looked round and a gleam of recognition came into her bonny eyes.

" Tommy, you shameless boy, is that you ?" she exclaimed.

CHAPTER IX.

WORKING UP INTEREST.

Miss Earle opened her eyes to their fullest extent in her astonishment at Sarah Leslie's greeting to her young brother. " Oh, have you met Stuart ?" she said.

" Stuart ?" Miss Leslie laughed. " No, I know no Stuart, but I know the shameless boy they used to call ' Tommy ' at Brighton last autumn. Do you know, that boy," she went on in teasing tones, "that boy walked about with me for a whole week, and then when little Violet, who was just sixteen, joined us, he quietly jilted me for her."

" Oh, Miss Leslie !" cried the object of their attack, "there was a long brute of a Guardsman, and you never so much as cast a glance my way after he came. What was the good of my hanging after you while he was to the front ? So I just slipped into the background, and, thinks I, ' I'll let

them get comfortably married, and then pernaps
there'll be a chance for me.'"

There must have been some shade of truth in this
assertion, for Miss Leslie flushed up in a very guilty
way, though she made believe that his desertion had
cut her to the heart.

Nancy Earle was only too delighted to see her boy
had met friends who were pleasant and glad to see
him. She watched him proudly, as he stood in the
midst of the handsome Leslie girls, shaking hands
and exchanging boisterous greetings with every one
of them. She was quite content to be passed over
with just a careless touch of his cheek against hers,
and to wait until it should suit his lordly pleasure
to give her the last details of her father's welfare.

How proud she was of him too, the handsome,
smooth-faced lad, who was the last of the Earles, the
last to count, that is. She had been well drilled in
her family duty, and honestly thought herself far
inferior to him in every way, and of infinitely less
importance ; for he was a boy, you know, a lord of
creation, and she was—well, in her own estimation,
nothing, as far as the family tree was concerned.

He was a handsome lad, very much like his sister,
but with much more importance of manner, and
none of her sweet, shy ways. Not for a moment did
it occur to him to study any wishes save his own,
and as soon as he had spoken to Lady Margaret and
the lovely Aileen, who was not one of his divinities,
he went off with the Leslies without troubling to
give his sister another word.

Lady Margaret had noticed it all, trust her for that, and she said sharply enough to Aileen, "Young Earle does not seem to have anything to say to his sister."

"It's the way he's been brought up," answered Aileen—as if a boy, and the last of the Earles, had a prescriptive right to lord it over his sister, who is only a woman, a sort of excrescence which the family tree would, if anything, be rather better without.

However, as Nancy herself seemed thoroughly delighted by the simple knowledge that her dear boy was within reach of her, it was no use for either Lady Margaret or Aileen to worry about it. As a matter of fact, they very soon had something else to do; for just then Lord and Lady Mallinbro' arrived, accompanied by a houseful of guests, and Lord Cardella, looking as moody and miserable as only a man with a settled trouble ever can look; and the ceremony of declaring the bazaar open began.

Lord Mallinbro' made the shortest and most appropriate speech that could be wished, and immediately afterwards went with Lady Mallinbro' on a round of the châlets and other attractions of the place.

"Polly," said Mrs. Antrobus, in a loud whisper, "have you seen Lord Cardella?"

"Yes, Mother," Polly answered.

"Did he speak to you?"

"No. I've not seen him speak to anyone yet."

"I think the least he can do is to introduce us to his father and mother," said Mrs. Antrobus with dignity. "If he comes to speak to me, I shall tell him so."

"As you please, Mother," said Polly.

Polly was not a good saleswoman, and was not as yet doing good business; if the truth be told, indeed, she utterly loathed the whole business, and was in hourly, at least momentary, dread of her future husband's arrival.

"Is Monty coming?" asked Mrs. Antrobus, who had no aversion or such-like feelings to fight against, and was looking eagerly forward to waddling round the various stalls with her son-in-law-to-be, covering herself with honour and glory out of his fat purse.

"I believe so," said Polly, assuming an indifference she was far from feeling.

"Did he promise to come?" persisted her mother.

"He said he would come," returned Polly.

"I hope he will; your clasps and ornaments are lovely," her mother whispered. "I have seen nothing like them so far. Really, it was most lavish of Monty to send to Switzerland for them after *all* the costly presents he had given you."

Polly gave a glance at her great silver clasps and ornaments, such of them as were visible, that is; but she did not answer. Truth to tell she liked the clasps well enough, for in themselves they were lovely. But after Eliot Cardella and Lord Cardella his brother, whom she had seen a few moments ago looking the very picture of misery, and after Lord Charterhouse, whom each moment she expected with dread to see, it was impossible to be particularly enthusiastic about the appearance of a Moses, or, as Mrs. Antrobus euphoniously and with affectionate familiarity called him, Monty Mandarin.

But there is a proverb founded on the probability of bad shillings turning up again, and, sure enough, Mr. Mandarin put in an appearance very soon after the opening ceremony was brought to a close. He made his way quickly to the stall at which Polly was helping, reaching it in fact just as Lady Charterhouse, followed by the unhappy Mr. Winks, approached it from the other side.

"Oh, that *is* pretty," exclaimed Lady Charterhouse, stopping to look at a pretty carved whipstand which graced the stall. "How much is it?" addressing herself to Polly, with undisguised admiration for her beauty. "Thirty shillings. Oh! I'll have that. Pay up, Charterhouse, please."

Thus bidden publicly, the unfortunate Mr. Winks had no choice but to go forward and doff his hat to Polly. At the same moment Mrs. Antrobus bore down upon them from behind, and greeted Lady Charterhouse with affectionate effusiveness. "And I must introduce my daughter," she said, indicating Polly, who would willingly have died at that moment if by so doing she could have escaped the ordeal through which she had to pass.

She tried hard to turn Lady Charterhouse's attention upon a pipe-rack exactly matching the whipstand, hoping by so doing to convey to her mother that she need not introduce Mr. Mandarin to anybody. But Mrs. Antrobus was much too proud of her wealthy son-in-law-elect not to make all the display she could of him; so before Lady Charterhouse could turn to look at the pipe-rack, she had done the deed.

In spite of her confusion and misery, Polly involuntarily looked at Mr. Winks, who was looking at the odd mixture of German-Jew and John Chinaman with unconcealed horror; then he looked at Polly, and saw that ere her eyes fell before his gaze they were filled with tears.

It was a miserable moment. Lady Charterhouse declined the pipe-rack, and with a pleasant word passed on. But as soon as they got out of earshot, she turned to him eagerly. "Charterhouse," she said, "is that girl going to *marry* that monster?"

"I suppose so," returned Mr. Winks, staring straight in front of him, and saying nothing.

"Good Heavens," cried his wife. "What a poor lot the men here must be to stand it."

Poor little Mr. Winks's heart gave a great sick throb, and his wife gabbled on.

"She is lovely, perfectly lovely. Did you know her pretty well?"

"Pretty well," he answered woodenly.

"Well, I can't understand it. Did you know her before you got engaged to me?"

"Oh, yes."

"Well, I tell you frankly, I can't think how in the world you came to think of me, when you might have married her; and to let that little monster——"

"That little monster is a new acquisition," said Winks, with a ghastly effort to be facetious.

"It's a sin," declared his wife with conviction.

Of course, she had not understood ; but there were other eyes upon the stall just then, who not only saw but understood precisely what had happened. They belonged to the Leslies, whose stall was in the next châlet, and who were all hovering about outside it, the better to waylay any likely-looking purchasers who might be passing along the street.

It happened that Beautiful Jim, who had come in about the same time as Mr. Mandarin, was brought to the Leslie's châlet just then by Nancy Earle, that he might make young Stuart's acquaintance, and he too saw more than Lady Charterhouse had done.

Nor was that all he saw, for just as Miss Earle pointed out her brother to him, that gay young gentleman was very busily engaged in fixing up a heavy plait of Violet Leslie's hair, which had escaped its pins.

"H'm—plenty of cheek," said Beautiful Jim to himself.

Miss Earle waited until the plait of hair had been properly fixed in its place, and then she went forward and intimated to her brother that one of the officers of his regiment was waiting to be introduced to him.

"Ah ! How-de-do ?" said Tommy, with perfect composure and a hail-fellow-well-met style, such as would have done credit to a general, just appointed to command the district, and to whom it would have been much more suitable than it was to him, a not yet joined subaltern.

They stood a few minutes making conversation, and parted with relief on both sides, for Beautiful Jim was in that frame which found everything but Nancy Earle flat, stale, and unprofitable.

Nor did he at any time particularly affect the society of youngsters; and in this instance he set down "Tommy Earle" (as he was called in the regiment from that day) as "an impudent young devil, who wanted licking into shape and his cheek knocking out of him."

Nor had Tommy any desire to stay. There were five bright and pretty girls close at hand, with whom he was on the best of terms, and he felt that he would like Mr. Beresford better in his proper place, that is, at the mess-table or in the barrack yard.

"What do you think of him?" enquired Miss Earle eagerly.

"He is rather like you," returned Beautiful Jim, in a tone which conveyed that if Tommy had been more like his sister he would have been more to his liking.

"Oh, he is far better looking than I," she cried— at which Jim laughed outright, and she protested further—"He is more of an Earle, you know. I am more like my mother's family."

"That is lucky for you," said Beautiful Jim, gravely.

Miss Earle chose to pass this compliment over without apparently noticing it.

"Do you think he will make a good soldier, Mr. Beresford ?"

Beautiful Jim laughed. "It is impossible to say," he answered. "I could better answer your question next year this time."

"Next year this time! Oh, we don't know what may happen in a year," she said quickly. "They tell me that Stuart will have a terrible time at first among the other officers."

"I daresay he may find the first few months pretty rough," answered Jim composedly.

"But what will they do to him?" she asked anxiously.

"They'll try his temper a good bit," Jim replied.

"Oh! Mr. Beresford," she exclaimed. "I don't know how he will stand it—he has *such* a hasty temper."

"He must have had a pretty fair test of his temper already at Sandhurst," said Jim.

"Well—I believe it was an awful stumbling-block to him," Miss Earle admitted; "and if I only knew that some one was looking after him, it would be such a relief to my mind—I can't tell you what a relief. And he is such a dear boy—quite the dearest boy I ever knew."

"I am sure he is," said Beautiful Jim, telling the lie boldly and promptly. "And, of course, if it will make you feel more comfortable, Miss Earle, I will keep an eye upon him; only, if you want to make a first-rate soldier of him, you must let things take their natural course."

But Nancy Earle, caring more in her steadfast and simple mind for the personal comfort and welfare of her precious boy, " the last of the Earles," than for the advancement of his qualities as a soldier, did not heed the advice. In truth, she scarcely understood it, and certainly did not realize sufficiently how valuable it was. To her, a first-rate soldier meant one who would dash proudly on through fire and smoke, who would storm a battery single-handed, and, if need be, die with a proud smile upon his lips—that was Nancy Earle's idea of a first-rate soldier. But to Beautiful Jim, who loved his profession as his life, though he could grumble with the best at an extra field-day or at a court-martial, and hated an inspection like poison, a first-rate soldier was something very different. It meant somebody who would learn to obey before he should attempt to rule, one who would follow as well as lead, one who had learnt patience and forbearance, and the value of that greatness which consists in ruling his own spirit—it meant, in truth, a good deal less dash and a good deal more sound plain common-sense.

However, Nancy Earle did not know all this, and Beautiful Jim was either too weak or had not the heart to tell her; so she got him to promise that he would be a sort of fairy—or at least a regimental—godfather to young Stuart, and try to keep him out of harm's way.

Pleasant task

CHAPTER X.

A FIRST FLIGHT.

TAKEN on the whole the bazaar was a brilliant success, and the funds of the hospital were considerably increased by the proceeds thereof. A great deal of pleasure and fun had been got out of it, too, by many persons, and if there had been some pain attending it—why nobody knew much about it.

Polly Antrobus, for instance, in spite of her brave attire and the lavish gifts of Mr. Mandarin, which had made her out and out the best dressed Swiss peasant in all the show, had suffered a very martyrdom of pain—but, after all, nobody was any the wiser, and only one or two people suspected what Polly never spoke of to a living soul.

And Lord Charterhouse, whom Mrs. Antrobus had once eulogised as being " so frank and open," to him also that Swiss Fair and Maske of Flowers was an ordeal, a period of such exquisite anguish, that on the second day, when my lady spoke of going again, he found out in sheer self-defence, that his leg was bad again and he would rather keep quietly at home.

So Lady Charterhouse, not unwillingly, went off by herself and had an uncommonly good time, much better than if Mr. Winks—who was, she made no secret of saying, a dear old boy but as slow as a top·—had been with her. But when she came home and enlivened him with a full description of everything, and of how that beautiful fair-haired girl, with the fat fussy mother and the lovely silver ornaments, had looked more beautiful that day than she had done on the day before, Lord Charterhouse found himself wishing that he had gone too, and made up his mind that he would go on the morrow. And sure enough on the morrow he did go, and finding his way to the stall at which Polly was helping, stayed there, his game leg giving him an excuse for a chair, and the chair giving him an excuse for remaining where he would be out of the way.

I think Mr. Winks hardly knew that he was inflicting positive agony on the girl he had once called his Mayflower. Polly was very quiet, making no effort to get rid of the various wares which she had come there to sell, and neither he nor anyone else guessed that there were times when she could have covered her eyes with her hands and shrieked aloud for the very anguish in her heart. Poor Polly!

I say poor Polly advisedly; for it was hard that after Blankhampton had seen her as the possible, aye and probable, bride of such men as had worshipped at her shrine in the days gone by, she should have to appear before her world acting Hermia to this Bottom—this monster—this Caliban. Nor was this all! She was in utter ignorance that Charterhouse had engaged himself to his cousin after he had known her and had done his best to make her like him. She believed that the marriage had been some family arrangement to which he had committed himself before he had entered the army.

She believed that he would have got out of it if he
could, and that in his heart he was just as desperately in love with her as he had ever been!
Yes, it must be owned that it was a very trying time
for poor Polly.

Perhaps the two persons who enjoyed the affair
most were Mrs. Antrobus and Mr. Mandarin. To
Mr. Mandarin it was joy unspeakable to flaunt
round buying anything that took his fancy, with a
loud-voiced remark to his mother-in-law-elect that
"Polly will be sure to like this;" and to Mrs.
Antrobus it was a delight beyond the expression of
words to waddle from one stall to another, making a
great show of patronage out of Mr. Mandarin's fat
purse.

And it had the desired effect. Blankhampton
had laughed at the unutterable pretentiousness of
poor little To-To's marriage, but Blankhampton
this time could not but believe that Mr. Mandarin
was as rich as Crœsus.

And how dear that was to Mrs. Antrobus's soul
it would be hard for me adequately to convey. She
loved money, and all the pomp and display and
flattery and adulation which the possession of
money enables you to enjoy. If Mrs. Antrobus had
thought it necessary to start a new religion, she
would certainly have set up the worship of Crœsus;
and I don't suppose, if her golden image had only
been big enough, that she would have had her joss-
house empty, or even ill-filled.

But there yet was another person who enjoyed the

week thoroughly—that was young Stuart, the last of the Earles.

On the whole, the young gentleman had a famous time of it—from the five blithe and bonnie Leslie girls he was passed on to the acquaintance of almost every decent-looking girl in the town ; his happy, good-form impudence stood him in good stead, and proved as fascinating as if he had been of a marriageable age, instead of, as he was, a mere slip of a lad nineteen years old. And one evening he went up to Mess, when he greatly edified Beautiful Jim, whose guest he was, and all the other officers of his new regiment, and laid up a goodly store of suffering for himself in the days to come by his frank and easy comments on men and manners alike, by the careless and friendly ease with which he took the lead, as befitted him who had been born the last of the Earles.

But, unfortunately for him, he was also the last of the Blankshire Regiment, and his future comrades were only able to check their disgust by remembering that he was as yet a guest, when, having perhaps had a trifle more wine than his young and unseasoned head could carry (I do not mean to say that the boy was drunk, far from it), he gaily undertook to chaff Urquhart, the commanding officer of the Black Horse, who was also dining there.

" Of course, I don't remember the stage as far back as yourself, Colonel," he began, in the tone of a man of the world. " I daresay you'll remember Macready."

"I never saw Macready," said Colonel Urquhart, giving the youngster credit for being a good deal more nearly drunk than he was.

" No ?—ah—I should have thought you'd be quite up in all that period," returned Tommy, flippantly. " But you'll have heard what an irritable chap he was."

" Heard what ? " asked Urquhart.

" You'll have heard what an irritable chap he was," Tommy repeated, tipping the wink to one or two of the less disgusted of the officers of the Blankshire Regiment, who were grinning with expectation.

Whether he had some joke or catch about Macready's peculiarities of temper or not, it would be hard to say, but if he had, Urquhart nipped them in the bud after a fashion quite his own. He looked up as courteously as if Tommy had been a fieldofficer instead of an unfledged subaltern, and fixed him with a pair of keen and clear grey eyes that seemed able to look right through him and out at the other side. " Yes," he said gravely, " I believe Macready was an irritable man. Some men are born bad-tempered—they can't help it, and, in fact, it is really not their fault. They are born so," he went on mildly, so mildly that Marcus Orford, who was dining there that night, looked sharply up to hear if anything more subtle and smart than usual was coming—"they are born so, and silly people irritate them by asking foolish questions."

To the surprise of the lad, who was not just then

clear enough in his head, nor at any time clever enough to understand a shaft of quiet sarcasm, every man round the table burst into a roar of laughter.

They would have laughed to a man at any joke of Urquhart's, whether they had seen it or not; in this case, however, they did see it clearly enough, and the officers of the Blankshire Regiment would each and all have thoroughly enjoyed "punching" the lad's head for being such a young fool as to bring so severe a snub upon himself.

Finally, when still highly pleased with his performance and on the best terms with himself, he said adieu to Urquhart, that gentleman paid him a somewhat doubtful compliment.

"Good night, youngster. Your new regiment ought to be very proud of having you coming among them."

"Tha—anks," replied Tommy, accepting the words and not understanding the spirit. "I hope I shall always—"

"Be a credit to them," ended Urquhart, with perfect gravity. "My dear lad, you've only to go on as you have begun, to find yourself hobnobbing with Lord Wolseley and the Commander-in-Chief in next to no time."

In the midst of the roar of laughter, Beautiful Jim, none too gently, hustled his precious young charge out to the cab which was awaiting him at the anteroom door.

"Get in, you young ass," he muttered, "before you do any more mischief."

But the last of the Earles, on whom the keen night breeze began to tell instantly, was too much occupied in steadying himself to catch the words which his host only spoke under his breath.

"Good night, old chap," he called out airily, when he had reached the comfortable haven of the back seat—"had a devilish good time. Urquhart's a blazing good fellow; only wish I'd gone into his regiment——"

But then the speech was cut short by the cabman starting off his old horse, and, as a matter of course, pitching Tommy violently backwards. Beautiful Jim wheeled round with a disgusted exclamation, and found himself face to face with Colonel Urquhart and Marcus Orford, who had said good night and were going to walk home together.

"Good night, Beresford," said Urquhart. "I suppose I ought to feel immensely flattered, but I must say I'm very glad you are going to have the licking of that young gentleman into shape instead of any of us."

"That young cub, you mean, Colonel," broke out Beautiful Jim, who had but little patience with short-comings of that kind, and was thinking too what *she* would say.

Colonel Urquhart, however, only laughed, and with another "Good night" passed on.

CHAPTER XI.

THE BELLS.

Happily for the credit of the Earles in general, and the last of the race in particular, the household at the Deanery was habitually an early one, and if no entertainment was afloat, the family were in the habit of disappearing at half-past ten o'clock.

Therefore, when Tommy had pulled himself together, paid the cabman, and straightened his somewhat unmanageable person and his decidedly refractory arms and legs, which somehow wouldn't keep in their proper places, he gave a pull at the bell.

The door was opened, not by the staid and respectable family butler, but by a young footman, who knew that the young gentleman had been dining at the Infantry Barracks and was perhaps sympathetic, knowing what singular effects night air sometimes has upon a person who has come out of a hot and noisy room.

Anyway, he shut the door and immediately lighted the candle, with a remark that "the family have retired for the night, sir, all but the Dean, who I expect every minute."

Now, this was enough to send Tommy off to his room as fast as his unsteady legs could climb the stairs; for, although he had felt perfectly equal to chaffing one of the keenest witted men in the

Service in the person of Colonel Urquhart, he did *not* feel equal, after a twenty minutes' ride in a jolting springless cab over the villainously quaint cobble-stones which pave the streets of Blankhampton (making him feel as if he had eaten ten times too much dinner, and as if, when he got settled in the Blankshire Regiment, he should have something not perhaps altogether to his liking to say to the President of the Mess-committee about the quality of the wines) to encountering the Very Reverend the Dean of Blankhampton; in fact, he had more than a suspicion that that gentleman would tell him in blunt outspoken terms that he was drunk.

Not that he was drunk, mind you! He pulled up short on the first landing, and glared at himself in a big square of looking-glass which was set against the wall, as if his other self in the glass had charged him with being drunk, and he meant to knock him down for the insult! So there for a minute he and his reflection stood, with one white face staring at another, with hair rumpled on end like a sulphur-crested cockatoo, and with candle-stick held with elegant negligence on one side, so that the hot wax ran down in a stream upon the handsome Axminster carpet beneath.

"D— bad wine that," he muttered, "I believe it's got into my head, or upset my digestion, or something;" and then he heard a quick, firm foot-step on the flag of the portico, followed by the rattle of the key in the door.

Oh no, he was not at all drunk; he blew out his candle and crept off to his room, only lurching once or twice against the wall on the way—that of course was because he could not see. Anyway, he gained his room in safety, and sat down upon the first chair he could find to recover his breath. It happened to be an easy chair, and his breath took a long time to recover; and, somehow, he dropped off to sleep, and slept like a top until the daylight was streaming into the room, and the bells high up in the great tower of The Parish were ringing for a saints' day celebration.

Tommy rubbed his eyes as the bright sunlight met them, and wondered what had happened.

"By Jove, I must have been fearfully tight last night," he exclaimed; and then he wondered if he had come in quietly, or whether he had been fool enough to make a noise and disturb the very reverend household.

The bells were pealing away right joyously in the tall tower just across the Close Gardens; but they gave Tommy no accurate idea of the time o' day, he not being well versed in the different peals, for in Blankhampton Cathedral the bells rang a different peal for every service—a new idea of the Dean's, which he had carried out to the intense disgust and no small annoyance of a great number of the townspeople, who grumbled and growled right heartily when the sound of the bells came floating into office or study, counting-house or sick-room, and they likened the dear Dean—whom they loved—to a child with a new-fangled toy, which he would, if the mercy of Heaven permitted, sooner or later weary of.

I always thought the good people of Blankhampton were a little hard up for something to find fault with. The Parish peal is an exceedingly beautiful one, and the tower in which the bells hang is so tall, and they so high up in it, that their silver throats never sounded to me in the smallest degree like a disturbing element—no, not even when they were ding-donging their hardest. But that might have been because it was my lot to live—while I called Blankhampton my home—under the shadow of another sacred edifice—not a cathedral, but a new parish church. It had one bell, and oh! ye gods, what a bell it was! Shrill, cracked, ear-piercing, maddening! They rang it at *all* times, in season and out. For services as a matter of course; for weddings, funerals, christenings and the like; but they did not end there! No, it rang for a quarter of an hour every Monday morning for the purpose of summoning the clothing club together—it rang for Bible-classes and Sunday-school teachers' meetings! Somewhere Charles Dickens speaks about the screw of a steamer, which he calls " the Voice." He ought to have lived under the sound of that bell! He would probably have called it " the Devil."

But after all, if one can generally better the best, we may be quite sure that sooner or later we shall be able to cap the worst. And now I live at Putney; just within sound of the bells of the twin churches which stand on either bank of the river by the bridge; and day by day, week in week out, from year's end to year's end, do one or other of those two peals of wretched, cracked, unmusical old bells keep going! If All Saints is not echoing out over the sound-carrying water, St. Mary is doing her best to make morning, noon or night hideous. I do not go to either church myself, but if the outward and visible sign of the bells is any indication of the inward grace to be found in the number of services held there, why both parishes must be uncommonly well worked! For they are at it, one or other of them, almost all day long. They must have services innumerable, and I believe they marry and bury more folk with the aid of those two churches than are married and buried by the help of any other half dozen churches in England.

Not that I mind that so much. What I do mind are the bell-ringers. I don't know, and it would be of little good to trouble myself to enquire, how many societies of bell-ringers are attached to each church; but I do know this, that many and many a week I have known one or other set of bells a-going for three hours every night, to be followed on the day of rest—save the mark, a day of rest at Putney—by the almost ceaseless clamour of both peals from seven o'clock in the morning until the same hour at night.

But then—it's good to be merry and wise! And some day I may find myself even worse off in the matter of bells, and may even look back to this period of my life as a perfect peace! Who knows? I might even come to be Lord Mayor myself some day, and then—why how charming it will be to realize that the bells of St. Mary's or All Saints, or both, will be pealing away as hard and fast as ever, their cracked and brazen throats will allow, waking the insignificant nobodies in Putney and Fulham out of their blessed morning sleep to apprise them of the fact! Aye, it will be a fine and glorious day for me, that same, and when it comes I shall get out of my bed in the small hours, and make a pilgrimage in the darkness to the very centre of Putney Bridge, where I shall doff my hat first to St. Mary's and then to All Saints, and cry "I forgive you!"

I do not seriously believe that the good people of Blankhampton resented the dear Dean's latest whim as bitterly as my neighbours resent our bells! But they did grumble pretty much among themselves, just as we do. And on that particular morning they were pealing out through the soft sunlit air in a way which somehow or other served excellently well to remind Tommy Earle of his recent sins and shortcomings.

He looked at his watch, but in staying the previous night to recover his own breath he had forgotten that essential process without which the best watch in the world will not keep going, and there it was in his pocket, as silent as the quiet dead whose mainspring has run down for ever.

He went to the window and pulled up the blind; but alas! the Close Gardens were always deserted, or nearly so, until towards mid-day, and the sight of the Dean disappearing with vigorous steps through the little North-door, did not help to give any better idea of the flight of the enemy.

Nor did the state of the room help him at all. His bath was set as usual in one corner, with a huge can of water standing in the midst of it. The clothes which he had worn the previous day were lying on a chair neatly folded up; and on the floor near was a pair of smart and newly-varnished boots.

It was no use to stand staring at any of these; he could only toss up his bed so that it might look as if it had been slept in, fling off his evening clothes, and have his tub—then dress himself as if nothing out of the common had taken place.

Then, in chippiness and doubt, Tommy went downstairs.

CHAPTER XII.

THE DEAN'S TROUBLES.

TOMMY went down feeling, as I said, far from well, and in great apprehension lest he might have brought home a little more of the mess-room element than his host would approve of.

Of course, it was natural that he should blame the mess-room for the weakness of his own head as a carrier of liquor: but as a matter of fact, in all that large company Tommy had been the only one who had in any way approached the border-land of that half-blissful, half-miserable state, which he had described that very morning as " fearfully tight : "

indeed, he had not had sufficient wine to have any excuse for it, for he had sat next to Beautiful Jim, who had kept a sharp eye upon him for his sister's sake.

The big clock in the hall was striking eight as he descended the stairs, and Tommy felt as if he had been fairly done into rising at such an unearthly hour. However, it was no use going back again to his bedroom, and moreover, the young footman was just coming out of the dining-room, and Tommy wanted to ask him a question.

" Oh !—er—what time was it when I came in last night—very late, eh ? "

" Oh no, sir, not very late. The Dean came in after you, sir. a good bit," the lad replied.

" Oh !—er—I had gone upstairs when he came in ? "

" Can't say, sir, I'm sure. We don't sit up for the Dean, sir, he lets himself in."

" H'm," said Tommy, vaguely.

He went into the dining-room and walked to the window, where he stood looking out, his eyes seeing none of the beauty of green trees and emerald turf, none of the glory of the golden sunshine ; hearing none of the beauty of the music from the little silver-throated singing birds uttering their morning hymn. No, his mind was harassed by that vexing question, had he or had he not come in the previous night without making a noise.

He beat his foot restlessly upon the carpet, but that did not help him to answer the question. He caught up a newspaper which was lying upon the window-seat, but flung it down again when he found it was one of the previous day, and relieved his feelings a little by swearing at Blankhampton because the London papers did not reach it until ten o'clock.   He added a little special oath, too, because the post was not yet in ; and then, when James, the young footman, did appear with the letters, which he laid out beside the plates of those to whom they were addressed, Tommy did another swear because there were none for him.

"I say, James," he burst out at last, unable to bear the suspense any longer, "was I frightfully tight last night ? "

"A little on, I should say, sir," said James, indulgently, as he laid the last letter in its place.

"I didn't make a row at all ? "

"Not as I heard, sir," said James, flicking an imaginary crumb off the cloth.

"Did the Dean see me, do you think ? "

"Not unless you sat down to rest on the way up, sir," returned James, with a delightful air of solemnity.

"Oh ! that's all right.   Thanks, James ; here's a tip for sitting up for me," said Tommy, slipping half-a-sovereign into the servant's hand.

He was glad when James had thanked him and departed.   He wanted to be alone, for a hideous recollection had come to his mind, a remembrance brought there by James's words—a remembrance of how he had stood, with his candlestick on one side and the fat from the candle spluttering down on to the carpet, staring at his own image in the glass on the landing.

" I don't think I was drunk," said Tommy, wisely. " It was the night air, after that hot room. And I have it on my mind," he ended, " that the wine was beastly ! "

Then, to his relief, he saw Lady Margaret come out of the little door in the north transept, followed by his sister and the fair Aileen, who took hold of her arm; then the Dean came out with the Canon in Residence, and they all stood for a minute or two talking together. And as they stood there an extraordinary-looking person came quickly along the path and addressed herself to the Dean.

Tommy thought he had never seen such a queer-looking woman before. She was very tall and large-made—her head-gear was at least a foot high, and made up of flowers and feathers and coarse black frowsy hair which all seemed to bob over her eyes as she shouted at the Dean, who turned his back five or six times in a vain attempt to be rid of her.

Her costume and general appearance was as odd and as unattractive as her head—her gown was of sky-blue silk, and over it she wore a short and wide velvet jacket, slit up the back to the depth of several inches, in the style that was worn about the year of grace 1869, and not only was it antiquated in shape, but it was hung about with many tabs and scraps of jet and lace; and, above all, she wore a huge white muslin tie, with elaborate lace ends,

7—2

tied in a broad bow. An odd figure, and with actions odder than her looks.

After turning his back five or six times, the Dean and his party passed on their way, and the Canon went his. But not thus easily did they get rid of the strange person, who had evidently a grievance and meant to air it. She followed them along the road, shouting at the top of her voice something which floated on the morning air until it reached Tommy where he stood, something about " my boy —wouldn't stand it—the utter injustice of it—my boy has rights and he means to have them, too—and I shall take every means to expose the whole shameful scandalous proceedings ! "

Tommy forgot all his doubts and fears, even his general feeling of chippiness, and fairly danced and chuckled with delight as he beheld the handsome Dean scuttling along like a ship before a storm, trying to escape from that terrible woman's terrible tongue.

" Fine old boy." He laughed as he watched Lady Margaret, who was scarcely so nimble on her feet as the Dean, hurrying along in her husband's wake —the girls, by-the-bye, had taken to their heels already. " Oh ! by Jove, I believe she'll collar him yet," he exclaimed.

The young footman came in just in time to hear what he said, and advanced to the window to see what was going on.

He took in the whole situation at a glance. " My ! " he exclaimed, " if she ain't at it again ! "

and rushed out that he might get the door open for his master's easier entry.

The first to gain the house were the two girls, who dashed in excited and laughing. Then the Dean appeared with a sigh of relief, followed by Lady Margaret, who was so breathless that she subsided on to a chair, and did not, that is could not, speak for full five minutes.

Tommy, with his hands in his pockets and his most jaunty air of impudence, turned from the window to greet the party.

"Why, Mr. Dean," he remarked—as if he had not seen the encounter in the Close Gardens and did not indeed at that moment hear the angry tones of the irate lady of odd appearance, arguing with the luckless James, who had not been able to get the door closed after the entrance of her ladyship, and who could not indeed close it now because a substantial foot in a very doubtful-looking boot was firmly wedged between it and the door-frame— "why, Mr. Dean, you seem very flurried. Is anything the matter?"

The Dean groaned. "That woman will be the death of me," he said, abjectly.

Aileen and Nancy crept out to see the battle-royal then waging between the lady and James.

"Who is it?" Tommy enquired, following them.

"A Mrs. Jonville. She's awfully mad," Aileen answered. "She was in love with the last Dean, I believe she worried him for years. Poor Father comes in for her attentions now."

“ Queer sort of attentions,” murmured Tommy. “ I say, James can’t hold that door long.”

James’s strength, never very great, was unmistakeably giving way before the fury of the besieging party, and Tommy went to his aid.

“ Be good enough to take your foot out of the door, ma’am,” said James, with painfully studied civility.

“ I want to see the Dean,” panted the lady, in gasps, for it is hard work trying to push a door open when there are two young men on the other side who wish to prevent you.

“ The Dean won’t see you, ma’am,” said James, leaving the work of holding the door to Tommy, and eyeing the lady through the crack; “ and I shall ’ave to send out at the back way for a pl’eeceman if you don’t take your foot out. We shouldn’t like to treat a lady——”

“ Is this treating me like a lady ? ” Mrs. Jonville retorted.

“ Ladies don’t put their foot in a door when they are told the master’s not at ’ome to them,” James explained.

“ Just hold this door, James,” said Tommy, “ I’ll get rid of her; ” and forthwith, James having got his shoulder once more against the door, he knelt down and took a box of matches from his pocket.

The girls, enchanted with the whole episode, had pressed forward to see what he was going to do. “ You’re surely not going to set fire to her frock, Stuart ? ” exclaimed Nancy, in horrified tones.

"Is it likely?" in profound contempt. "I'm
going to make her take her foot out of the way.
that's all. Now, James, let the door slip an inch."

James did as he was bidden, and Mrs. Jonville
uttered a gurgling yell of satisfaction, fancying the
door was giving way. Thus the foot in the unlovely
boot thrust itself further in than before, and presented a fine large surface for Tommy's plan of
action to be carried into effect.

It was an old barrack-room joke, but it answered
its purpose well; for Tommy just lighted a match
and laid it very gently on the instep of the foot.
For a moment there was no effect. Mrs. Jonville
was evidently gathering her energies together for
another effort. Before she could do it, however,
the match began to take effect on the foot, and
with an agonised shriek it was withdrawn and,
the next moment, the door was shut and securely
barred.

"What was the matter with her, Mr. Dean?"
Tommy enquired, when he went back into the
dining-room.

"Oh! she is not right in her head, I believe,"
said the Dean; "but she is not quite mad enough
to be put away, or, at least, nobody likes to do it.
The present grievance is that her boy did not get
a scholarship which he tried for at Henry the
Sixth's School. However, we cannot go on having
such scenes as these. Something must be done to
stop it."

And probably something was done, for that was

Mrs. Jonville's very last affair with a Dean of Blankhampton.

CHAPTER XIII.

TOMMY EATS HUMBLE-PIE.

THUS Tommy got uncommonly well over the episode of the dinner at the mess of his new regiment. But he thought he ought to go up and call, so that if he had in the faintest degree upset his commanding officer that was to be, he would be able to set it straight, and not start, as it were, with a black mark against his name.

So he went up to the Infantry Barracks and asked for Mr. Beresford, who was, he found, in his own room, whither he went in search of him.

Beautiful Jim was lying in a big chair with a novel and a pipe, enjoying the first half-hour of rest he had had that day. He looked up and laughed as Tommy entered.

" Hollo, youngster, is that you ? How are you ? " he remarked, speaking in a more friendly and civil tone than his feelings would have indicated had they been on the surface.

Tommy sat himself down on the edge of the cot and informed Beautiful Jim, with a man-about-town air, that he felt " a bit chippy."

" And I don't wonder at it," returned the other curtly. " You made a regular splash here last night."

It might have been the accent of rebuke in Beresford's tone, I know not, but certain it is that Tommy turned brazen all at once.

"That's a good thing," he remarked airily. "I never like putting myself forward, but anything's better than mediocrity," and with that he got up and shook himself out as it were, swaggering to the glass above the fire-place, and standing there just in front of Beautiful Jim's disgusted nose, preening himself as you may see a peacock preening his feathers in the sun.

It is safe to say that at that moment he fairly stank in Beautiful Jim's nostrils!

"It's all very fine, youngster," he said, in a tone which he tried hard to make fairly civil; "but the sort of splash you made last night won't do you any good in the regiment—not any good, but a great deal of harm. Why, d——— it, mediocrity will stand you in good stead long after that kind of splash has sent you to the devil."

Tommy turned round with an innocent face.

"What did I do?" he asked. "I didn't stand on the table, did I?"

"Worse than that," returned Jim.

"I didn't call anyone a d——— cad, did I?"

"No; but you might have got over that in time if you had owned that your head wouldn't stand liquor."

"Then what did I do?" Tommy was beginning to get alarmed, and showed it. "I didn't shy the knives about, or anything of that sort, surely?"

Beautiful Jim burst out laughing. " Look here, young 'un," he remarked. " You've got a very fair notion of your own qualities, your position, your appearance, your—your everything. You're the last of the Earles——"

" D—— the Earles," put in Tommy, who had no sort of respect for his position as the last of a proud race, though he liked others to have—none better.

" With all my heart," said Jim. " It will do you no good in the Blankshire Regiment ever to re-member it again. But you're a youngster, a new idea, a scrap, a wart, as yet—and for you to give your opinion among field-officers on subjects of which you are totally ignorant and about which your opinion has not been even asked, is not the way to become a popular officer when you join. And then to back it all by trying to chaff Urquhart, of the Black Horse, who's got the levellest head and the clearest judgment and the keenest wit and the most stinging tongue of any man in the British Army, take it from one end to the other ; Urquhart, who's the coolest, pluckiest beggar that ever lived— for a scrap like you to try and best him with your tongue—why it's just ludicrous, and it won't do, Tommy, and the sooner you make up your mind to that the better."

It must be owned that Tommy's brave and brazen front had given place to utter dismay and consterna-tion long before Beautiful Jim had come to an end of his remarks. His smooth young jaw fell to the length of a fiddle, and he looked in truth the picture of abject misery.

" What an ass I must have been ! " he ejaculated.

" Well, you were," returned Jim with delightful candour.

" And what a consummate fool the fellows must have thought me," he went on, never being above blaming himself when he found himself fairly cornered.

" They did," said Jim, promptly.

" And as for Colonel Urquhart——" he continued in a tone of despair so intense that Beautiful Jim relented somewhat and took pity on him.

" Oh, well, as to that," he said in a tone of judicial deliberation, " as to that, I don't know that it matters very much what Urquhart thinks. Of course he's a devilish clever chap, and one it's best to keep on the right side of; but at the same time Urquhart ain't your chief, and if he felt inclined to forget the fact we should very soon make him remember it. It ain't so much what Urquhart 'll think of your cheeking him, as what our fellows 'll think of your cheeking Urquhart. D' you see ? "

Tommy did see, and was comforted on that point; but he was still terribly distressed in mind at what he had done.

" I don't know what I can do," he repeated for about the twentieth time. " Oh, I think I'll send in my papers at once. I won't join at all."

" You young duffer ! " laughed Beautiful Jim, " what rot you talk ! Why, man alive, if you're going to sneak away from every mistake you make by making a clear bolt of it, how do you ever intend to make a decent soldier, or anything else ? ”

“ But what must I do ? ”

“ Live it down, of course. You’ll get chaffed about it for ever, but you must make up your mind to bear it ; and, after all, there was not another man at the table, not even including ‘ old Jane ’ himself, who would have dared to do it ! ”

“ *Jane?* ” repeated Tommy, taking rather a brighter tone ; “ and who is ‘ Jane ? ’ ”

“ Oh, we call the Colonel ‘ Jane,’ ” replied Jim, with a laugh.

“ I see. Well, do you think I’d better just go away and come to join as if nothing had happened ? ”

“ Of course I do. Why——” but there he turned his head as some one knocked at the door. “ Come in,” he roared, and then the door opened, and the officer commanding the regiment, that is, Colonel Barnes, entered.

He came in with a cordial, “ Oh, Beresford, I wanted you to ”——when his eyes fell on young Tommy, and he broke off with something very nearly approaching to a glare.

Tommy got off the cot and said, “ Good morning, sir,” in his most modest tones—and mind you, when Tommy was modest, he looked as if the proverbial butter would not melt in his mouth.

“ Oh ! Good morning, good morning,” returned the Colonel, in a series of snorts, and in a tone which conveyed to Tommy that, if anything, Beresford had understated rather than overstated the enormity of his offence.

He felt that his time was come—that if he did not speak then, he would be, as it were, socially damned in the Blankshire Regiment for ever; but it was not without an immense effort that he broke the ice within which Colonel Barnes had frozen himself. He looked at the big, fierce, red-faced, burly man, with his haughty red nose and his long, bristling moustache, each end of which was waxed—soaped, if the truth be told—to a formidable spike, and his heart—yes, even his brazen heart—failed him! Still he felt that delay was dangerous, and at last he spoke! And if only his sister Nancy could have heard the last of the proud race of Earles eating humble pie with that shrinking air, she would have declared that her dear boy's degradation could go no further, and sink no lower.

"If you please, sir," he began, "I'm afraid"—— and then he stopped short, awed into silence by the astonished stare with which the Colonel was regarding him.

"WELL?" said the Colonel in a loud voice; it was a very big "well," and Tommy felt more shaky about the legs, and, if the truth be told, more inclined to cry than he had felt for many and many a year.

However, he had to go on. "Well, sir," he said, very humbly, "I—I'm afraid I made an awful ass o myself last night."

"H'm!" remarked the Colonel drily; "and when did you make that discovery?"

"Well, sir," returned Tommy, apologetically, " Beresford here tells me I was awfully drunk; and —and--I'm sure I didn't drink much, sir, but," a happy inspiration suddenly occurring to him, "you see. sir. I'm beastly young yet, and my head gets knocked over in next to no time."

Probably never in all his years of service had Colonel Barnes ever had made to him, or heard given by any one else, such an excuse for an indiscretion at the table ; in fact, it was so new that he did not in the least know what to say. And whilst he was still staring at Tommy, speechless with surprise, I must confess that Beautiful Jim, whose sense of humour was not small, went off into smothered agonies of laughter such as at last bade fair to choke him. And the more he tried to disguise it by the help of a big pocket-handkerchief and a make-believe cough, the more and more infectious it became, until at last Colonel Barnes got up from his chair with a dignity that was exceedingly shaky.

"Well, Earle," he said, in a voice as shaky as his dignity, "I am very glad to see that you have sense to know and to honestly own when you've been in fault. If you keep up that spirit, my boy, there will be no fear of your not doing well in the Blankshire Regiment. We will say no more about it. Beresford—I'll—look—in——" probably the chief had meant to say "again," but before he had finished speaking his laughter had got beyond his control, and his only way of hiding from the offender that he was laughing himself, or that he had taken notice of the agonies that Beautiful Jim was suffering, was by edging off towards the door, and getting himself out of the room without the delay of a moment. As a matter of fact, he simply could not have uttered the last word without going off into roars of laughter, even to have saved his life. And Colonel Barnes had a very proper idea of the dignity of his rank and position, and the due effect of both upon his junior officers.

Beautiful Jim, relieved from the necessity of hiding his laughter, simply laid back in his chair and laughed weakly until the tears stood in his eyes, and his sides ached so that he could scarcely breathe.

"I can't see what you find to laugh at," said Tommy, blankly.

"Tommy, Tommy—you'll be the death of me," Jim gasped.

"Can't see why. As for the Colonel," Tommy remarked, "I believe he's gone off to have a fit of apoplexy."

"I shouldn't at all wonder," declared the other in a feeble voice. "I know if he'd stayed five minutes longer in this room I should have had one for certain. 'You see, sir, I'm beastly young, and my head gets knocked over in next to no time.' Tommy, can't you see the joke of it?"

"No, I can't," said Tommy, tartly. "You told me to patch it up if I could, and I have patched it up, and even now you aren't satisfied. I don't know what you want, nor what you would be at !"

"Then I can't enlighten you, my son," Jim declared, "and as I live, I am due at the office! Ta, ta, old chap. See you later in the day, I dare-say," and Beautiful Jim jammed his cap upon his head and rushed off, buckling on his sword as he went.

———

CHAPTER XIV.

PROGRESS UNDER DIFFICULTIES.

As soon as he was free to get out of the barracks that afternoon, Beautiful Jim betook himself off to the bazaar, which was open for the last day. He found a great crowd there, for it was market-day and nearly all the country people had con-trived to go to it for an hour or so before they went home.

The ladies were all very busy; for in spite of a week's good sale there was still a large quantity of things to be disposed of, and they were taking almost any price they could get for them so as to effect a clearance. Miss Earle was especially busy, her pleasant winning manner and fair bright face bringing her many and many a customer who otherwise would not have cared to spend a far-thing.

Beautiful Jim, however, suffered by this popu-larity, for he could not manage to get a word with her, or hardly one. He knew that she and Tommy were going home on the Monday morning, and he knew, too, that he could not hope by any chance to get even a two days' leave on this side the 1st of September.

So Beautiful Jim, despite the gay and giddy throng of which he made one, was as nearly miserable as he could be while he had still the privilege of watching his divinity.

"I shan't see you after to-day, Miss Earle," he said disconsolately, when at last she had ten minutes to spare, and he had the felicity of taking her off to the refreshment châlet for a cup of tea.

"Why not ? " she asked.

"Because I'm on duty to-morrow, and I can't get any of the other fellows to do it for me," he returned mournfully.

"Oh !" she cried, in dismay, "and Mrs. Trafford is having a tea after the Parish."

"Yes, I know," said he, wretchedly. Then after a moment he exclaimed in a brighter tone, "There's one fellow I haven't asked, so there's just a chance yet for me."

"Then I shall not say good-bye to-day," said Miss Earle, with decision. "I hate saying good-bye. Don't you ? "

"It depends," said Jim, guardedly. "It depends a good deal on the other person. Now, if I was saying good-bye to you," he said, in a desperate tone—and just as Miss Earle was beginning to

show the prettiest of danger-signals in her cheeks
and a droop in her sweet eyes, some—some—*idiot*,
Jim said to himself savagely, came clumsily along
and knocked a heavy tea-tray against her arm,
making her shriek out in unmistakable pain.

"Now then! Where are you going?" Jim
thundered, looking daggers at the luckless individual.

After many apologies and regrets the poor
wretch went away forgiven; and then, just as
Jim was going to be tender and lover-like over
the poor arm, a great stream of people came in,
among whom were two of the Leslie girls and
Tommy Earle.

It is to be hoped that the recording angel does
not put down all the naughty words that rise in
the heart and never pass the lips; if he does, he
must have had a busy ten minutes that Saturday
afternoon, for Beautiful Jim's unspoken thoughts
were—well, far from saintly.

Thus reminded of her duties, Nancy Earle went
back to her post, and never another chance did Jim
have of uttering the words which, if she would only
hear and heed, would have made him the happiest
man in Blankhampton that day! But for all that
he hung about Lady Margaret's châlet with the per-
sistence and fidelity of a dog, and once or twice
when Nancy sallied forth to dispose, by the unlaw-
ful and sinful means of raffling, of some rather
large article of upholstery which hung on hand, he
was privileged in being allowed to carry that same.

to stand by while she enlarged on the beauties of sofa-cushions which nobody wanted to buy, and descanted on the merits of banner-screens which were a mockery and an abomination.

"I may come and see you when I am in town?" he asked.

"Oh! yes, Mr. Beresford, we shall be delighted if you do," she replied, heartily.

"Ah! I shall not be able to get leave until well on in September, or perhaps even October, and you won't be in town then," he said, in dejection and gloom. "You're sure not to be in town then."

"I am not so sure," she said. "True, we always go to the country for several months and *intend* to stay all the winter—only somehow, my father likes our house in town better than our country place, and we generally find ourselves home again 'n Hans Place early in October. We may stay in the country longer this year, because Stuart may care to bring friends for the shooting. I suppose my father would like to be there if he did—only he does hate the country so. The country people bore him, and he says the house is a draught-trap. And then he likes his paper at breakfast-time, and he likes his club and his whist and all that. Oh! I daresay you will find us at home if you happen to be in town in October, or even at the end of September."

"It's a tremendous time from this to September," said Jim, feeling a little mollified by her information.

8—2

"Yes," said Miss Earle—"it is a sofa-cushion, worked by the Duchess of Blankshire—only sixty chances at a shilling each—and I only want three to make up the number."

Beautiful Jim stood still and cursed at fate, the cushion and its noble maker the Duchess, at the inquisitive person who desired to see it, at everything, in short, excepting Miss Nancy Earle.

"Look here," he said brusquely. "Need you hawk that thing about any longer? I hate to hear you wasting blandishments over these people I'll take the remaining chances."

" Oh ! that is sweet and lovely of you," Miss Earle said. " Two shillings, please. I do hope you'll get it, for I'm real tired with trailing about trying to get rid of it."

"If *I* get it," grumbled Jim, "I shall take it back to barracks and burn it."

"But why ? "

"Just to revenge myself on the Duchess for making such a hideous thing," he answered.

However, he did not win it, for after a long and tiresome process the raffle was conducted in much solemn state up in a corner, the Dean himself holding the bag ; and the cushion fell to Miss Earle herself. She took it with very doubtful satisfaction.

" Mr. Beresford," she said, suddenly, as if a really brilliant idea had struck her, " you've been as good as gold helping me to get rid of it—I'll give it to you.'

" To me ? " cried Jim.

"Yes; it will help to brighten your room. Will you accept it?"

"Miss Earle," he said, "I will keep it for ever."

"Then," said she, with her pretty laugh, "I think I will take it back and find you something prettier for a keepsake; for if you have such a thing as that in remembrance of me, it will not be very long before you say, or at least think, 'What a hideous thing that is. Why did I buy it? Oh! a girl gave it to me. Yes, young Earle's sister; it was at a bazaar, at Blankhampton.' And then you'll only remember the girl by the cushion, and you'll get to associate me with the cushion, and——"

"I will keep it," Jim declared stoutly, keeping the uncomely cushion fast under his arm. "You gave it me—it is exquisite. I would not part with it for the world."

Miss Earle laughed again, and just then Lady Margaret beckoned to her. "Nancy, my dear, Aileen has had to go home. She has given in at last, poor child."

"Oh! poor Aileen," cried Nancy.

"Is Miss Adair faint? Can I do anything for her, Lady Margaret?" Jim asked, in great concern.

"No. She is overtired, that is all; thank you so much, though. This long week has been too much for her," Lady Margaret replied. "She has gone to lie down, but I hope she will be able to come down for supper."

For each evening there was supper at the Deanery for the workers at Lady Margaret's stall, and for such of those helpers as came from a distance.

"Oh! I do hope so," Nancy explained. She was very fond of the beautiful Aileen.

"Meantime," Lady Margaret went on, "she told me to ask if you would finish off the raffle for this," holding out a child's little velvet pelisse, handsomely trimmed with lace.

"Oh, of course," Nancy answered readily.

Beautiful Jim would fain have raised the objection that Nancy was almost as worn out by her labours as Miss Adair; but Nancy saw what was coming, and checked him by an imperative pat on the arm.

"That is good of you," exclaimed the Dean's wife, gratefully. "Then see here, dear. There are thirty-five shilling chances, and Aileen had already got seventeen taken up. Here is the bag with the names and the money. It will leave you eighteen still to get."

Beautiful Jim fairly groaned within himself—eighteen shillings to be wheedled out of eighteen unwilling pockets — eighteen men or women to captivate by all the pretty persuasions and graces which he wanted to keep so badly for himself—eighteen—oh! it was too cruel not to give her a moment's rest, and he would like to have burnt the thing.

"Very well," Nancy answered. How ready and willing she was, worn out and weary though she must be, to take up the burden again and keep working still.   "Here, Mr. Beresford, will you carry it for me?"

"With pleasure," returned Jim, not very truthfully, it must be owned, "and after this you too will knock off work, won't you?"

"Oh yes, it will be time," answered Lady Margaret for her.   "And, Nancy, be sure you tell the people how it happens to be so expensive. It is made of the best velvet, the lace is very good, and the linings are silk. In fact, there is no profit on it whatever, for Mrs. Bateman made it for me for nothing."

"I'll tell them," said Nancy, and she started away at once on her mission.

But Beautiful Jim could not stand any more of it.

"Miss Earle," he said, "please don't hawk that thing about any more, will you?   I'll buy the chances remaining."

"But, Mr. Beresford," she said, "*you* don't need a little child's pelisse."

"No; but I'd like to buy the other chances if you've no objection," he returned meekly.

"But what can you want with it?" she said.

"I don't want it, of course," he said. "Who would?" he asked, eyeing the little garment with huge contempt. "But I don't like to see you killing yourself over the thing, and—and—please do let me have the rest of the chances."

"But eighteen chances—and, if you get it, what will you do with it?" she asked.

"Oh! give it to someone or other," he replied--"anything, so that you don't go about any more, wasting yourself on such a crew as this," moving his head impatiently from side to side so as to indicate the crowd gathered in the street of the Swiss village.

So Nancy Earle gave way, and allowed him to fill up the eighteen places on her card with his initials; and then he drew her away from the glare of the lamps until he found a cosy and retired seat under a wide-spreading tree.

CHAPTER XV.

WHAT MIGHT HAVE BEEN.

IN spite of the pains and trouble at which Beautiful Jim had been in order to secure a quiet half-hour with Nancy Earle, they were not long left undisturbed under the shadow of the wide-spreading tree beneath which they had taken refuge. For hardly had they settled themselves there in comfort before little Violet Leslie, followed by the incorrigible Tommy, pushed aside the branches and invaded their retreat; and the incorrigible Tommy, it must be understood, was quite too full and overflowing with his own importance to dream for a moment of betaking himself out of the way for the convenience and pleasure of his senior officer.

Thus Tommy got very much the best of the

situation, for being like a young bear with all his troubles to come, he had yet to undergo one of the most important parts of his education. Let but a single year pass over his head, and he would know better than to coolly appropriate a couple of chairs within a couple of yards of the senior subaltern of his regiment—under the particular circumstances of that evening, at least.

But Tommy had much to learn yet, very much, and this bit of ignorance was laid up in store against him, and he would suffer for it by-and-bye, never fear. Of course, if he had been a boy blessed with a fair share of common-sense, he would have departed at once and left the field clear for Beautiful Jim; but Tommy did not happen to have much sense, and never gave Beautiful Jim a thought! He only saw that Nancy was sitting there with some fellow or other, and as all his life long he had been taught to look upon Nancy as a distinctly inferior being to himself, it never occurred to him to put himself out of the way for the sake of considering her. Really, it was not so much the lad's own fault—it was the way he had been brought up.

Still, in Her Majesty's Service the seniors are not in the habit of making much allowance for the defective early training of the juniors; and as Beautiful Jim drew Miss Earle impatiently out into the glare of the gas-lights again, he registered a vow on the most lasting tablet of his heart that Tommy should pay dearly for this night's work, and before long. Ah! well, well, one Franklin says: "Experience keeps a dear school, but fools will learn in no other, and scarcely in that;" and Franklin generally knew full well what he was talking about, thoroughly well in that instance.

Nor did the events which followed his expulsion from what was neither more nor less to him than an earthly paradise tend in any way to soften Jim's wrathful feelings towards the incorrigible Tommy, for that happened to be the very last chance he had of a quiet quarter of an hour with Nancy Earle before she left Blankhampton. For no sooner did they emerge from the shelter of the branches than they were seized upon by two of the Leslie girls, who demanded, in their friendliest tones, what was the state of business at Lady Margaret's stall?

Now, in Beautiful Jim's opinion, as in that of many another man, the Leslie sisters were quite the most brilliant and attractive girls in the town, but, as a truthful chronicler of Blankhampton life, I must own that, at that moment, he found himself wondering what in the wide world he could ever have seen attractive about any one of them. Poor Jim! From that moment until they were summoned into the Deanery for supper, he did not get rid of them, and by that time his last chance of a quiet talk with Nancy was gone.

The Leslies did not go into the Deanery, having a little festivity of their own that night; but as they parted from Nancy at the door, some suspicion of the truth dawned upon Sarah.

"Norrie," she exclaimed, as soon as they were

out of earshot, "did you notice anything unusual about Beautiful Jim to-night?"

"I thought he seemed uncommonly flat—for him, that is," returned Norah, promptly.

"It's that Miss Earle," exclaimed Sarah, "and he is as gone on her as possible. What a joke—and oh! poor old fellow, what a shame we couldn't leave them together; she's going away on Monday."

"Oh, there's the Parish to-morrow," said Norah easily.

"Oh, but he is on duty to-morrow," Sarah cried. "Young Towers told me so, because Jim wanted him to do it, and he wouldn't. He said old Jim was in an awful way about it."

"Then I think he might have taken it, nasty little wretch," said Norah, who had but little love for Towers. "Let us snub him all we know to-morrow."

But all the snubbing in the world did not alter the fact that Beautiful Jim had found no one willing to do his duty, or that he was eating his very heart out in barracks on Nancy Earle's last day in Blankhampton.

As for Nancy, all the sweetness and light of the place seemed to have gone out, and out of her life too, so far as that went. She sat a long time beside the open window of her bedroom that night thinking—thinking—thinking! First how savage he had been when Violet Leslie and Stuart came under the tree—as if poor dear Stuart would ever dream that they had gone there for more than five minutes'

rest from the noise and turmoil of the Fair. And
how, when he had espied his servant in the crowd,
he had given that hideous cushion to him, and bade
him take it back to barracks with great care. Then
how he had sat beside her at supper, and how tender
and gentle he had been, and how he had held her
hand at parting and looked at her—why, positively,
her cheeks were burning as she thought of it. And
then another thought rose up in her mind, a thought
of which, owing to her training and the traditions
of her house, she felt more than half ashamed.

" If only Stuart had not chosen just that spot and
just that moment to take little Violet Leslie out of
the crowd—ah ! how different all might have been "
—and then her eyes fell upon the child's little
velvet pelisse which Jim had won and left behind
him.

CHAPTER XVI.

IN NEW QUARTERS.

AT last the time of young Stuart Earle's first long
leave was over, and he went to Blankhampton to
join his regiment—when for several months his life
was certainly not of the most pleasant kind, and
was very different from any experience he had had
before.

For one thing he had made a bad impression at
his very first appearance among them on each and
all of his brother-officers, from his commanding-

officer down to the latest joined subaltern, so that every one of them was on the look-out for the smallest sign of that "cheek" which every man of them felt it was his personal and particular duty to try to eradicate. A difficult task even for the united strength of a whole regiment, for Tommy's native bounce was apparently of unlimited quantity, while in quality, as bounce, it was of the very first water.

So far as his manners in the mess-room were concerned, he was in an incredibly short time what Beautiful Jim called "licked into shape," but in other ways Tommy proved himself to be simply incorrigible ! For instance, he never could be brought to see that in Blankhampton society he was in any way inferior to his senior officers, and even in the Palace of the Lord Bishop himself, he made no more ado about openly chaffing Beautiful Jim or telling an absurd tale at the Major's expense, than he did of flirting desperately with little Violet Leslie, who was barely out of the school-room. Indeed, before six months had gone by, Tommy had the name of being the most impudent young cub who had ever graced the Blankshire Regiment or the old city of Blankhampton by his presence.

It must be owned that the women had had a good deal to do with it—they utterly spoilt him, for they allowed him to take almost any liberties that he chose, partly because he was so young, partly because he was so actually beautiful in person, partly because he was the last of a very old and rich and eminently distinguished race. And Tommy, as Beautiful Jim truly said, was utterly spoilt by all the adulation and flattery which was lavished upon him, simply because his head would not stand it, any better than it was able to stand a single extra glass of wine at dinner.

It was strange that this foolish child did not realise that his best interests for the future lay with the officers of his regiment, rather than with the ladies of the town in which he was quartered. Yet it was so! Not a day passed, if he was not on duty, that as soon as he was free from work he did not go flying off to some feminine charmer, and he neither could nor would understand that "the fellows" objected to going to tea-parties where Tommy was the central figure, to dinners where Tommy monopolised the whole of the conversation, and to dances where Tommy's audacious flirtations made him the observed of all observers.

But though Tommy did not become very popular in his regiment, he was popular enough in the town to satisfy any ordinary craving after the approval of the many. He became, after the first few weeks, the intimate friend of all classes—he was "Tommy" from one end of Blankhampton to the other.

Beautiful Jim did his best, but his influence went a very short way, for his advice was anything but palatable to the last of the Earles, and it must indeed be a very strong and firm will which can follow the most excellent advice in the world if it is unpleasant, to the exclusion of all that makes life worth having, a much stronger will than Tommy was blessed with. In truth, all Tommy's strength of purpose went in an opposite direction, that of serving his own ends and gratifying his own sense of pleasure.

"Look here, you young beggar," said Jim one day to him, being moved thereto not by any desire to do Tommy good, but by an uncomfortable feeling that *she* would be grieved if she could see all that went on in Blankhampton society, "if you go on like this, what do you mean to come to—hey?"

Tommy looked up with his own unabashed gaze.

"What on earth have I been doing to upset you now?" he demanded.

"Well, I saw you myself kiss no fewer than three women last night," Beautiful Jim growled. "The greater fools them to let you."

"Like to have been there yourself, eh?" remarked Tommy flippantly.

If Beautiful Jim felt half as contemptuous as he looked at that moment, he must have attained to the very furthest limits of disdain, for his ugly face seemed petrified with unutterable disgust.

"Like to have been there," he repeated. "Why, you young idiot, do you suppose there's a single woman, married or maid, in the whole of Blankhampton, that would give you so much as a look if *I* took the trouble to be civil to her? Bless you, child, don't flatter yourself. Why, it's because these women think you're such a baby—such a nothing—such a non-dangerous scrap of humanity—that they let you make the young show of yourself that you do.　But what I want to know is, what the devil do you mean to come to?"

"Well really, Jim," Tommy replied, with a certain "last-of-the-Earles" haughtiness in his tone, "it seems to me you're troubling yourself in a very unnecessary way about my private affairs, and——"

But Beautiful Jim had broken into shouts of derisive laughter.　"Tommy, Tommy, you'll be the death of me yet—you will, indeed," he said.　"Your private affairs—why, bless me, child, the last-joined sub hasn't got any private affairs except in applying for leave.　Private affairs, indeed!　Well, it's too lovely, that—simply too lovely."

Tommy looked blandly blank.　"I daresay it's very funny, Jim," he said, airily, "but where's the joke?"

"The joke?　In yourself, Tommy, my child, and you can't be expected to see it."

But, after that, Jim gave up trying to keep the lad from making a fool of himself with the Blankhampton women, and gained nothing whatever by the attempt he had made—except to make Tommy firmly believe, from that time forward, that the senior subaltern was eaten alive with jealousy of him. And if he had only known that Beautiful Jim's whole heart and mind was wrapped up in his own sister! If he had only known that, to him, he—Tommy— was simply nothing but an impudent young cub whose only claim to interest, or even notice, lay in the fact he was the brother of the insignificant and not-to-be-counted creature, Nancy Earle—well, it would have helped to take down the young gentleman's idea of his own greatness and his own importance marvellously.

Unfortunately, however, Jim had not during all those months the ghost of a chance of furthering his position with Nancy, for almost immediately after Tommy joined the regiment, Mr. Earle was seized with a somewhat severe attack of bronchitis, and by the orders of his medical advisers was on the very first opportunity ordered off to the sunny shores of the Mediterranean, there to stay until the very last east wind of our ungenial spring-time should have taken its departure from his native shores.

It had been a bitter blow to him, but it was useless to fight against fate, and though he tried hard for foreign leave, he was, owing to various rumours of disturbance floating about the country at the time, unable to get it.

So the—to him—dreary and profitless winter days dragged over, and he only lived in anticipation of the good and joyous time to come, when he would have put a certain question to Nancy Earle, and she would have said " yes," and given herself to him for ever. Some men might have had a doubt lest she might say " no," but Beautiful Jim had no such misgivings, and it never entered his head that it was possible she might refuse him—never once.

At the beginning of March, a certain part of the Blankshire Regiment was sent from Blankhampton to Walmsbury, there to remain for at least six months. The officer in command was Owen, who had lately got his troop, and with him went Beautiful Jim, a youngster called Manners, and, to his own unutterable and inexpressible disgust, the last of the Earles—Tommy.

Just at first he was rather elated at the prospect of a change. There was something jaunty and soldierly about marching out, colours flying, band playing, and a dozen broken hearts behind them; and for a few hours Tommy went airily round announcing that they were off to Walmsbury next week, with a "fresh-fields-and-pastures-new" air about him that was irresistibly funny to those of his brother-officers who knew what manner of place Walmsbury really was.

But the elation of this young Alexander, longing for more worlds to conquer, did not last long. From "the fellows" he learnt nothing; indeed, for any information he would have had from them he would have remained in the ignorance which is bliss, doubly so in this case, until he reached Walmsbury itself; but in Blankhampton it was different.

"Going to *Walmsbury*," cried one lady to whom he told his news with a very "girl-I-leave-behind me" sort of air. "Oh, you poor dear boy, what a shame! Why, you'll be buried alive in Walmsbury. There's nothing to do and nowhere to go, and not a soul in the place that you can possibly know. No society whatever."

"Oh! I don't know, Mrs. Fairlie," said Tommy, trying not to look as if his jaw was dropping perceptibly, yet with an uncomfortable sort of feeling that the lady, who was quite a small social celebrity in her way in Blankhampton, was right in what she said, " there must be plenty of good people round about."

" My dear boy, *none*," returned Mrs. Fairlie, with an emphasis which killed the last remnant of jauntiness left in him. " Not a soul who will take the very smallest notice of you."

" Take the smallest notice of *me !*" echoed Tommy, feeling as if an earthquake had suddenly rent the ground under their very feet.

" Yes, of you ! Everybody who is anybody in the neighbourhood of Walmsbury," Mrs. Fairlie answered with uncompromising straightforwardness, " is so horribly rich that they only count incomes by millions, and daughters *dots* by hundreds of thousands. Old families like your own they only regard as useful in having got together fine country places for them to buy; and as for any one of them ever asking you to dinner—why, they would almost as soon ask their sweep. Oh ! my dear child, I assure you that in going to Walmsbury, you'll find yourself in no bed of roses."

It occurred to Tommy at this moment that Mrs. Fairlie was rather what he called " piling it on." So she was, but not for the reason that he suspected. In truth, having set up for being quite the professional beauty of Blankhampton, and having been attended here and there by her own particular " mash " (I must use the slang of the day sometimes, for what other word, or combination of words, express so fully and clearly the exact sort of friendliness conveyed by the word " mash ? "), in the shape of Colonel Coles, she had, since stern duty had sent that gay and gallant old gentleman off to other climes, been without, or almost without, that desirable article of modern feminine equipment, and it was rather hard on her that the blithe and bonny Leslie girls should invariably go about the quaint old city with men in attendance galore! Tommy Earle, with his good old family, his beautiful ingenuous young face, his happy impudence, and his devil-may-care air, would have suited her down to the ground, not as a substitute for but as an improvement on, the gallant old gentleman removed— and she had expressed, or at least intimated, her decision to Tommy at a very early stage of their acquaintance. But Tommy had greatly preferred the bonny young Leslie girls to the middle-aged lady of provincial fashion, who had once been pretty and now posed as a beauty in consequence, and so she " piled it on " as high as she possibly could in recounting the disadvantages of Walmsbury as a military quarter.

" But, Mrs. Fairlie," said Tommy, when he could get his breath so as to speak, " have you ever been to Walmsbury ? "

" *Never*," returned the lady promptly.

" Then how do you know all this ? " he enquired, triumphantly.

" From the unfortunate men who have been quartered there," she replied immediately, and Tommy was crushed forthwith.

But Mrs. Fairlie was only the first of many who condoled with him on the misfortune of being sent to a place so uncouth, so unattractive in every way as Walmsbury. Thus the young Alexander's thoughts and ideas underwent a complete revolution, and by the time half the week—the last week in Blankhampton—was over, his indignation and disgust at his fate had positively reached their furthest limits. And then when they got to the hated place and he found himself in his own miserable deserted quarters, he became simply abject. When he saw the dirty unattractive streets, the pokey little shops, the ill-looking men and women, and the utter absence of any and every sort of rank and fashion, he fell into a settled misery of regret.

For the first time since he **had** joined his regiment, Tommy regretted sincerely that he had not, when he had the chance, made himself more popular with his brother-officers than he had done. For he found Walmsbury no better than a prison, the very end of the earth, the abomination of desolation! Moreover, he was fairly thrown on his beam ends for the lack of feminine society.

It would be difficult for me to truly describe how his soul sickened and yearned for the crowd of pretty and well-dressed women whom he had known in Blankhampton, the women with aristocratic and pretty drawing-rooms, in which he had had his own especial seat, and where he had been waited on like a young god—how he missed the good balls, the luxurious club, the grand old Parish with its tall towers and its stately ceremonious services—how he missed the gay shops and the pleasant dinners, and the innumerable tea-parties! Yes, he pined for them all with a fierce resentment such as made Walmsbury and everything in it hateful to him, and many were the unfavourable comparisons which he drew between them as he stalked sullenly through the narrow and dingy ill-kept streets of the little manufacturing town to the club, where there was never a soul excepting a few millionaires playing whist for shilling points, who took no more notice of him— the last of the Earles—than if he had been one of their own factory hands, and displayed none of that adulation which they would have shown him if he had been one of those same factory hands, who had been hard-headed enough and close-fisted enough to scrape a fortune together!

"And these people live here from one end of their lives to the other," Tommy cried one day as he crossed the road from the barracks to the Commis- sariat-office, encountering on the way a stream of oily hot-looking factory-hands just let out of the mills. "Go on from year's end to year's end, know- ing nothing different. Good God! what an end to live for "—and then he had to go on his way and sign a report that the bread for the day was sour and not sufficiently baked, and then, oh! poor Tommy, to sit down in his bare and hideous room— for he had never had the heart to try and make it

look even habitable—and write a duty letter to his
sister Nancy! Poor Tommy, it was a long fall and
a hard fall, from the cosy drawing-rooms and the
charming women on which his memory dwelt so
fondly, to the stern reality of life at Walmsbury, of
which the chief incidents were insufficiently baked
bread and a duty letter to his sister Nancy!

And, as the natural result of all this, it was not
very long before Master Tommy Earle got into very
unmistakeable mischief indeed.

CHAPTER XVII.

A TERRIBLE DREAM.

IT is not often that I wish my readers to follow me
through a very close description of bricks and
mortar, of stairways and rooms, of doorways and windows ; but it is really necessary that they should
know something of the plan upon which the mess-
rooms and officers' quarters at Walmsbury were
arranged.

It was not a barrack intended for the accommo-
dation of a regiment, but only for a detachment of
such regiment as might be quartered at Blankhampton. On the left of the principal entrance gate
stood the larger of two blocks of buildings—this
contained the guard-room and cells, the men's
rooms, and the married and sergeants' quarters ; on
the right was a second block, which contained on the

ground-floor the orderly-room and office, the mess-rooms and some other rooms used either for married officers' quarters or as quarters for staff-officers, such as the doctor or paymaster, if one happened to be needed. On the floor above were seven good-sized rooms, and a large kitchen used in common by all the officers' servants on that storey.

This kitchen overlooked the road, and was of irregular shape, owing to the fact that the well of the staircase was taken out of it. On the side of it furthest from the entrance gate was an empty room, and on the other were the two rooms usually appropriated to the officer commanding the detachment, though, in this case, Owen had not troubled to furnish both rooms, and had only brought a portion of his goods and chattels from head-quarters. Thus the room on either side of the kitchen was empty, while on the other side of the corridor which cut that floor of the building in halves, were the quarters occupied by the doctor—who preferred to be on the upper storey—Beautiful Jim, Tommy Earle, and young Manners.

Thus Beautiful Jim's room was exactly opposite to the kitchen; and it happened that one lonely evening at the beginning of May, after he had spent an hour with a pipe and the pleasure of dreaming about his sweet Nancy Earle, he was just beginning to think it was time to dress for mess, when Captain Owen opened the door unceremoniously and walked in.

That something serious had happened to disturb

Owen, Jim saw at once by the unusual cloud on his solemn good phiz—which was to him the dearest in the whole regiment.

"Hollo! old man, what's up?" he demanded.

It was still chilly enough, in spite of the lovely spring weather, for all the officers to have their fires blazing halfway up their chimneys, and Owen, with the usual freedom of barrack-life, began to tell him what was the matter by possessing himself with the poker and vigorously smashing the big lumps of coal.

"What on earth is it?" Jim asked, his curiosity now thoroughly aroused; for Owen was a man of quite unusually equable temper, and this display of mental disturbance betrayed that something greatly out of the common had happened to ruffle him.

"That young ass, Tommy," Owen burst out in contemptuous disgust.

"What—has he been at it again?" Jim asked, not much surprised, except that Owen should think enough about Tommy to be annoyed by anything he might take it into his empty young head to do. "And what's he been after? Mischief, of course," with an amused laugh.

"Mischief! I believe you! The young fool— the idiot—the——just look here," holding out his hand.

"Why, that's Tommy's flashiest ring—beats all Evelyn Gabrielli's rings to fits," Jim exclaimed. "Where in the world did *you* get it? Surely, young Tommy hasn't been 'reduxed' so as to pay visits to his avuncular relative?"

"If that was all, there wouldn't be much harm done," returned Owen. "No, it's much worse than that. You know that pert little barmaid at the Duck's Tail?"

"Yes."

"I went in there this afternoon to get the address of that horse-dealer that Whittaker told me about, and I found my lady dusting her bottles and counters and so on with this blazing on her hand. Knew the ring in a minute, and, by Jove, I was down upon her like a terrier on a rat. 'Where did you get that ring?' I asked.

"'What's that to you?' she said, with as much cheek as even Tommy himself could have shown.

"'You got it out of Mr. Earle,' said I.

"'And what if I did?' she returned, pertly.

"'A good deal,' said I; 'in fact, just this. You're a good many years older than Mr. Earle—ten at least—you're anything but a reputable woman, and, in fact, if you were as good as an angel out of Heaven—which you are not—you're just about the last woman in the world that his family would ever receive if you bamboozled him into marrying you. I see you're wearing it on your engaged finger, and I suppose that means that you have inveigled him into promising to replace it by a plain one. But he will do nothing of the sort, and you will just hand that ring over at once to me. We don't allow our young officers to go about marrying any one they like, particularly such a woman as you are.'

"'And if I don't?' she asked, insolently.

" ' If you don't ?   Well, I happen to be Mr. Earle's commanding-officer just now, and unless you at once give me that ring and your solemn promise to make no further attempt to get him to marry you, I shall simply put him under arrest and keep him there until his father comes, and his father will very soon straighten him up, I promise you.   Remember, he is not nineteen yet—that he's an infant—a minor—and can't even make a legal marriage without his father's consent until he is one and twenty.   He is absolutely dependent upon his father, too, for every farthing he has, or ever will have ; so just hand me over that ring and I will settle the matter with him.' And the end of it all was," Owen wound up, " that she gave me the ring and her solemn pledge to have done with the young fool for good and all. Of course, it was pretty nearly all bounce that I said, and would not have borne a moment's reflection if she had been a better educated woman ; but it has served its turn, and it seems to me that *anything* is justifiable to save a young fool from coming such a cropper as that."

" Yes, that's so," murmured Jim, turning the ring over, and thinking what *she* would say if she knew about it.

It was a valuable and very beautiful ring, the finest one of many possessed by the object of Owen's righteous indignation.   In the centre was a large sapphire of great price, on which was engraved the crest and motto of the Earles.   Surrounding this were diamonds of much beauty, which flashed and sparkled as the firelight fell upon them.

"Have you seen him?" Jim asked at last, looking up from the ring.

"No, I went into his room, but he has not come back from Blankhampton yet; he is due to-night, though," Owen answered. "I think if he makes any fuss about the matter I had better write to the Colonel and tell him about it, and get him to send one of the other fellows here and let the young ass go back to the Regiment. What do you think?"

"I think he'll get into the Devil's own mischief wherever he is," Jim replied, his faith in Tommy having been shattered long before.

"Perhaps! Still there are plenty of ladies in Blankhampton to keep him out of harm's way, and if he were to go and get engaged to one of the Leslie girls, her father would soon choke him off; or, if he wouldn't be choked off, old Earle couldn't possibly object to anything in the engagement but his son's youth and general idiocy. Well, I suppose I must be off to dress; it only wants ten minutes to mess now "—then, without waiting for a reply, Owen went out, shutting the door with a bang, and leaving Beautiful Jim with Tommy Earle's ring still in his hand.

And Jim sat quite still, thinking.

"The girl at the Duck's Tail," he muttered. "I've seen her; little sharp-nosed thing, with golden hair that don't anyhow match her complexion, and enough strong Blankshire in her accent to knock you down—just a little vinegarish shrew— and he, the last of the Earles—the one that counts.

Good God! what will *she* say when she hears of it?"
—for, although he admired old Owen greatly for the
pluck and presence of mind he had shown in dealing
with the affair, yet he had little faith that opposi-
tion would in any way damp Tommy's ardour, or
that the bounce of which the dear old chap was so
unmistakably proud would have more than a tempo-
rary effect as a deterrent upon the young lady at the
Duck's Tail.

"Well, I must be quick, only seven minutes to
dress in," he exclaimed, getting hurriedly out of his
chair as he realised how late the time was. "By
Jove, old Owen's left the young fool's precious ring
here. I suppose I had better lock it up. Oh, Lord,
what a fool that lad must be. 'Pon my word,
though, I thought he'd a better idea of his own
value than to look at that little cat at the Duck's
Tail;" and then he locked the ring away in safety,
and shouted for his servant, who was in the kitchen
just across the corridor, to come and help him to
dress.

With the help of that individual, who was one of
the handiest of his kind, he managed to get downstairs just in time, and went into the mess-room the
last of all the little party.

They had a sort of guest-night that evening, for
in addition to the three officers of the Blankshire
Regiment and the doctor, who messed with them,
they had a young fellow staying a mile or two away
who was not of the millionaire type common to the
Walmsbury neighbourhood, the officer in charge of

the Commissariat Department, the clergyman who acted as chaplain, and the R. C. Priest of the district.

Thus it was quite a dinner-party; and although Beautiful Jim looked once or twice across the table at Owen to see whether he had got over his annoyance, he very soon entered into a discussion, on a more interesting subject than Tommy's delinquencies, with his neighbour the Priest, and speedily forgot all about the matter.

Nor did he remember it till Tommy himself came on to the scene some hours later, apparently utterly tired out with the short journey from Blankhampton, where he had been spending a two-days' leave. It struck him more than once that the lad looked very white and fagged, and he put it down to his having tried to cram too much into the few hours he had had to spend in the old city.

"Any news from Blankhampton, Tommy?" he enquired, civilly.

"None in particular," returned Tommy, in a very absent wooden sort of a voice.

"See the Leslies?"

"Oh, yes. Sarah's engaged to be married," Tommy answered.

"Sarah? Really. H'm—who's the man?"

"Oh, some fellow or other. I don't remember the name," indifferently.

"Don't remember the name," thought Jim. "That looks fishy! Always thought little Violet was the attraction there—seems not. H'm—poor

Tommy looks as if he didn't feel very elated at his return to the young lady at the Duck's Tail. In that case, old Owen's task will be all the easier to carry out. Yes," laughing to himself in his amusement, "I should think the contrast between her and the Leslies must have given Tommy a regular sickener."

"Is Miss Antrobus married yet?" he asked presently.

"I think so. I didn't call there," Tommy answered, in the same mechanical voice.

"Did you call on Mrs. Seton?" Jim enquired.

"No. I don't like Mrs. Seton much," returned Tommy, then got up and moved away as if he had heard enough on the subject of Blankhampton, and did not want to be questioned any further about it.

"Poor lad," said Beautiful Jim to himself, "he has evidently had an awakening to the real value of the charms and fascinations at the Duck's Tail. What a good thing for him! Poor old Owen will find the business easier to manage than he thought."

He looked across the room at his friend, and found his thoughts running away to his little cousin, Nell Marchmont! Jim had never said a word, and Nell had never said a word either—yet he knew that Owen had spent the greater part of his leave in London, and guessed that he had tried his fate and that Nell had said no. Suspecting this, he had purposely spoken to her of Owen more than once, and she had flushed up a little at the mention of his name, and

a certain dewy tenderness had come into her eyes, a
tenderness so tinged with sorrow that Jim gleaned
all the information that he wanted from it. Well,
it was a pity, and Jim wished to the very bottom of
his heart that it had been otherwise; but still, if
Nell did not see it in that light it was no use his
thinking any more about it.

And by-and-bye their guests went away and the
four officers went off to their rooms, Owen going
into Jim's for a last pipe instead of turning to the
left towards his own. And for an hour or so they
sat together smoking and chatting, and Jim told
his friend his suspicions about Tommy's disenchant-
ment, to his extreme satisfaction, it need hardly be
said.

"And, by-the-bye, Owen, you left the young fool's
ring with me—I'll give it to you. Now, what the
deuce can Leader have done with my keys? 'Pon
my soul, Leader's infernal tidiness is the very curse
of my existence. *I* don't know where he has put
them."

"Never mind, old chap, you can give it to me to-
morrow," answered Owen, who was getting tired.
"Good night, old fellow."

"Good night, old chap," returned Jim, cheerily.

It is safe to say that he was not five minutes in
throwing off his clothes and tumbling into bed, and
in less than a minute after that he was sound asleep
and dreaming—dreaming that he had committed
some terrible misdemeanour, and that Owen—old
Owen, his own especial chum—ended with—"Con-

sider yourself under close arrest. Go to your room at once, and I will send for your sword."

The dream was so real that he awoke trembling from head to foot, to find the fire still blazing cheerfully, and the sound of footsteps going along the corridor outside.

"Gad, what rot a fellow can dream," he said, and turning over fell asleep once more.

CHAPTER XVIII.

MURDER!

NOT once again did Beautiful Jim stir or move during the rest of that night; but soon after seven in the morning he was roused by Leader coming into the room—Leader, with a face like chalk and ashes, and hands shaking like aspen leaves in a gale of wind, who shook him up with less ceremony than he had ever done before during all the time he had served him.

"Mr. Beresford—sir—for God's sake wake up!" the man panted. "The awfullest thing has happened, sir—for God's sake wake up!"

"Eh—what?" muttered Jim, sleepily. "Mr Manners is on duty to-day."

"It's not duty, sir—it's *murder!*" cried Leader desperately, shaking him harder than ever.

The ominous word was enough to rouse Beautiful Jim completely. "Hey—murder—oh, is that you, Leader? Why, has anything happened?"

" Happened!   Yes, sir.   Mr.—Captain Owen, that is, is lying dead in his quarters this minute," the man gasped out as well as his chattering teeth and shaking lips would let him speak.

Jim sat bolt upright in his cot.   " Captain Owen *dead!*   Good God! Leader, is it true, or are you mad, or am I dreaming ? "

" True enough, sir," returned Leader, sadly. " Jones went to call him ten minutes ago, and found him—dead and stiff."

By this time Jim was out of his cot and getting rapidly into the first clothes that came to hand, and in less than a minute from the time he realized the information which Leader had brought him he was across the corridor and in Owen's room.

But up to that moment he had scarcely believed that it was quite as Leader had said, that Owen was really dead.   Still there was no mistaking the evidence of his own eyes, for poor Owen was lying just as they had found him, half on the floor and half on the cot, his hands still clutching the bed-clothes, which were stained darkly and deeply by a great pool of blood which had oozed from a frightful gash at the back of his head.

" My God!" gasped Jim, staggering back, " then it's true ; " and then the doctor came hurrying in, as pale and scared-looking as the others, yet keeping his presence of mind admirably.

" Great Heavens! what an awful thing," he exclaimed.   " Here, Jim, help me to lift him over and see if anything can be done."   Then, as they simultaneously touched him, he shook his head. "Ah! no, poor chap—it's no use—he's been dead for hours."

Aye, it was true enough; there could be no mistaking the ashen-grey face, the parted lips, the blank stare of the dimmed eyes, even by the most inexperienced there in the room; and besides, as they had found him, so he remained when they laid him on the cot, with knees bent and hands stiffly clutching at nothing. Oh! awful, awful sight!

"The best friend I ever had in my life," cried poor Jim Beresford, the big tears chasing one another down his cheeks.

He was so blinded by his grief that he never noticed that Tommy Earle had come in, and was standing looking with horror stamped on every feature at the awful thing on the bed, all that was left of what twelve hours before had been a living, breathing, gallant man of honour.

"Who did it?" the lad asked, shaping the words with his lips rather than speaking them.

It was Owen's servant, Jones, who answered the question.

"We don't know, sir. Some dastardly coward what struck him from behind;" and then he dashed the tears away from his eyes, and turning from the cot, began tidying up the room in a dazed, mechanical sort of way, as if he hardly knew what he was about.

"You'd better not touch anything until the police come," said the doctor, who had kept his senses about him better than most people would have done under the circumstances. "They will be here in a few minutes now. Mr. Beresford, I should advise you to have the room cleared and a guard mounted over the door. It is no use our stopping here now— we can do no good."

Thus reminded that he was now the officer commanding the detachment, Jim gave orders to have the room cleared, and having locked the door, set a double guard upon it. Then he went back to his room and dressed himself, being already in his undress uniform by the time the police arrived from the town, half a mile away.

And although the entire barracks seemed to be paralyzed by the awful deed which had been committed in their midst, Beautiful Jim found himself with plenty of work on his hands. First, he had to be with the police while they made a close examination of the room and of the dead man, together with the army-surgeon and a civilian doctor, who had come up with them from the town.

"'Ere's the thing that did it," said one of the men, suddenly stooping to pick something off the floor.

The others all pressed forward to see what it was, Beautiful Jim among them ; the man held in his hand an iron dumb-bell of about seven pounds weight, which Jim at once recognized as one of his own.

" That's mine," he exclaimed instantly.

The Inspector of police looked up sharply.

"You'd better say nothing, sir; anything you say now is liable to be used in evidence against you."

"Against *me!*" repeated Beautiful Jim, staring at the man as if he were mad, or drunk, or both. "Why, you don't mean to say that you suspect me of murdering the best friend I have in the world?"

"Be quiet, old fellow," put in the doctor, soothingly. "Of course the Inspector does not suspect you, except as he suspects us all until he gets at the truth. He only warned you to say nothing that might lead to suspicions being thrown upon you. But, Inspector, I suppose there would be no harm in my asking Mr. Beresford how the dumb-bell came to be here?"

"Not the least, sir."

"I am sure there cannot be," said Jim, rather haughtily; "nor in anything I may say. I wish my conscience was as clear of everything as of having lifted a finger against that dear old chap. As to the dumb-bells, that is simple enough. I lent mine to him weeks ago, for I've never been able to use them since I broke my collar-bone last year. Captain Owen's own are ten pounds weight, and he fancied they did him more harm than good, so he used mine for some time before we left Blankhampton."

"I can answer for that," put in Jones, who had been admitted during the examination: "and there's the other one by the door there. My master always had them stand there, close by where his bath was set."

There was no doubt whatever that the dumb-bell in the policeman's hand was the weapon with which the foul deed had been done, for it was dabbled with blood, to which a good many short dark hairs were still sticking.

Then the Inspector having announced that they could do nothing further at present, locked and sealed the door, and went away, leaving the sentries still on guard in the corridor.

And as I said, Beautiful Jim had enough to do— send telegrams off to head-quarters, and to various members of Owen's family—to be interviewed by newspaper reporters and shoals of people who flocked from all parts to learn the details of the terrible event—to carry on the work of the entire detachment, and make all manner of arrangements in connection with the inquest and funeral, the like of which had happily never fallen in his way before. It was an awful time for them all; the men stood about the barrack-yard in groups, and the few women clustered round their doors and talked and talked it over until there was positively no light left in which they had not looked at it. The three officers, with such guests as had gathered about them, discussed the matter in the ante-room in much the same way—asking over and over again " Who could have done it ? " and " What motive could anybody have had to murder the dear old chap, who was everybody's friend, who had never been known to have an enemy in the world."

“And he was hit from behind,” Beautiful Jim wound up bitterly after the question had been repeated for about the fiftieth time. “That’s the hardest rub of all, that old Owen, who was straightforwardness and honesty itself, should have been hit from behind. But it will all come out—mark my words, it will come home yet to the hound who did it.”

“God, who is above us, grant it,” said the Chaplain, solemnly, “and rest assured Mr. Beresford, that if He does not see fit to grant it in this world, the murderer will meet with his reward in the next. ‘ *Vengeance is mine: I will repay, saith the Lord.*’”

Beautiful Jim took off his cap and bared his curly head. “Amen,” he said, solemnly, and one by one every man in the room followed his example, until the turn came to young Earle, who, with the slightest perceptible hesitation, took off his cap also, with a hand that shook so violently that he scarce could hold it.

“Amen!” said he in a voice that was hardly above a whisper—and then there was a moment’s dead silence, one of those solemn pauses in life’s journey when we seem able to hear the very hearts of those about us beat.

It was the Doctor who broke the silence.

“Tommy, my lad,” he said, with rough kindness, “all this terrible affair has sent your nerves to pieces. Did you have any breakfast this morning ? ”

Tommy shook his head, and, if possible grew yet paler and more ghastly than before.

" I couldn't touch it," he said.

" Well, I don't suppose any of us did," the Doctor returned. " I know I feel myself as if I shouldn't be able to touch food for a month. But you're such a youngster, you'll be giving way altogether if you don't eat something. Here, Simpson," addressing a man-waiter who appeared at the door at that moment, " bring Mr. Earle a glass of strong brandy and water, cold, and get him a basin of good soup or beef-tea as soon as possible."

The man departed, and in an incredibly short time appeared with the beef-tea and brandy, whereon the Doctor just stood over the lad and insisted on seeing him dispose of both.

Of course he had to do it! Doctors in general are not accustomed to stand much nonsense for a mere matter of disinclination, and it was useless for Tommy to protest that he was not hungry, that he couldn't swallow a morsel, that the brandy would be safe to go to his head, and that he would make an utter and complete fool of himself in consequence.

" Stuff and nonsense! Drink it off at once without any more argument," replied the Doctor, " if you don't, I'll just get these men to help me pour it down your throat. Why, you'd better be down-right drunk than look as you look this minute," and thus pressed, Tommy did the Doctor's bidding.

CHAPTER XIX.

SUSPICION.

PRIVATE EDWARD LEADER, batman to Mr. James Beresford, of the Blankshire Regiment, sat in the kitchen of his master's quarters looking and feeling that a more miserable devil than himself did not exist upon the face of the whole earth that day.

He was not a young man who had enjoyed the advantages of a liberal education; in truth, he could just read and write sufficiently well to be able to scrawl notes to his sweetheart, and to make out the addresses on his master's letters, but certainly not sufficiently well to trouble to make himself acquainted with the contents of the epistles which came to, and were sent off by, Mr. Beresford. Had he been a better educated young man, he might have known and felt the wisdom of a certain very sensible remark which comes to us from the Italian:—"The word that once escapes the tongue cannot be recalled: the arrow cannot be detained which has once sped from the bow;" but alas, Private Edward Leader was blessed with no wisdom of that kind, and only acquired it after the fashion of most blundering fools, by the aid of the expensive school of sad and bitter experience.

Now that the mischief was done and the effect of his blabbing tongue had passed beyond his control, he saw but too plainly the extraordinary value of silence; but it was too late—the mischief was done

—the word had escaped his tongue—the arrow had sped from the bow, and its progress could not be stopped by him who had let it fly—no, not even though it should lodge in the very heart of the one who in all the wide world least deserved it.

For, during the excitement of that fearful day on which Captain Owen was found stiff and stark in his own quarters, done to death by the dastardly hand of a murderer, Leader had, in talking over the events of the previous night with his comrades, let slip that his master and Captain Owen had had a "shindy" in Mr. Beresford's quarters immediately before dinner.

"Some'at must have 'appened to put the Captain out," said Leader, shaking his wooden head with a great air of wisdom, "for in general he's such a quiet sort—ay, dear, *was*, I mean—'pon my life, it's hard to believe that 'e's really gone."

"And they had a row?" asked one of the by-standers.

"Yes; of course, you know, I wasn't there in the room, but the Captain, 'e come up the stairs and banged into my master's room; and then I 'eard 'igh words, and at last the Captain banged out again and into his own room."

"But you don't mean to say, Leader," exclaimed another listener, "that you think Mr. Beresford did it?"

"Course not; but it looks rum that they should 'ave 'igh words that very night," returned Leader stubbornly.

Naturally, after this, it did not take very long for a rumour to spread throughout the barracks that Leader had good reason to believe that Mr. Beresford was the murderer of Captain Owen; and when the London detective, who came down from Scotland Yard to watch the case for the Owen family, appeared on the scene, almost the first information he received was an account of Leader's remarks, an account doctored and heightened in such a way that the unfortunate young man scarcely recognised his own story when he heard it again.

Poor wretch, when he realised what his blabbing tongue had done, what mischief he had wrought, he made every effort in his power to minimise the impression which he had given.

"My master murder anyone!" he exclaimed in unmitigated horror, when the detective's meaning first dawned upon him. "No, no, master, you're on a wrong scent this time. Mr. Beresford ain't one of that sort—'e ain't capable of it."

"I don't say he is, my man; but at the same time I'll trouble you to give me an account of the row that you say took place between the two gentlemen on the night of the murder," said the detective calmly.

"I never told you any row had taken place at all," returned Leader, in a vain attempt to fence the question.

"I never said you did, did I?" said the detective contemptuously. "But you told it to others, and I'll trouble you to tell it to me."

“ Then I’ll be damned if I tell you anything ! ” shouted Leader in a blind rage of fury.

And not a single word more could the detective coax or bully out of him ; and the immediate result was that Beautiful Jim was a few hours later arrested on suspicion of being the murderer of Captain Owen.

It cannot be said that Jim was half so seriously disturbed about the matter as his now abjectly-repentant servant was. He felt, with the assured consciousness of innocence, that the detective had blundered, and that close investigation would very soon set the whole matter right so far as he was concerned. It was a bore going off to the county gaol, of course, but beyond this inconvenience he did not mind very much. And before this had happened, Colonel Barnes had arrived from Blank-hampton, full of distress at the terrible tragedy, and desperately anxious that the offender should be brought to justice.

It literally took his breath away when he returned to the barracks, after transacting some business in the town, to find that Jim Beresford had been actually arrested on suspicion of being the culprit, and he hastened off to the prison at once to try if he could not see him. The Governor raised no objection, and he was at once ushered into Beautiful Jim’s presence.

“ Well, Beresford,” said he, suiting his voice and manner to the occasion, “ this is a very terrible business. I——”

"I hope it's not necessary for me to protest my innocence to you, sir," said Jim gravely.

"My dear lad, I need not say that nothing short of your own confession could make me believe you capable of an act so cowardly," said the Colonel kindly; "but at the same time, Beresford, it would be a satisfaction to me to have your positive assurance that all was right between you."

"Colonel Barnes," said Jim, solemnly holding out his hand, "I give you my word, on the honour of an officer and a gentleman, that I am absolutely innocent of this charge, and as utterly ignorant of the truth as you can be yourself."

"I believe you implicitly," said the Colonel, taking the young man's outstretched hand and gripping it hard.

"It was the greatest blow to me," Beautiful Jim went on wretchedly. "In fact, Colonel, I could scarcely believe my own eyes when I went in the next morning and found him. Oh!" with a shudder, "to think it could be poor old Owen, the best friend I ever had in all my life—the dear old chap who smoked his last pipe with me only seven or eight hours before——"

"He was with you the last thing?" the Colonel cried.

"Yes, Colonel, he generally turned into my room on his way to bed, and he did that night."

"But what is this story about you having had a quarrel with him?" the Colonel asked.

"A quarrel—with Owen—*I?*" repeated Jim, in

accents of such unmistakable astonishment that the Colonel saw an explanation was necessary, and began to make one at once.

"Yes; there's a tale going about, which I suppose accounts for your being here at all, that you and Owen had a quarrel that evening just before dinner."

"Never!" exclaimed Jim, indignantly. "Never, either then or at any other time. Owen and I never had a wrong word in our lives."

"I confess it seemed to me incredible, knowing the fast friendship which had existed between you ever since you had been in the regiment," the Colonel said; "but such is the tale, and from what I could gather during the few minutes I was in the barracks after hearing the news of your—your——"

"Arrest," put in Jim, who was too anxious to hear what the Colonel had to tell to be above calling this very unpleasant spade anything but a spade. "Yes, sir. Well?"

"I gathered," the Colonel went on, relieved about having to use the obnoxious term, "that it was your servant who set the idea afloat. It seems that he was in the kitchen just before mess that night, and saw Owen dart into your room, and heard very high words between you afterwards. He seemed to have the impression that you were quarrelling, and blurted it out after Owen was found."

"Oh, Leader's a bit of an ass," said Jim, carelessly; "but I shouldn't have thought he would have imagined I was ready to murder my best friend. Utter fool as he is, he might have known better than that."

"Leader don't think it at all, poor devil," said the Colonel promptly. "He swore through thick and thin that he had never said it, and I left him blubbering like a school-boy kept in on a cricket-match day. But I'm afraid it will prove a troublesome business; and, by-the-bye, Beresford, how could Leader have got such an idea?"

"Well, Colonel, in one way he was right enough," Jim answered. "Owen did come into my room that evening in a towering rage, but not with me, nor in any way concerning me. I can't tell you what about, as it is connected with another person who could not have been mixed up in the later events, for he was and is absolutely ignorant that Owen knew what he did know and was so affected by it, as I happened to know. Leader was right enough about there being high words, only they were not between us. In fact, it was simply that the poor old chap was full of disgust, and therefore came and poured it all out to me. Of course, all the other fellows will be able to speak to the fact that Owen and I were on the best of terms during the whole evening."

"Oh, of course, it won't hold water for a moment, Jim," said the Colonel, kindly. "It will all come right, there's not a doubt about that; only it was so unfortunate that Private Leader should have aired the idea that there were high words between you, more particularly as you say the matter about which

Owen came to you could not in any way be connected with the after events of the day."

There was a moment's silence, but then Beautiful Jim looked up at his commanding-officer, who, by-the-bye, had never called him Jim in all his life before.

"I'm very glad that you believe in me, Colonel," he said simply, "because it puts new heart into me; but I do hope that, while these fools of detectives are trying to fasten it on me, they won't let the real man slip through their fingers. I've an idea that it will all come out—a dim and confused sort of feeling that I ought to be able to put my finger on the villain, and yet, though I've been thinking and thinking night and day ever since it happened, I can't hit it."

"It will come out, never fear," said the Colonel; "and meantime, your great object must be to prove your own innocence. Better far that the poor fellow should go unavenged altogether so far as this world is concerned, than that the wrong man should suffer for it. I'm sure Owen himself would be the very first to say so, more especially as they have picked out *you* as the wrong man."

"Colonel," said Jim solemnly, "he was the best and truest friend I ever had in my life, and "— speaking slowly and clearly—" I give you my word that I would sooner suffer the worst myself, if it would ensure the murderer being brought to justice, than that his cruel death should go unpunished and unavenged."

"Hush!" said the older man imperatively, "you do not realise what you say! The issues of life and death and justice lie in higher hands than yours. 'Vengeance is mine. I will repay, saith the Lord,'" and as the words which the Chaplain had used on the previous day fell upon his ears, the hardness died out of Jim's resolute face, and he let his hands fall to his side.

"You are right, Colonel," he said humbly. "I'm unhinged and unnerved altogether. I—I—hardly know what I am saying. Don't stay here any longer, sir; you'll do me more good by looking after my interests outside."

CHAPTER XX.

THE VERDICT.

THE hour of the inquest had come, and all Walmsbury and the adjacent neighbourhood was in a state of the wildest excitement.

The great criminal lawyer who had come down from London to watch the case on behalf of Beautiful Jim, had given him as his cue two words—"absolute silence;" and upon that line his client behaved.

There was a stormy scene with one Private Leader, who swore and forswore himself until he was threatened with contempt of court, and was finally bundled unceremoniously out of it as a witness who was nothing better than an idiot; and his unwilling and confused evidence was the only evidence which bore in any way against the character of the dead man's friend, James Beresford.

On the other hand, there was the testimony of the officer commanding the regiment that since the time Captain Owen and Lieutenant Beresford had been in the Service, they had been on terms of unusual intimacy; that, on his oath, he believed they had never either quarrelled, or had any approach to a quarrel, during all the years they had been officers of his regiment, and that so far as he knew, Lieutenant Beresford had never had any quarrel or unpleasantness with any other of his brother officers.

Then came the evidence of the other officers whose quarters were on the same landing, namely, the Doctor, young Manners, and Tommy Earle.

The Doctor stated that he occupied a room overlooking the barrack-yard, and next to that of Mr. Beresford. He was, therefore, the furthest away from the room in which the murder had taken place. It was Captain Owen's invariable, or almost invariable custom to spend the last half hour of the evening in Mr. Beresford's room. He frequently joined them there, but on that evening he was very tired. He had had a dangerous case under his care for some days previously, and had not had much sleep the two nights before.

"But you were invited to enter Mr. Beresford's room?"

“Certainly.”

“And by whom?”

“Well—practically by both of them.”

“Can you give us the exact terms of the invitation?”

“Oh, yes,” answered the Doctor quietly. “I went up the stairs with Captain Owen; Mr. Beresford was immediately behind us. I said, ‘Well, I’m off to bed; good night all of you.’ Whereupon Captain Owen returned, ‘Oh! don’t go to bed yet, come in and smoke a pipe with us.’ Mr. Beresford supplemented the invitation by taking hold of my arm. ‘Yes, come in for half an hour, there’s a good chap,’ he said.”

“But you did not go?”

“I did not. I told them that I was dead tired; that I had been up the greater part of two nights with a bad case in hospital, and wanted to get to bed while I had the chance,” Dr. Foster answered. “So I bade them good night and went into my own room.”

“And that was the last time you saw Captain Owen?”

“Alive,” replied the Doctor.

“And you heard no quarrelling or any dispute between them?”

“Not a word.”

“Could any such quarrel have taken place in Lieutenant Beresford’s room without your knowledge?”

“I think not.”

“ But, being very tired, did you not fall asleep immediately? Did you go to bed at once ? ”

“ I did; but not to sleep. In fact, I heard Captain Owen go to his own room.”

“ How long after was that ? ”

“ I should say about half an hour.”

“ And they were apparently on good terms then ? ”

“ Well, I heard them laughing several times. In fact, it was their laughter which kept me awake. And then I heard the door open and Captain Owen say, ‘ Well, I daresay you’re right. Good night, old chap.’ ”

“ Did Lieutenant Beresford make any reply ? ”

“ Yes; he said ‘ Good night, old man.’ ”

“ You heard Captain Owen go to his own room ? ”

“ I did, and close the door behind him.”

“ Did you hear Lieutenant Beresford moving about his room after that ? ”

“ Yes. Well, I heard him, to the best of my belief, get into bed.”

“ How could you hear that ? ”

“ Because I heard him moving about the room precisely as I had heard him move every night for weeks past—once or twice across the floor, then one boot dropped off after the other, and then I heard his cot creak.”

“ Through the wall? ”

The Doctor smiled.

“ The walls are not particularly thick, and there is, I believe, only a lath and plaster partition between his room and mine, and as our cots stand in the same position, with only the partition between, I can hear it creak very distinctly."

"You can hear voices plainly through the partition?"

"I have often called out to Mr. Beresford from my room, and received an answer."

"And what more did you hear after you believed Lieutenant Beresford had got into bed?"

"Nothing."

"How was that?"

"I suppose because I went to sleep; at all events I heard nothing more until I was called in the morning to Captain Owen's room and found him dead."

Then followed some medical evidence and the examination of the Doctor was at an end.

Mr. Earle was called next and sworn. He haa very little to say. He deposed that he occupied the room on the other side of Mr. Beresford to that occupied by Dr. Foster. Yes, it was on the same side of the block, and overlooked the barrack-yard. He could not say whether Captain Owen and Mr. Beresford were on good terms at the time or not, as he had been at Blankhampton and only reached Walmsbury late in the evening. He had been present in the ante-room about half an hour before they all retired for the night. Was rather tired and had not especially noticed either officer.

At this point Dr. Foster was re-called.

"Did you hear any dispute between Captain

Owen and Lieutenant Beresford immediately before dinner ? "

" Not a dispute.   I heard them talking."

" Were they talking loudly ? "

" Captain Owen was speaking rather loudly; but as I heard Mr. Beresford laugh more than once, it did not occur to me that they were quarrelling."

" Thank you, that will do," and the Doctor stood down again.

Then young Manners was put up, but he had less even to say than any of the others. Apparently he had noticed nothing and suspected nothing, and he had got into bed as soon as he went to his room, and he had gone to sleep immediately.

Yes, he had noticed, while in the ante-room after dinner, that Captain Owen and Mr. Beresford kept pretty close together, and that they were laughing a good deal at some joke between them. Yes, he saw them go upstairs as Dr. Foster had described, and he saw Captain Owen go in Mr. Beresford's room.   He had never heard of Mr. Beresford's having a quarrel with anyone in the regiment— he was a great favourite.   He (the witness) had not been quite a year in the service.

There was a moment's pause in the proceedings, and then the name of Lieutenant Beresford was called, and Jim stood up.

" You are a lieutenant in the Blankshire Regiment ? "

" I am."

" What length of service have you ? "

" Eight years."

" The deceased was in the regiment when you joined it ? "

" Yes ; he was."

" You and he became friendly very soon ? "

" Yes ; he was my best friend."

" You are on friendly terms with all your brother officers ? "

" Yes ; and I have always been so."

" You have never had any quarrel or misunderstanding with a brother officer ? "

" Never."

" When the deceased came into your quarters before dinner, did any dispute arise between you ? "

" No."

" He was very angry about something ? "

" He was *annoyed*," emphasizing the last word.

" With you ? "

" Oh ! no.   He was never either angry or annoyed with me in all his life."

" What was he annoyed about ? "

" I am not at liberty to say."

" You must answer the question."

" I cannot.   It was an official annoyance, about a person not in Walmsbury or very near Walmsbury at the time, and who could not possibly have been in any way connected with Captain Owen's murder."

" How was that ? "

" Because that person never knew, and to the

best of my belief does not know now, that Captain Owen had any cause for annoyance."

" And you say it was not a personal matter ? "

" Not in the very least."

" Then why cannot you disclose the particulars ? "

" Because they were given to me in confidence, and I decline to break it."

" Did Captain Owen say where he had been during the afternoon ? "

At this point Beautiful Jim raised his honest eyes and beheld staring at him, with the fascinated gaze of a bird attracted by a snake, the girl who was barmaid at the Duck's Tail; her small sharp features were strained and anxious, her dark skin was of a greenish pallor, which contrasted horribly with her profuse and unnaturally golden hair. Jim looked at her steadily for a moment and then turned his attention back to his questioner.

" Yes ; he had been into Walmsbury."

" Did he tell you where ? "

" Yes ; he went to the Duck's Tail."

" The Duck's Tail ? What to do there ? "

" To get the address of a horse-dealer, who had been recommended by Major Whittaker."

" Did he get it ? "

" I don't know ; he did not say."

" Was the annoyance connected with this horse-dealer ? "

" Not in the very least."

Then there followed a long and close examination on the after events of that day and evening, to all of which Jim returned answers precisely corroborating the evidence which had gone before. Then at last he was told to stand aside, and the name of Rose Meeking was called.

Somewhat to Jim's surprise, Rose Meeking proved to be the sharp-visaged young person from the Duck's Tail; and, if fright was any sign of guilt, Miss Meeking must have had the credit of being very guilty indeed.

She deposed that rather late in the afternoon Captain Owen had come into the bar of the Duck's Tail. There was no one else there. She did not know the exact time, but the landlord and the family were at tea. She was busy tidying up the bar for the evening. She always did that the last thing before she went to her tea.

Captain Owen enquired the address of a certain horse-dealer, a Mr. Johns. She knew Mr. Johns's address and gave it to him. She also told him that Mr. Johns had been in the hotel that morning and had gone up to London for two or three days, upon which Captain Owen remarked that it was no use his writing or going to him for a week or so. Captain Owen stayed a short time, talking to her about other things, and then left. She did not know which way he went. There was no one else in the bar during the time he was there.

She was then asked whether Captain Owen had often been in the hotel before, and whether she knew him at all intimately ?

And to this she replied that she had never seen

him in the hotel but once before, when he had not
spoken to her. The day of the murder was the first
time she had ever had any conversation with him.
She was not the least intimate with him. No, he
had not shown the smallest wish to be intimate with
her.

After this, Miss Rose Meeking was put down, and
several minor witnesses were put up, from none of
whom could any evidence worth mentioning be ex-
tracted. There were various officers' servants, and
the men who had been on duty that night, two
mess waiters and the gentlemen who had been
guests at the mess-table. If their united evidence
was worth anything, it was towards clearing Jim
Beresford of the suspicion which Leader's unfortunately long tongue had caused to rise up against
him ; and then they all sat down to await, with what
patience they might, the decision at which the jury
would eventually arrive.

"You are safe enough," said the great criminal
lawyer to Jim. "There's not a jot of evidence
against you."

" I have never been afraid there would be," said
Jim coolly.

And presently the jury were ready with their
verdict, and, amid a breathless hush, it was given
to the public—when it is safe to say that the only
person in that assembly who did not tremble was
the one on whom the darkest suspicion had fallen,
Beautiful Jim. While the eyes of all were dimmed
with fear of what the next moment might bring

forth, he stood up in his place straight and true, and awaited the verdict with the assurance of complete innocence. And the decision of the jury was :—

"Wilful murder against some person or persons unknown."

And, oh! what a cheer burst out then, and how they all—or nearly all—pressed forward to take Jim by the hand and tell him that they had never, never believed him guilty for a moment. And then poor Leader came, shaking and pale as a ghost, to tell him if they had given a verdict against him he should have gone out and hanged himself like Judas; and then when Jim, with rough kindness, told him not to talk rot but to get back to barracks, he burst out sobbing like a great baby and cursed himself for a blubbering fool, who had risked the neck of the best master man had ever served under.

But it was all very delightful, nevertheless, to Beautiful Jim. It is easy and well to make little of a danger when it is over; yet this danger had been very real while it had lasted, and more than once Jim, in spite of his innocence, had caught himself furtively stroking his throat and wondering what the feel of the rope would be like, if it should come to that! Oh! without doubt it was very very pleasant to be free once more.

On account of the dead man still lying in the room above the mess-room, who had been so great a favourite with them all, there were no open demonstrations of satisfaction and joy at Beautiful Jim's release that evening. But immediately after dinner the Colonel filled his glass to the brim, and turning to Jim, who sat in the place of honour beside him, drank to him in silence, an example which was followed by every other man at the table in turn.

"By-the-bye, where is young Tommy?" asked Jim, suddenly becoming aware that Tommy was not in the room.

"Gone to bed, or in his room. Seedy, I fancy," returned the Doctor, who sat on his left. "The young duffer's not up to much; he's just about as weak as a cat. In fact, there's no stamina at all about him, and all this business has knocked him over completely."

"H'm—there's no reason why it should particularly," remarked Jim.

"No; but it has, and that's very certain," said the Doctor decidedly.

Suddenly it occurred to him that it was just possible that young Tommy might have been down to see his charmer at the Duck's Tail; that that young lady, feeling herself released from silence by poor dear old Owen's death, might have disclosed to him the episode of the afternoon, when Owen had coolly taken possession of his ring. Further, that Tommy might all this time be in a mortal funk lest his well-known ring should be found among poor Owen's belongings, and some very unpleasant enquiries be set afloat in consequence.

"I should think the sight of that beauty in the

witness-box to-day must have cured him completely," Jim thought, with a certain amount of compassion for the lad's foolishness. "Well, I must go up as soon as I can get off and talk to him like a father; and then I'll set his mind at rest about his precious ring."

Accordingly, as soon as he could get free of the Colonel's ponderous efforts to show his pleasure at his favourite's freedom, Beautiful Jim betook himself upstairs, his eyes turning with a look which was in itself a reverence to the door before which two sentries were stationed, and with a rap upon the panel of Tommy's door, opened it without further ceremony and walked in.

The lad was sitting in an easy chair, his pipe in his mouth, his elbows resting on his knees, staring into the fire. He looked up listlessly enough at Jim's entrance, but when he saw who his visitor was, sprang up into an attitude of haughty resentment.

"To what," he asked, "do I owe *the honour* of this visit?"

CHAPTER XXI.

"YOU WON'T TELL HIM?"

"To what," asked Tommy Earle, with icy formality and politeness, "do I owe *honour* of this visit?"

For the space of quite a minute Beautiful Jim stood still and stared blankly at him, as if he had not understood the meaning of his words. At last, however, he pulled himself together, and spoke. " What on earth do you mean ? " he asked.

" Exactly what I say," returned Tommy Earle, curtly.

Most men would have grown furious under such an attack from a lad of Tommy's years and regimental standing; but Beautiful Jim, just freed from the shadow of a violent and ignominious death, with the weight of his best friend's cruel murder still pressing upon him, did not lose his temper in the least—on the contrary, he became perfectly calm and still.

" Tommy," he began—when Tommy interrupted him passionately.

" Earle, if you please, sir," he cried.

" *Mister* Earle," said Jim with a half smile, and strong emphasis on the word. " Tell me plainly what you mean by this extraordinary behaviour."

" The inference is obvious," said Tommy coldly.

" Yes," in an enquiring tone—then finding that the lad did not speak, went on—" and I am to infer ——what ? " but even as the question passed his lips the full light broke in upon him, and he grasped Tommy by the arm with a grip that made him wince and shrink.

" My God, do you mean to say that you believe *I* murdered him ? " he cried.

Tommy turned away his head and tried to force his arm from the grip of the other's strong fingers.

" Answer me ! " thundered Jim.

" Let go my arm and go out of my room, if you please, Mr. Beresford," returned the lad.

But Jim stood still and stared straight into the lad's handsome eyes, as if he would force out of them the plain words which apparently Tommy's tongue refused to speak; and as they stood so, an awful thought flashed into Beautiful Jim's bewildered mind—a confused recollection of something gone by, something like a dream, and yet, oh ! what was it ? What was it ? A memory crowded over by the mist of intense drowsiness; and yet, if he could only grasp it, a memory that had something so utterly real and vivid about it that it would show the whole truth to the light at once.   But what was it ?

Aye, what was it ? And what was there in young Earle's eyes which gave him the clue he sought ? I know not, and assuredly Beautiful Jim, to the end of his days, would never know it either ; but during those terrible moments of doubt and anguish the mists were suddenly lifted off his mind, and he remembered—remembered the dream he had had *that* night, a dream of Owen, his dear old friend, being in anger with him, and the momentous words, " *Consider yourself under close arrest. Go to your room at once and I will send for your sword.*"   In an instant everything was perfectly clear to him, and he gripped young Tommy's arms closer and faster than ever.

" You—young—hound !" he exclaimed, between his set teeth. " I suppose you mean to come your ' last-of-the-Earles ' rot over me in this instance.

The last of the Earles, and a pretty ending for the Earles—to be snuffed out by the hangman's rope!"

Young Tommy's white face turned to a sickly yellow, and Jim felt a tremor run through him.

"What do you mean, sir," he cried, trying to pass it off with a high hand and succeeding very badly.

"I mean that *you—you* murdered Owen, and I know it—you dastardly young hound; and you tried to fasten it on me—you scoundrel!" and forthwith Beautiful Jim set to work and shook the lad, much as a terrier shakes a rat and with as little mercy, until in fact the teeth seemed to rattle in his head, and his very knees seemed to knock together. Then, with a last burst of fury, he flung him from him into the big chair, where he lay gasping and livid, more like a limp rag than a smart young officer—to say nothing at all of his being the last of the Earles.

But even then he did not altogether give in. "You shall answer for this!" he panted.

"Answer for it!" echoed Jim, with mighty scorn. "Yes, by the Heavens above us, I will answer for it. I will answer *you*, you damnable cowardly hound. I say you murdered Owen, murdered him in cold blood, you struck him from behind. I have the most convincing proofs against you. I have only to disclose the subject of Owen's conversation with me that afternoon, and to show the ring that he insisted on having from that woman, to put the rope round your neck without a chance of escape."

" Ring ! " gasped Tommy, in a different tone. " What ring ? What woman ? "

" *What* ring ? *What* woman ? " Jim repeated in disgust. " Do you come that humbug over me still ? Then, *Mister* Earle, I will enlighten you. I mean the sapphire and diamond ring, engraved with your family crest and motto, which you gave as a pledge of affection to that sharp-nosed little hussey at the Duck's Tail ! Ah !—You know what ring I mean, do you ? " as a groan of **utter** and abject despair burst from the lad's lips.

Jim went on without mercy—" Now, I see it all —all. You went to see that woman on your way back to barracks from Blankhampton, and she— like the double-faced, designing little jade she is— told you Owen had been there, that he had seen the ring on her hand and insisted on her giving it up. Then you came back and bided your time, and after Owen left my room, you followed him to his. And then, you came your ' last-of-the-Earles ' air with him and demanded your ring, and Owen refused to give it to you until he had communicated with your father——"

" He did not," broke in Tommy eagerly.

" Ah ! those were not the precise words, I dare say," said Jim, carelessly, " but I can give you the precise words which were the last the dear old chap ever spoke—they were these : ' *Consider yourself under close arrest. Go to your room at once and I will send for your sword !'* and then," said Beautiful Jim, speaking very slowly and distinctly, " you—went—back—*and killed him !*"

The lad had been lying helplessly back in the big chair, staring at Jim with a fascination piteous to behold, but as the last words fell upon his ears he sprang up, trembling in every limb.

"I never meant to do it—never—I swear it! I had no thought of harming him; it was done in blind rage; it was, indeed."

"H'm. Was it blind rage which prompted you to try and palm off your dastardly cowardice upon me?" Jim demanded, contemptuously. "Was *that* blind rage?"

"I have been mad ever since," replied the lad abjectly. "God above only knows how and what I have suffered. I have not known what I've been doing. I haven't, indeed."

"Ah! there's been a good deal of method in your madness, though," returned Jim in disgust.

"But, Beresford—Jim——" Tommy began, when the other interrupted him sharply.

"Jim to my friends only—Beresford to my equals," he said curtly. "To you, now and for always, Mr. Beresford, if you please."

The miserable lad made no reply, but he hid his face upon his arms, shivering and shrinking away from the blaze of his comrade's righteous indignation. What a contrast they made, the two; the one so straight and strong and honest, the other so wretched, so pitiable, a miserable, guilty thing, driven up in a corner, without even strength to stand at bay.

At last he looked up. " What are you going to do ? " he asked hoarsely.

" Do ? " Jim repeated. " Why, what should I do but tell the Colonel the whole truth at once."

Young Tommy shuddered and buried his face in his arms once more. " They will hang me," he moaned.

" And a good thing too," returned Jim coolly. " The sooner the better, before you have time to do any more mischief. And one thing is very certain, which is that you'll thoroughly deserve it."

" No, no ! " Tommy cried. " My family; my father. Oh ! no, no, Beresford, don't hang me,—for the sake of my name, don't ! "

" And what the devil has your name to do with it ? " Jim returned roughly. " Did the fact that you are the last of the Earles keep you from compromising yourself with a little slut that you knew your father would have died rather than receive as his daughter ? Did being the last of the Earles keep your hand from murder ? Did it keep you from trying to fasten the blame of that murder upon an innocent man ? No ; don't talk to me about your family. Show me something your family has done for you before you expect that claim to have any weight with me. No, 'pon my soul, when a long and honourable name comes to an end with such an infernal young scoundrel as you are, the sooner it is blotted out altogether the better."

12—2

"I never meant to kill him," Tommy protested, shrinking over the word as if the word was really more than the thing. "I had no such thought in my mind. I hadn't, Beresford, upon my honour."

"Your—— *what?*" asked Jim, in genuine amazement.

The lad turned scarlet. "You think I haven't any honour," he said bitterly. "Well, I suppose I've forfeited any right to that for ever. Anyway, you may believe me or not, as you like, but I'll tell the whole truth. I had no thought or intention of harming Owen in the least, but I was furious at his interference with a matter which did not in the least concern him; and Owen was frightfully sarcastic and bitter about the whole affair. If he had spoken to me reasonably, and told me I was a young ass, I should have seen the justice of what he said. But he didn't—he jibed and jeered at me; taunted me with my youth, my family, my general idiocy; and I couldn't get back my ring. No; he meant to keep the ring until he saw my father; and he swore that nothing should induce him to keep quiet about it. I had disgraced my name, he said, and myself and the regiment, and everything and everybody connected with me, and my father should know about it at once. And, of course, I was frightfully angry about it, for it isn't pleasant to have one's doings canvassed over to one's father; and I daresay I did answer pretty cavalierly—in fact, I believe I told him to go to the devil. Anyway, he put me under arrest, and—and—and then I went back and chucked that dumb-bell at him; but, Beresford, upon my soul, as sure as I am alive this moment, I had no thought of doing him a serious injury, let alone of taking his life; I had not, indeed. I was just blind with rage. I didn't know what I was doing."

"You were not blind with rage when I came in here to-night," said Beautiful Jim, who was not in the smallest degree moved by the lad's story, though he implicitly believed every word of it.

"I was worse than that, I was desperate," Tommy answered humbly. "I—don't——," and then all at once he gave way entirely and broke down into violent weeping.

And Beautiful Jim stood looking at him, at the convulsively shaking shoulders and the fair, lovely head, so like *hers*—the one who did not count, but the one who was all the world to him. It was with an awful shock he realised that the news must reach her sooner or later; that, young scoundrel as he was, he was *her* brother, and if disgrace touched him, it would of necessity touch her also.

Quick as thought his mind put into ideas all that would happen—he saw the almost certain death of the frail old man, bearing his good old name with honour to the last, but crushed completely beneath the shame and degradation of his son's end; he saw Nancy, with her pure, noble mind and her sweet dove's eyes, left alone, quite alone—for he knew that even for justice tender Nancy would never forget that his had been the hand to bring him to punishment. "And, oh! God forgive me—Owen, dear old friend, forgive me," his heart cried within him. "I *cannot* be the one to break her heart—I cannot do it."

He knew that it was wrong, he felt that it was weak, he felt that it was little short of madness to leave himself under even the faint shadow of suspicion which still hung over him, and which might, and probably would, cling to him as long as he should live; and yet he could not force himself to follow a course which, under any other circumstances, probably he would have followed— that of simply laying the whole story before his commanding-officer, and leaving him to do what he thought best in the matter. No, he had practically no choice—either he must shut his eyes to the suffering which the exposure of Tommy's guilt would bring upon two innocent persons, give up all hope of ever being anything to the girl he loved, or he must lock this dreadful secret in his breast and trust to time and chance concealing it for ever.

But was this *a choice?* Scarcely! His heart and soul were wrapped up in Nancy Earle. She was the one woman that the world held for him. No, there was no choice about the matter. The vision of Nancy decided the question, and the wretched, sobbing, craven-hearted lad in the big chair was safe—or if not actually safe, he was safe, at least, from Beautiful Jim's vengeance.

Having once come to a decision, Jim was not the man to let the grass grow under his feet. There

was much to be done, for if Tommy was to be
shielded he must be shielded effectually. " Here,
stop that howling, you miserable young cur," he
said, breaking the silence at last, and speaking in a
sharp, authoritative tone. He had any amount of
the tenderest and most touching pity for Nancy ;
but for the boy, none. He would let him, for his
sister's sake, go scot free, but he was troubled by no
sickly sentimentality about the lad's abject terror
and expressions of sorrow. " Quite right if the young
devil does feel it," he told himself as he watched
Tommy's efforts to regain composure ; " I hope he'll
go on feeling the same way for the rest of his life.
I sincerely hope it."

" Come ! What good do you think that will
do ? " he demanded roughly. " I'm not going to
expose you, though I tell you candidly, if there was
no one but yourself to think of, I should have called
for the Colonel long before this. But there are
others to think of besides yourself ; there's your
family—no, I don't mean the family pedigree that
you are so fond of bragging about, but your old
father, and the sister who has had to play second
fiddle to you all her life—the Earle that doesn't
count. Just you remember, will you, that it's for
her sake I do you this service, not in the very
smallest degree for your own."

By an immense effort, Tommy pulled himself
together and looked up at Jim. And Jim thought
that a more pitiable object than the lad's white and
haggard face, with its wild and staring eyes, he had

never seen. He strode to the door, and turned the key in the lock.

"Look here, youngster," he said sharply; "this sort of thing won't do! If the truth has to be kept between you and me you must manage to pull yourself together and hide your feelings a bit better. The best thing for you to do is to get a stiff glass of brandy and tumble into bed at once. And then the sooner you get out of Walmsbury the better."

"But I *can't* get out of Walmsbury," Tommy exclaimed fretfully.

"You get to bed, as I tell you," returned Jim. "I'll manage that—I'll speak to the Colonel about it."

"But you won't tell him, Beresford?"

"Tell him *what?*" contemptuously. "Get to bed, and stop there. Foster is impressed with the fact that you are seedy, and you had better keep it up—it will simplify matters. Besides, you cannot go to the funeral to-morrow—I couldn't quite stand that." He turned to leave the room then, and Tommy followed him a step or so with an eager expression of gratitude on his lips. Beautiful Jim, however, promptly cut that proceeding very short.

"Look here," he said. "You had better understand clearly from the beginning that I am not doing this in any way for you. If there was no one but you to think of, I would very cheerfully see you hanged to-morrow. You richly deserve it. But there happen to be others to be thought of, and I think of them—it's lucky for you that it is so, perhaps, though being such a thorough-paced young scoundrel as you are, I don't know whether hanging would not be the best thing that could happen to you." With these words Beautiful Jim went out of the room and, as the night was yet young, down into the ante-room again.

As for Tommy, he sat down before the fire again and thought it all over; but his first thought was —"I always did dislike the fellow—I hate him now."

CHAPTER XXII.

A PAINFUL HOUR.

THE Colonel, who was staying at a hotel in Walmsbury, had betaken himself away from the ante-room by the time Beautiful Jim returned to it, so for that night he could do nothing further to promote the scheme he had prepared for getting Tommy Earle sent back to headquarters. Therefore he had to wait until ten o'clock in the morning, when Colonel Barnes arrived in barracks.

The funeral was arranged to leave the door of the officers' quarters at two in the afternoon, so as soon as the Colonel appeared, Beautiful Jim went into the office with him and asked him for ten minutes' private conversation before he saw any of the others.

" Certainly, Jim, certainly," said the Colonel kindly. " Now, tell me, what is it ? "

" Well, sir," said Jim, gravely, " young Earle

won't be able to go to the funeral—he's ill in bed,
but of course the Doctor will tell you about that.
Still, I wanted to speak to you about him. The lad
is ill—in fact, he's been ill and unlike himself ever
since we came here. The place does not suit him,
physically or morally, and I am perfectly certain if
he remains here he will go to the dogs, nothing
else."

"But I don't quite understand," said the Colonel,
looking puzzled.

"No, sir, but I'll explain," said Jim. "It's just
here. Young Earle is very young as yet, his mind
is of the smallest, and the lack of society in this
place is driving him to seek society that will be the
ruin of him. In short, he has got mixed up with a
very dangerous designing sort of woman, and if I
could induce you to get him away out of this it will
be the salvation of him, nothing less. Owen, poor
fellow, was very anxious about this, and almost the
last thing he said to me was that he should try to
get you to transfer him back to headquarters."

"Was *that* the subject of conversation which you
would not disclose?" the Colonel asked.

Beautiful Jim hesitated for a moment. "Well,
sir, frankly, it was. I thought it best to keep it to
myself, because I was certain that the lad did
not know that Owen had found out what was
going on, and it seemed hardly fair to him to
tell it."

"I understand. I will respect your wishes," the
Colonel said hastily.

" Thank you, sir," said Jim. "Apart from the fact that this woman will certainly marry him if she gets the chance, or, rather, if she does not find herself circumvented by us, Walmsbury is about the worst place in the world for a lad of his temperament. With proper bringing up he might have been, and probably would have been, a very fine fellow; but he has not been properly brought up, —quite the contrary in fact. He's the last of a good old family and the child of his father's old age, and in consequence has been taught from his cradle to think himself a young god—nothing short of it. Now the lad isn't a young god; he's a very ordinary addle-headed young ass—as you saw for yourself, sir, the night he first dined with us—as full of self-importance and conceit as it's possible to be. Therefore apart from this entanglement, this is a very bad atmosphere for him to be in; he is a most important person, and being only one of four men practically isolated—for there is literally no society here, and I fancy the people hereabout look upon us as so much dirt than otherwise—he is able to give his opinion far more freely than is good for him. Now, with the regiment he is scarcely able to open his mouth at all, he is regularly at school, and a pretty sharp one too, and is made every hour to feel himself to be not of the very smallest importance whatever."

" Well, I'll see what I can do about it," said the Colonel.

There was not much sympathy in his tone; but then, as Beautiful Jim knew, he did not particularly like Tommy, and when Colonel Barnes did not like a person he was never very gracious.

"I suppose," said the Colonel, after a moment's silence, "that you would like to go back to head-quarters yourself, Beresford?"

"Just as you like, sir," answered Jim indifferently. "It is pretty much all the same to me. *I* shall not get entangled in Walmsbury, and though of course the place *is* dull, one place is very much the same as another to me. But when all this terrible affair is over, sir, I should like a few days' leave. I should indeed."

"That is easily managed," returned the Colonel kindly—then hesitated, stammered a little, opened his mouth as if to speak, and flushed scarlet under his bronzed skin—"Er—the—the—er—well, my dear boy, the fact is I—I thought perhaps after all that has happened—the—the mistake of your arrest and all that, you might find it a little painful to—to remain here."

"Not a bit, sir," said Jim promptly. "It will be painful to me ever to think about Owen, no matter what part of the world I might be in, for he was the best friend I ever had in my life; but about the matter of arresting me—well, the police thought they had a clue, and they were quite right to follow it up. I am not at all tender on that point, sir, I assure you; and besides, everybody who knows me, who knew what friends he and I were, would laugh outright at the idea that I could have murdered him."

" Very well.   We will see—we will see," said the
Colonel, in a tone which signified that the interview
was at an end.

So far as poor Owen was concerned the day was
soon over.   At two o'clock precisely the sad procession left the officers' quarters, and went slowly
towards the cemetery on the outskirts of the town.
The coffin was carried on a gun-carriage and the pall
held by officers of the dead man's regiment, Colonel
Barnes being on one side and Beautiful Jim on the
other.   In front was the band—or the greater part
of it—which had come over from Blankhampton,
and behind were the mourners, all members of
Captain Owen's family.

These last had been especially demonstrative to
Jim Beresford, showing him by every means in their
power that they had no part whatever in the suspicion which for a few hours had been cast upon him.

" It is very good of you to meet me like this, sir,"
Jim said to his dead friend's father, when that old
gentleman held out his hand before everyone
assembled in the ante-room, and shook it heartily.

" All I can do for my poor lad now is to stand by
his friend," returned the old man sadly.

" Thank you, sir," said Jim, gratefully.   " I shall
never forget that you did stand by me, never."

And then they had to take their places and the
sad procession started on its way, to crawl at a foot's
pace through the crowded streets, with arms reversed
and the band playing the mournful strains of the
Dead March, while hundreds of eager heads were

pressed forward to get a glimpse of Jim as he paced first on the left of the gun carriage, and to point Jim out as " him as was took up for it, you know, but they couldn't prove naught again him." It was a painful hour, but Jim held his head up high and straight, and bore himself like the brave soldierly gentleman that he was.

" I'll never believe that he did it," cried a woman in the crowd at the grave side. " If he'd had a hand in sending the poor chap there, he could never have looked into the grave so sad and sorrowful as he did. No, I'll never believe it of him."

" Well, he's not clear of it yet, and won't be until something more is found out about it," was the answer of her companion.

And then the service came to an end, and the last volleys were fired over the open grave of one who had been a universal favourite among his fellows.

So they turned away and left him to his quiet sleep for ever, marching away with brisk and jaunty steps to that smooth and swinging air, which has jarred so often on hearts harrowed by a great and irreparable loss.

> Love not—love not,
> The thing you love may die.

CHAPTER XXIII.

TEN DAYS' LEAVE.

As soon as Beautiful Jim had a spare hour to himself he went down to the Duck's Tail and asked for the landlord, who came to him, looking a little frightened.

"Mr. Brown," said Jim, going straight to the point at once, "I want to have ten minutes' private conversation with Miss Meeking. Have you any objection to it?"

"Not the least in the world, sir," returned Mr. Brown, civilly, "and, perhaps, Mr. Beresford, you won't be offended if I make so bold as to say I never was so pleased in my life as I was when the jury gave their verdict—never."

"That's very kind of you, Mr. Brown," said Jim, and forthwith held out his hand to him. "And now if you can let me see Miss Meeking for ten minutes, I shall be more than obliged."

"You shall, sir," said Mr. Brown, and immediately hurried away to carry Jim's wish into effect.

In the course of a minute or two the barmaid appeared, evidently in almost as great a fright as she had been on the day of the inquest.

"Good day," said Jim, civilly—"er—do you mind shutting the door?"

Miss Meeking shut the door and advanced very slowly and unwillingly towards the fire-place, keeping her terrified eyes fixed on Jim the while.

Jim handed her a chair. "You had better sit down, had you not?" he said in the same civil tone. "I shall not keep you long, but you look ill. You had better sit down."

Miss Meeking sat down. Jim, on the contrary,

stood up with his back to the fire; there was a moment's silence.

"You are perhaps a little surprised at my wishing to see you"—Jim began—"and I daresay you will be more surprised still when you have heard what I have to say to you. I wanted, however, to see you about the evidence you gave at the inquest the other day."

"What about it? I told all I knew," the barmaid flashed out.

"Excuse me," said Jim, very politely—"but you did nothing of the kind—you told very little and, as it happens, you know a great deal."

Miss Meeking started up from her chair, but Jim motioned to her to sit down, motioned with a gesture so imperative that she was compelled to obey.

"You did not tell the truth, Miss Meeking," said he severely, "and, though it is possible you do not know it, they call false evidence by the ugly name of perjury."

"And what did I say false?" She framed the words with her pallid and trembling lips rather than spoke them.

"You implied a great deal. You suppressed all that passed between you and Captain Owen about a ring you were wearing at the time. You did not tell the jury that you had given your word to Captain Owen that you would have nothing more to do with Mr. Earle, or that the self-same night you broke your word, while it was almost yet in your mouth, and actually told Mr. Earle what sent him straight back to barracks in a blind passion, and——"

"Sir," said she, rising and going towards him, "as there is a God in Heaven above us I did not break my word at all. I told him—Tom, that is—that I'd have no more to do with him, that I'd seen how set against a marriage his people would be, and how it would be the ruin of him. I told him his father would never overlook it or receive me, and that we couldn't be married without his father, for we couldn't live on nothing. And then, Tom went into a fury—poor boy, he is that passionate—and asked for the ring. So I had to out and tell him that I'd given it to Captain Owen, and that he could get it from him. And with that he just cursed me and Captain Owen too, and went, and I never saw him again till I saw him at the inquest."

"Is that true?" Jim asked searchingly.

"True as that God is above us," Rose Meeking answered solemnly. "Mr. Beresford, I've no idea of his going back and murdering him, and if I shielded him it was because I believed in my heart the poor lad was beside himself when he did it."

"And supposing that suspicion had grown against me?" said Jim. "Would you have shielded him at the cost of my life?"

"No, Mr. Beresford, I would not. If you had not been cleared that day, I should have given him the chance of getting away, and then I should have spoke out. It was that that made me so nervous and frightened before the jury. I was terrified lest I should clear one at the expense of the other."

"But do you know that I am *not* clear ? " said Jim, gravely. "So long as this mystery remains, I may be brought up again at any time and charged with my friend's murder."

"I should speak for you in that case, Mr. Beresford," said the barmaid with dignity.

"Miss Meeking," said Jim, "I have done you a wrong. You're a better woman than I thought you."

The barmaid breathed a sigh of relief. "I'm glad you think so, Mr. Beresford. I've been nearly out of my mind the last few days, for it's one thing to have a handsome young fellow making love to you, and it's quite another to have murder on your mind. I've never been mixed up in anything of the sort before, and it's what I've no liking for, I can tell you."

"Nor I," returned Jim, with sympathy.

"Then, Mr. Beresford," said Miss Meeking, as he moved to the table where he had laid his hat and stick, "I suppose you are not going to tell of this poor lad ? "

"Miss Meeking," said Jim promptly, "so far as the poor lad is concerned, I have neither feeling nor pity. I would willingly see him hanged to-morrow, for I think he richly deserves it. It is very well for you to excuse him by saying that he did not know what he was doing, that he was not himself when he did it, and for him to say he was in a blind passion and never meant it. On your part it's a mistake, but on his it's a lie. If I had suspected on the day of the inquest what I *know* now, nothing on earth, not even the considerations which will keep me silent now, would have induced me not to disclose the subject of that conversation between Captain Owen and myself (which was a full account of his interview with you, and his annoyance at Mr. Earle's proceedings). As it happened, he left the ring with me, and I have it now, so that I have but to speak the word to put the rope about the young scoundrel's neck. As I tell you, if it were only for him I would not hesitate; on the contrary, I should do everything to help the law. But when I declined to speak, it was because I did not believe he could have had anything to do with the matter, and it was only last night that I discovered the truth. Yet, although he persists that he was in what he calls a blind passion, and did not know what he was about, even last night he tried to my face to make me believe that he thought me guilty of this horrible crime, and it was only by the merest chance that I happened to be able to unmask him."

"Then why do you spare him?" asked the barmaid, in a tone of genuine wonder.

"Because there are others to think of. His father is a very old man, infirm, and in bad health. Such a blow would be his death. His people are all very good, and would be crushed for ever by a shame so horrible; he has a sister who is an angel, who has always been taught to stand aside because he is the boy, the heir, the last of the name. It is for the sake of these and these alone that I mean to keep silent, though I know that I ought to speak."

" It's good of you," said the barmaid admiringly, " for it will cost you a good deal, I've no doubt. I'm afraid, Mr. Beresford, that you'll find a good many people who'll be ready and willing to throw it at you —the murder, I mean. But I hope you and the young lady will be happy. Oh! yes, I guessed at once. I hope she'll never know it, poor thing, I'm sure."

"Miss Meeking," said Jim, "you have my best wishes for the future. I will write to you by-and-bye, when matters are a little more settled, and if I send you a little present, in return for your straight-forwardness to me this afternoon, I hope you won't refuse it."

" Indeed I won't, Mr. Beresford," she said, quickly.

" And if ever there is anything I can do for you, be sure I shall be ready to do it," Jim went on, and then he held out his hand and she laid hers in it. " And I needn't say, need I, that I'm very sorry I misjudged you at first."

" Not a word," said the barmaid, heartily. And then they shook hands again, and they parted. How relieved he was it would be hard to tell. Of course he knew that he ought in strict justice to go and tell the Colonel everything, and simply leave Tommy to his well-deserved fate. But he had taken the wrong upon his own conscience for *her*—for her and the old man who was so proud of his good old name and his own unstained honour.

For the old man's sake? Ah! and not out of much consideration for him, for was it not all for the sake of one who was only a girl, the Earle who did not count?   Assuredly, yes.

It was not many days before young Tommy Earle was ordered to return to headquarters, and another officer came to take his place; also one of the senior subalterns came to relieve Beautiful Jim, who was to return to headquarters, and one Captain Moore came to take up command of the detachment

And as soon as Jim found himself once more in Blankhampton, the Colonel told him that he could have ten days' leave at any time that he liked. Naturally enough, he replied that he would like to have it at once, for, in the course of his conversations with Tommy he had elicited the fact that his father and sister had returned to England, and were in truth at their town house at that very time.

Therefore, Beautiful Jim packed up his traps—or had them packed up, which amounts to the same thing—and took himself off to London Town, there to see the lady of his love. In his excitement he almost forgot the dread secret which he carried about with him—I say *almost*, because night or day he never could altogether put it out of his mind, for with the return to headquarters he had found less relief from it than he had hoped; there were so may things to remind him there of the friend he had lost—the barracks themselves, the familiar figure in his quarters, the roads and houses and shops, all reminded him so forcibly of him who had been there when he saw them last, but who would never be with him there or elsewhere any more. It was a painful coming back, and Beautiful Jim was heartily glad to get off to London, where the associations and remembrances would be far more few than in any place where they had been quartered together.

The journey to London seemed to him a terribly long one, although the train by which he went was the fastest express in the kingdom; but to Jim's impatient heart it seemed to crawl, although when he reached the terminus he found that they were in to the minute, and that his watch had neither gained nor lost. And then, being nearly eight o'clock in the evening, he had to wait until morning before he could venture to show himself at the house of his divinity. First he had to think of his dinner, after which, for the sake of killing time, he dressed himself and went out—very late—and what he called " looked in " at the Savoy Theatre. He had some sort of vain hope that *she* might be there—but she was not. He was lucky enough to get a stall, the only one vacant, and scanned the house narrowly, but alas, there was no such lovely saint's face and dove's eyes as hers, although there were lovely women in the audience by the dozen.

So he went back to his hotel and straight to bed, only because the sooner he got to sleep the nearer he would seem to morning and to *her*. And in the morning, ridiculously early, that is to say between eleven and twelve, he started off to Hans Place, and

was told that Miss Earle was at home. Better still
she was alone, and best of all there was a something
in her face and manner as she rose to greet him
which made Beautiful Jim forget all ceremony and
take her in his arms. "Oh, my darling, my
darling," he cried, "my own darling——"

CHAPTER XXIV.

"I LOVE YOU."

IT was some little time before either Nancy or
Beautiful Jim could collect their senses enough to
say a single word. Then Nancy made a remark
which fairly took Jim's breath away, acting on him
very much like a pail of iced water might do on a
cold and frosty morning.

"Oh! you don't know. I've been nearly mad,"
she cried; "nearly mad! They all said you had done
it, and then Stuart wrote——"

"What did Stuart write?" he demanded sternly.

She looked at him half frightened and with
doubtful eyes.

"Ought I to tell you? It is all over now and
proved to be a mistake."

"I insist upon knowing," he returned harshly.

In spite of the anger in his face, the sunshine
broke out over the girl's lovely countenance.

"Oh! my dear, don't put that word 'insist'
between you and me," she said gently. "It sounds

ugly, and it looks uglier, but it *feels* the ugliest of all. There is no need for it, for I will tell you if you wish it, without any insisting."

Jim was penitent in a moment.

" Forgive me, my dearest," he said beseechingly. "I have had a good deal to try me since I saw you last, and the worst of it all was that I wasn't sure that you cared a button for me. It would all have been so easy if I'd only been sure of that ! "

Nancy gave a great sigh, not entirely a doleful one, for a distinct thrill of satisfaction ran through it.

"And I was just the same. As soon as I heard the awful news that suspicion had fallen on you— *you* of all men in the world—I sat down and wrote to tell you that *I* for one did not and never would believe it.   And I——"

"You wrote to me ? I never had the letter," he broke in impatiently.

" Because I never sent it," she answered quickly. " I—I—remembered that I wasn't sure whether you cared about me or not, and the letter I had written was rather affectionate, and it seemed hypocritical to write a stilted one ; and besides, I couldn't think of anything to say in such a one, or what reason to give for writing at all.   And then Stuart wrote, and—and he seemed so prejudiced against you, said everybody believed you had done it, and that so far as he could see there could be no doubt at all about it, and that he was very sorry I'd ever met you, and all that sort of thing, you know. But still, it wasn't that which made me not write, for *I* didn't believe a word of it—not a word."

"God bless you for that, my darling," cried poor Jim passionately. "But tell me just what it was that kept your sweet letter from me?"

"Well, Stuart said—of course, I daresay it was only gossip that was floating about in the regiment at the time," she added apologetically, "but he said it was very well known among the officers that though you and poor Captain Owen had always been great friends, that he had lately cut you out with one of your cousins of whom you were awfully fond, and that it was undoubtedly this that was at the bottom of it all; and I thought if you were fond of her that you wouldn't care anything about a letter from me."

"The young hound!" muttered Jim, between his teeth.

The girl tried to withdraw herself from the clasp of his jealous arms.

"Jim!" she exclaimed.

"Forgive me, dearest," he said, softening instantly. "I forgot for the moment that young Tommy was your brother—we don't call him 'Stuart' in the regiment, you know," he ended with a sad smile—"but by the unromantic name of Tommy; and it is rather a blow to me to find that he of *all* the fellows has been the one to blacken me, and to you."

"I daresay it was only what he heard," she answered, still clinging to the old habit of shielding her boy, though all her love and sympathy were with Jim.

Jim shook his head.

"No, my darling, Tommy *knew* when he wrote that to you that I was absolutely innocent; and I'm afraid he trumped up all the story about my little cousin out of his own head and to suit his own ends."

"But why? How could he know? Then there is a cousin," she cried.

"Yes. I have two cousins, great friends of mine, and poor dear Owen was utterly gone on one of them," he answered. "I should have been enchanted if she had taken him, but she didn't, or rather I believe she didn't, for Owen never said a word to me or I to him about it. As for her, I've never seen her since the week I was in London before I met you."

"But how could Stuart know?" she persisted.

Beautiful Jim's face turned like a stone.

"He *knew* that I had no hand in it—that I was absolutely innocent," he replied. "Don't ask me any more, darling. The subject is too painful to me, for you know old Owen was the best friend I ever had in all my life."

For some minutes Nancy stood looking at him, her sweet dove's eyes filled with a light such as he had never seen shining in their clear depths before.

"I believe," she said slowly, "that you know who committed that murder."

Beautiful Jim returned her searching gaze with one as steady and as true, but he kept silent.

Apparently Nancy took it as an answer, for she made no attempt to press the question—for a question it was, though not put in the form of one—further; instead, she put another, and one much more difficult for Jim to answer.

"Does Stuart know also?"

The words rang out clear and sharp, as such words might fall from the lips of an accusing angel.

Jim said nothing, and she repeated the question imperiously. Then he spoke.

"Nancy, my dear, if you love me and trust me, ask me no more about this miserable affair," he said imploringly. "If I keep silence when I know, will not you, who trusted me when appearances were dead against me, trust me still?"

"It is not that I do not trust you implicitly, utterly, absolutely," she said gently; "but if you know anything and are shielding a guilty person, let me beg of you, for your own sake, for *mine*, to hide nothing. Jim, my dear, do you realise that you are not safe yourself so long as this crime remains unpunished? At any moment matters might take a fresh turn against you and you might be—hanged."

Jim shook his head and smiled at her fears.

"No; I could always speak."

"And you would?" eagerly.

"In that case—yes."

"Then let me beg and pray of you to speak *now*," she cried earnestly. "Jim, believe me, it can do no good to shield the guilty. It is kind of you— but in such a case silence, even from the kindest motives, becomes a crime. Jim, dear, it is the first thing I have asked of you."

The sadness in Beautiful Jim's honest eyes turned to distress.

"My dear," he said, "you don't know how hard it is for me to refuse you anything. If I had done it myself I would go and give myself up at once; but as it is, if I speak, the blow will fall the heaviest upon those who are perfectly innocent, who do not even guess that such a shadow has or ever could come near them."

"They would probably be the first to say 'Let justice be done,'" she cried.

Jim looked at her keenly. He saw that she had no suspicion of the truth, that it never entered her mind that it might be over her that this black and shameful shadow hung! He knew that she had been from her cradle taught to look upon honour as before all; that the traditions of her house contained many and many an example of fair and gracious women who had bidden the men they loved go forth to battle and, cost them what it might, had never flinched in the hour of parting; who, even though the one life dearest of all on the earth to them had been laid down, had yet, heart-broken as they were, gloried in their own fortitude. He saw that she was of the same race, this girl he loved so dearly.

"Supposing that such a test came to yourself?" he asked.

"If it was my own brother I would deliver him up to justice!" she cried proudly.

"And your father?"

"My father! Ah! I might hesitate for him," she admitted, "though, mind, he would not hesitate himself."

"That decides me," said Jim, heaving a great breath of relief. "This man has a—a parent too, who is old and without reproach. That is why I have stained myself with a crime, Nancy; for a crime it is, though I hope it will not go hard with me hereafter, being committed through mercy."

The girl was conquered.

"Jim, you have a better heart than I. You are more merciful by far. I will take back my request, but only on one condition."

"Which is?" he asked.

"That if personal danger from this silence should ever threaten you, you will speak out."

"I promise you that."

"And you are sure it is safe?" anxiously.

"From the worst—yes! I shall be severely blamed, and probably severely punished, if it ever comes to light that I have hidden my knowledge, when my allegiance to the Queen commands me to speak; but there will always be sympathy for me I think."

"And you actually have the proofs? There is no mistake about that?" she persisted.

"I hold the proof myself," he answered; "and shall do so as long as I live, or until the truth comes to light."

She professed herself satisfied—gently said that she would have been better pleased if no such mystery had been hanging over him; nor could he in any way blame her for that.

"You will see my father when he comes in?" she asked. "He is at his club now, but he will be in to lunch."

"Oh! yes. I would like to see him and get it all settled as quickly as possible," Jim answered with alacrity. Poor fellow, the prospect of seeing her father was a much more congenial topic of conversation than the details of poor Owen's cruel murder and the likelihood of his bringing the murderer—young Tommy, be it remembered—to justice.

"I don't think he can object to me," he said cheerfully. "My family and income are all right, and my Colonel will give me a good character if he needs it. I'm glad, my darling, and more than ever now, that I always went in for a good character. It's a tie sometimes, when you can't do things that you see other fellows doing and apparently none the worse for; but going straight pays in the long run —nothing like it. Not, all the same, that I ever calculated on any end at all—I don't want to blow my own trumpet in the least—but I've gone straight simply because I hate everything that's crooked."

"And I love you," said Nancy Earle softly.

CHAPTER XXV.

A REASONABLE OBJECTION.

IT was not more than half an hour after this that Mr. Earle returned from his club, and entered the little room where his daughter and Beautiful Jim were sitting.

And who his daughter's visitor was, Mr. Earle had not the very smallest idea, until she introduced him by name.

"And Mr. Beresford has waited to see you, dear Father," she said; "he wants to ask you something, so I will leave you a few minutes before lunch."

This implied that her father was to invite the visitor to join them at that meal, a hint that was not lost upon him.

"Well, Mr. Beresford," he said, as the door closed behind Nancy's retiring form, "you wanted to ask me something?"

He settled himself with his back to the fire with the air of a man who was accustomed to be asked favours and had no objection to granting them in a pompous sort of way. Evidently he had no suspicion of the nature of Jim's request, and indeed, his daughter had given him so little trouble in that way that it was hardly likely that he should know just what was coming, as he would undoubtedly have done had he been an aristocratic old lady instead of being an aristocratic old gentleman.

" You wanted to ask me something ? " he repeated blandly.

" Yes, sir, I did," said Jim.   " It is for your consent to my engagement to your daughter."

" To my daughter ! " Mr. Earle echoed, looking as he felt, simply thunderstruck.

" Yes, sir.   I met her frequently during the time she was staying at the Deanery at Blankhampton, and I should have come up to see you about it then, only I felt it was a little hurried—a little premature.   Besides, I was not by any means sure that Miss Earle would be inclined to listen to me—and I intended to be in Town during the autumn and thought I might see more of her then.   I was in Town, but you and she were abroad, sir, and I could not get foreign leave, so I had simply no choice but to await your return."

" And you have spoken to my daughter ? " the old man asked stiffly.

" This morning, sir," Beautiful Jim replied.

" Mr. Beresford," said Mr. Earle, speaking in the most formal tones possible, " I am very sensible of the compliment you have paid my daughter in wishing to marry her ; but in her name and my own I must decline the honour."

" But, sir," said Jim aghast, " what reason have you for this ?   My family is irreproachable—I am the eldest son, or rather the head of my house.   My income is between three and four thousand a year, and I don't owe a farthing in the world, not even a tailor's bill."

Mr. Earle waved his hand impatiently and yet with a lofty air.

"It is not a question of family, nor yet one of income," he said.

"Then, sir, what is it?" Jim cried in infinite distress. "Not my character, I hope—for as to that, my commanding-officer will speak for me, and I have been eight years in his regiment, so he ought to know."

"Mr. Beresford," said the old man gravely, "it is very painful for me to have to speak with greater plainness; will it not be best for us to consider the conversation at an end and your proposal declined?"

"I would rather hear your reasons for declining it plainly, sir," said Jim, with admirable coolness.

"Is that so?" asked Mr. Earle.

"Yes, sir," returned Jim, "that is so."

"Then I must speak out," said the old man with a sort of groan. He hated everything unpleasant, and made a rule of shirking all disagreeables whenever possible. "Well, Mr. Beresford, I must tell you frankly that if you had come to me last autumn and asked for my daughter, I should, if my daughter had been willing, have considered yourself, your family and your income a perfectly desirable and suitable match for her; but since that time a great deal has happened. You, for instance, have been arrested since then on a suspicion of murder."

Jim fairly staggered back as the words passed the old man's lips.

" Mr. Earle," he said, hoarsely, " you don't—you surely can't believe that I committed that foul crime ? "

" If I *believed* it," Mr. Earle answered, " I should have asked you to go out of my house some minutes ago. Yet there is the fact—*you* were arrested on suspicion, and a verdict of wilful murder against some person or persons unknown is returned. Do you not see that until the case is set at rest one way or the other, you are not and never can be free from suspicion? At any time it is liable to rise up against you, not a mere suspicion but a hideous danger which may overwhelm you ! Do you think, Mr. Beresford, that I could or would let my young daughter go headlong into such a danger as that? No, sir, a thousand times, no; and let me tell you that although I may have antiquated ideas of love and honour, I think you show your wish to love and honour her very poorly indeed by even dreaming—dreaming of subjecting her to even a remote chance of such a misfortune."

Beautiful Jim looked as he felt, more staggered than ever; and, worst of all, he felt that from his point of view the old man was right.

" You are right, sir," he said. " I—knowing my own innocence—forgot that all the world did not know it also. Do you mind telling me one thing— suppose that this mystery is ever cleared up, and Miss Earle is still willing to be my wife, will you give your consent then ? "

" Certainly I will," the old man replied.

"And you will not forbid me to see her?" Jim pleaded.

"I will not *forbid* you, Mr. Beresford. No, on the contrary, I will show you willingly that I trust you as an honourable gentleman, by simply asking you not to attempt to marry her without my permission, and not to compromise her by being seen about with her. If she likes to correspond with you, well and good. If you care to come here now and again when you are in Town, I will not prevent it or forbid it. I daresay, under the circumstances, this is a somewhat unusual way of proceeding; but I have always given my daughter the most absolute trust and she is worthy of it in every way. I believe you to be innocent and I believe you to be honourable, for I see you had not thought of the danger to which such a marriage would expose her—so I will trust you also."

"Mr. Earle," said Jim, holding out his hand, "this has been an awful blow to me—one I never expected. But you have spoken to me fairly and well, and I thank you. You may depend that I will never betray your trust. Miss Earle shall be as safe from any persuasions of mine as if I were a Malay Indian and could not speak a word of English."

"It may all work out smooth enough," the old man said kindly.

But Jim shook his head. "I have very little hope of it, sir," he answered sadly. "I have very

14—2

little hope of it; but I thank you all the same for
the consolation."

After a moment of silence, Mr. Earle spoke again.

" My daughter must be told," he said, uneasily.
" She is so sensible, so clear-headed, that I feel sure
she will see perfectly the advisability of the objection, or rather stumbling-block, which I have been
compelled to raise. But it will be a sad blow to
her, I fear, poor child, and—well really, Beresford,
on the whole I think the news had better come
from you."

" It will be a hard task for me," said Jim.

" I don't doubt it," returned the old man; "but
the question is, from which of us will she take it the
best. She will see then, even if she does not see it
already, that you are convinced of the truth of what
I urge; and—yes, I think it had better come from
you, Beresford, I do indeed. I will go out and
lunch at my club and leave you a clear field, so that
you may tell her and get it over. Yes, that will be
the best, I am sure. You see, my dear fellow, I
trust to your honour absolutely."

Before Jim could say a word against this plan,
the old gentleman had shaken his hand again and
had slipped out of the room. So he had no choice
but to await the meeting with Nancy, and the necessary disclosures which it would entail with the best
grace that he could.

Not that he waited very long; he heard the hall
door closed behind the master of the house, and
then, as Nancy did not come, he rang the bell and

asked the servant who came in answer to his summons, if he would ask Miss Earle to be good enough to see him? And in less than two minutes she came—with her dove's eyes all alight with love and the sweetest and brightest smile upon her lips,—the lips that were his and yet not his.

"Well?" she said gaily, as she crossed the room to his side.

Beautiful Jim took her outstretched hand in his.

"My dearest, I am afraid I have the most sorry news for you," he said humbly.

"Sorry news?" sharply. "Then where is my father?"

"He has left me to tell you—gone to his club."

"To tell me—*what?*"

For a moment Jim could hardly speak.

"To tell you that our engagement is impossible; for the present at least," he answered with an effort.

"Father said that? But why? What do you mean, Jim—that he refuses?"

"At present."

"At present—oh! do tell me the worst at once. What do you mean by at present?"

"My dearest, your father is quite right, though it is hard upon us," said Jim gently. "He does not forget that I have been arrested on a suspicion of murder, and that while the affair remains in mystery I am not free from further suspicion."

"But he does not believe it, surely," she cried, with blazing eyes and lips tightly compressed.

"No, he does not *believe* it, thank God!" Jim replied quickly.

"But if he does not believe it, why let it affect us?" she exclaimed. "I have never known my father influenced by the opinion of others in all my life, never. And to think that he should begin to be so when the consequences are so serious for me is too hard, it's too hard!"

"But you don't understand," said Jim gently. "It is not the opinion of others he is thinking of at all—only, that as I am not cleared yet, the suspicion might at any time rise up against me and overwhelm both of us."

"But you are innocent."

"Innocent men have been hanged before to-day, my darling, and your father feels it," said he, more full of pity for her than of sorrow for his own broken hopes.

"But Jim," she cried eagerly, "did you not tell Father that you could prove yourself innocent at any time?"

Beautiful Jim shook his head. "No, I did not tell him that."

"But why?"

"Because he would insist that I should speak."

"Oh, no! I shall tell him. Yes, it is no use trying to persuade me against it. I have made up my mind to do it. It is all very well to be generous and merciful to others; but *I* ought to be your first thought, and it will be but a poor sort of generosity to secure others their peace of mind at the cost of breaking my heart."

" But he will certainly deliver that person up to justice," Jim persisted.

" And if he does, does not that person deserve it ? " she said passionately. " Why should the innocent have to suffer for the guilty ? Or if some such must so suffer, why should it be you and I ? Why not the —— No, Jim, I have made up my mind. I will not let you lie under this suspicion a day longer. In fact, I tell you, frankly and honestly, that I cannot understand your being so weak about the whole affair."

For a moment Beautiful Jim did not say one word. The little clock on the chimney-shelf beside them ticked loudly and cheerily on, and Nancy was restlessly tapping her foot upon the fender. Jim felt that he must speak, at least that he must convey to her the necessity for not speaking to her father further than he had already done, yet he hardly knew how to begin.

" Why don't you say something ? " she asked at last, puzzled by the expression of his face, and guessing that there was yet something else for her to hear.

" I don't know how to say it," he said unwillingly.

" But there is something to tell me," she cried. " Oh, Jim, don't spin it out—tell me quickly ! Don't stop to pick and choose your words. Do tell me ! "

" Nancy," he said, thus urged, " you know you are making it horribly hard for me. Oh ! my dear, my dear, why can't you or won't you understand that it is impossible for me to say a word about my power to clear myself to your father, and imperative that you should not do so either?"

She had not fully grasped his meaning, and yet she realized that there was truth in his words. Her face grew pale and her lips stiff and strained as she stood looking straight into his honest eyes, so full of love and sadness.

"What is it?" she whispered.

Jim put his arm around her and held her closely to him.

"Must I speak more plainly?" he asked. "*Yes?* Oh! my darling, I am so sorry, so grieved to say it —but he is the one person in the world to whom I could not tell it, except in the face of the most dire danger."

"*It—was—not—our—boy?*" she whispered painfully; and for answer Beautiful Jim did not speak, made no gesture, no sign—only he looked at her with an infinite and tender pity shining through the love which filled his eyes.

CHAPTER XXVI.

FOR THE OLD MAN'S SAKE.

UNDOUBTEDLY it was the most bitter moment which had ever come into Nancy Earle's life, when she stood tight clasped in the arms of the man who loved her, the man she loved, and learned the true story of the terrible murder which had taken place in Walmsbury Barracks; when she learned with shame and anguish that it was no other than the last of her proud race who had done this damnable and cowardly deed.

She was so ashamed! That was the key-note of her thoughts—shame, only shame. Although she had not known it, she had been proud of her faith and trust in the man she loved—she had unconsciously been thrilled with a delightful sense of pleasure in her own brave faithfulness, which could stand up, though all the world should be against him and all the evidence of circumstances might conspire to do him to death, and yet say—"I love this man—I believe in him—he is incapable of this vile thing that is laid to his charge."

Yes, there had been something grand and noble in her love, and she had felt that, come what might in the after years, he could and would always feel that the woman he loved had never wavered in her trust of him! And then, after all, to find out that he had kept silence for her sake and for that of the old father who had borne his good name as a bright jewel to be guarded and treasured, that he had kept silence in the face of a charge which could and most probably would cling to him all the rest of his life. Oh! it was a bitter, bitter blow to the girl who had been reared in pride, and whose training had been one of honour.

In those few minutes of reflection she went back over the years of the past, the years during which

she had willingly stood on one side for her younger
brother, because he was the last of the Earles,
because he was a boy and she was only a girl, a girl,
a thing of no particular importance, and though she
was an Earle like him, yet she was an Earle who did
not count.   There was no thought, or room for such
in her mind, of pity for any temptation which
might have led him to do this horrible thing—she
had no feeling of mercy towards him.   Oh! no, only
a wild indignant sort of rage possessed her that he
should have stained and sullied the fair name he
bore, and have put upon his living relatives a shame
which they must carry with them to the grave.

She broke from the clasp of Jim's arms and turned
to the window, where she stood looking out upon
the Square, speechless from anger, and a whirl of
hot indignant thoughts chasing one another through
her mind ; and at last she turned back to where he
was still standing.

"You must tell my father," she said decidedly.
"Yes—yes—I know all that you would say.   But
I am doing what I know he would like best if he
knew.   It will be an awful blow to him, but he
would never forgive me if he found out that I had
kept such a thing from him."

Beautiful Jim shook his head.

"I will not tell him," he said firmly.   "In the
face of suspicion he has trusted me, and I will not
reward him in that way.   I could not, my darling,
even for you."

"But if he were to find out," she began.

"Then he never must find it out," rejoined Jim firmly. "Who is to tell him?"

"I will," said Nancy.

"It will be his death-blow—it will kill him! He has always been the best of fathers to you, and for the sake of that young——"—he broke an ugly word off here and substituted a milder one for it—"that young idiot, would you reward him thus? No, my child, I am sure you will see that it cannot be! Besides, he is so old and we are young. We can wait a little for each other."

"And *he* is to go on in his wickedness unpunished, holding his head as high as he will?" she exclaimed.

Jim could not help smiling as he remembered Tommy's piteously abject air on the evening before poor dear old Owen's funeral at Walmsbury.

"The poor young beggar is not holding his head very high, my dearest," he said gently. "Besides, for the sake of your father, we can leave his punishment to a higher Will than ours."

"Is it possible that you have any pity for him?" she cried incredulously.

"Yes, that I have," Jim answered. "It is no light matter to have murder on your mind, and he doesn't look as if he found it so."

"Ah! you don't know him," Nancy cried. "I do. He is like an india-rubber ball—while you hold him tight he is crushed and quiet, but once release your grip of him, and he is as full of bounce as ever. If he knows that you know, I can well believe that he is humble and abject *to you*. That has been his way out of difficulty and danger ever since he was a boy—a baby; but now that he is out of your sight, I would not mind staking my very life that he is flirting with one of the Leslie girls at this moment."

"Not at this moment," said Jim, smiling sadly, "if you would be very accurate, that is—but likely enough he is thinking about it."

She flushed up angrily all over her fair face.

"I cannot understand you," she cried. "He was your friend, your best friend—and you yet willingly let his assassin go free—you——"

"Don't you understand that *your* brother is sacred to me?" Jim asked gravely. "For *himself*, for his sake, I would not have held my hand one moment, and he knows it. Right willingly and cheerfully would I see him hanged to-morrow— nay, this very day."

Nancy shuddered at the dreadful word, but she did not attempt to speak, and Jim went on.

"But he is *your* brother—that made him safe from me in the first instance; now, since your father has shown me such trust and generosity, I could not betray him except to save my own life; even then it would be a hard task for me to be compelled to speak."

And then poor Nancy broke down altogether, and began to weep bitterly and passionately, and somehow Jim got his arms round her again and drew her head down upon his breast, soothing her as if she were a weary child in distress.

"There, there, my darling, don't cry so," he murmured. "At least let us wait a little while and see what happens. We are young, and it may only be a little time to wait, and if we love one another always, it will soon go past; and it is not as if we were to be kept apart altogether."

"It's so hard," she sobbed; "and are you to be under this hideous suspicion while *he* flaunts about as 'the last of the Earles'? And is my father to put all his trust and faith in him blindly and believe in him still? Oh! I know how good, how unselfish you are, Jim, to do this; but it is a cruel deception on an old man—it is indeed. I am sure no good will ever come of it. And what am I to say if—if —oh! I mean *when* they say that you did it? And people will say it, Jim, I know it."

"But their saying it won't make it true," he said quietly. "And, after all, you can always say that *you* believe in me, you know. And, Nancy, my dear love, do you think that *I* shall ever forget that when all the world might have been justified in being against me you were my own brave, loyal-hearted darling, who believed in me apart from all the evidence that seemed to be against me—do you think that I shall *ever* forget that? Oh! my love, my own darling, how little you realize what my love for you is if you can think so for one moment."

And thus Beautiful Jim won the day, conquered in the battle, against his own interests, against all that would have made him the happiest man upon

God's green earth that day, and after a little while, Nancy got over her first burst of indignation against young Tommy, and became more calm and collected. And then she was in a measure able to realize Beautiful Jim's real worth, to have some idea what a brave, true-hearted, honest gentleman she had won for her own.

"But," she said suddenly, and in a stern, determined voice, "there is one thing, Jim, that you need never ask me to do, for I never will. That is, as long as I live to acknowledge Stuart as my brother. When you go back to Blankhampton you must tell him that I know the truth, and that so far as is necessary to blind my father I will behave to him as I have always done; but out of my father's presence he must distinctly understand that he is, for the future, dead to me. I have consented—unwillingly, as you know—to help to hide his crime for my old father's sake, and for that alone, but I have not yet sunk so low as to have any dealings with a criminal. So make that absolutely clear to him, and tell him too that I am bound by no promise of secrecy—and if he in the smallest way presumes upon the knowledge that we wish to keep it from my father, I shall have neither hesitation nor compunction in speaking out at once."

"Very well, I'll make it clear to him," said Jim quietly.

On the whole he was not sorry that Nancy had taken the news in the way she had done. Mercy for young Tommy he had absolutely none, and if his sister—who had always had to play second to him—helped to make his life from that time rougher to him, why Jim thought it would only be a just portion of the retribution that the young scoundrel deserved. Besides, Jim had every hope and confidence that one day Nancy would be his wife, that something or other would happen to make the way straight for their happiness long before the old man should be gone to his rest, and he would not at all have relished young Tommy being on intimate, or even on frigidly intimate, terms with them.

And presently she asked him to tell her the precise details of the terrible event; and, after a good deal of persuasion, Jim complied and did so. Then, for the first time, she learned all there was to know about Rose Meeking, the barmaid at the Duck's Tail, and the part which she had taken in the tragedy.

"I must see her," she said. "I must do something for her; I wonder what it is possible I can do? She must be a good woman, a very good woman, or she would have used her knowledge to marry him before this. Anyway, I must see her. It will not be easy unless she comes to Town, but it must be managed somehow."

It was not very long after this that Mr. Earle returned from his club—if the truth be told, in a very uneasy frame of mind as to the manner in which Nancy might have taken his decision. He went into the room where they still were together, and Jim got up with a sort of apology for his presence.

" I am here still, sir," he said, by way of excuse.
" You see, we had a good deal to talk over, and——"

" As long as you like—as long as you like, my dear fellow," the old man cried. " I am only very sorry that——"

" Father," broke in Nancy, "I want to say something.   I have never disobeyed you in my life, but I want you to give me my way now.   I shall never marry any other man but this," laying her hand on Jim's arm; " and although we will wait for your consent to our marriage, I must be able and free to see him as often as I like."

CHAPTER XXVII.

A TRYING INTERVIEW.

MEANTIME, society at Blankhampton was greatly edified by the return of " the last of the Earles " to its midst.

Just at first he had not been inclined to avail himself of the privileges which it afforded him; he had been dazed and crushed by events which had happened recently, and had moreover suffered a good deal from Beautiful Jim's continued presence. Somehow, he never seemed able to get out of sight of the accusing look in Jim's eyes, or away from the accusing tones in his voice, or from the accusing meanings in everything that he said.

Jim had no thought of this at all—-in truth, he

had conceived such a profound contempt for, and
such an aversion to, the young scoundrel, that if
he could possibly help it he never addressed him,
or even allowed his eyes to rest upon him. Still,
as I have said, so it seemed to Tommy; and it was
not until Beautiful Jim went off for his short leave
that the lad began to breathe with anything like
freedom. But as it is but a step from the sublime
to the ridiculous, so it was but a step for Tommy's
light and buoyant nature to slip from the depression
which was the result of Jim's presence to the gay
and airy lightness of his usual demeanour; and then
it was that Blankhampton society was able to welcome him to itself again.

Now mind, it was not that Tommy had in any
way got over the horror and distress which the
Walmsbury tragedy had caused him—not at all; it
was only that he had a very singular and adaptable
disposition, and after the first great dread of discovery was over and he realized that, for his people's
sake, he was safe from Beautiful Jim's wrath, he
began to smooth the irrevocable past over, to
whittle away a motive here and to heighten an
aggravation there, until he at last came to feel
that, so far from his having committed a crime in
being the actual cause of Owen's death, Owen had
behaved with really vindictive and remarkable shabbi-
ness to him in being knocked over by the dumb-bell.

Of course, he was awfully sorry that poor old
Owen had come to harm, but undoubtedly Owen
had always had a particularly disagreeable way of

interfering in matters which did not in the smallest
degree concern him, and, of course, as all the world
knows, when fellows will do that sort of thing, they
often come in for more than they bargain for.   All
the same, he was sorry enough about poor old Owen,
whom he had liked very well on the whole, and he
would have given worlds to have undone or averted
such a deplorable accident—yes, Tommy always
now thought of Owen's death as a pure *accident;*
it was such a much more palatable word than
murder, which had something coarse and revolting
about the very sound and look of it—but since that
could not be, he had come to the conclusion that
it would be simply useless to worry himself into a
lunatic asylum, or even into his grave, by fretting
about it.

So you may believe, after Tommy had arrived at
this decision, that it was not very long before he
took to the old ways, and the pretty drawing-rooms
of the pretty women in Blankhampton knew him
as of yore.

With regard to the young lady at the Duck's
Tail at Walmsbury, it can only be said that Tommy
had already come to look upon the recent events of
the past as a distinct intervention of Providence
to save him from the consequences of the dull and
dreary life into which he had been mercilessly
thrust.   And the odd part of it all was that he
had meant seriously enough to marry her, to make
her the mistress of Earles Hope, and the possible
mother of the Earles to come.

Well, that had been an escape for which he could never be sufficiently grateful, never; and although he had no doubt that she could, if she chose, make herself uncommonly disagreeable, that sort of person is always open to being " squared," and happily he would always have the power to settle matters with her in that way.

So when Beautiful Jim, in great disappointment and yet not wholly sad, went back to Blankhampton, he found young Tommy once more in the full swing of social popularity, just the spoilt pet he had been afore-time; and after the first gasp of disgusted surprise, Jim promptly went for him.

" By-the-by, Earle, I want to speak to you," he said to him the day after his return from town.

" All right," returned Tommy, " will you come to my room or shall I come to yours ? "

" You can come to mine," said Jim, shortly.

So to Jim's room they went, and its owner turned the key in the lock so as to secure them from interruption.

Just at first Tommy tried on the old air of jaunty equality. " Well," he said, settling himself in the most comfortable chair that the room contained, " I suppose you've nothing especially pleasant to say to me, eh ? I don't expect it in the least, so I'm prepared."

" That's as well," said Jim shortly, not looking at Tommy at all but at the pipe he was filling, " for what I've got to say you'll find devilish unpleasant—I should, at least. You probably don't know why I went up to Town."

" Not in the least, except for the usual thing," returned Tommy, trying hard to keep cool and unconcerned, and only succeeding in looking thoroughly ill at ease.

" Ah! I thought so," said Jim, drawing hard at his pipe. " Well, I didn't happen to go for the usual thing at all. I went to ask your sister to marry me."

For a moment young Tommy simply gasped; all the " last of the Earles" pride seemed to stiffen him, and mingled with it was a curious contempt that any fellow should be thinking seriously of marrying his sister. Then the advantages of the connection flooded in upon him, and he made haste to reply.

" H'm—well. I can't understand any fellow wanting to marry Nancy, though she's pretty and good, and all that. However, I'm sure I hope she accepted you."

" I quite admit your sister's inferiority to the young lady at the Duck's Tail," said Jim brusquely, " but you see you were beforehand with me there. However, your sister did accept me."

" I'm awfully glad—let me congratulate you, old chap," cried Tommy effusively, holding out his hand. " And when is it to be ? "

" When I am free from any fear of being charged with Owen's murder," replied Jim coldly, and taking no notice of the out-stretched hand.

Tommy sank back into the big chair again.

"What do you want me to do?" he asked, growing white with fear.

"Nothing," Jim returned. "For myself, I don't know that I should have told you about it at present, only your sister charged me with a message for you."

"Yes?" said Tommy, breathing more freely. "And it was——"

"About this business. I had to tell her, you know," said Jim, looking straight at him.

All the fear came back into the lad's eyes again.

"You told her—Nancy!" he gasped. "Good God! You must have been mad!"

"I don't think so," said Jim icily. "And I would leave that name out of the question if I were you—it doesn't sound well. Well, as to telling your sister, as a matter of fact I did not tell her—she found it out."

"How?" Tommy hardly spoke above a whisper, and his heart began to beat so fast that he was nearly suffocated.

"Well, I naturally told her that I was not the man who murdered Owen.

"Well?"

"And then she expressed great anxiety lest I might fall under suspicion again. So, in order to re-assure her, and not in any way to let light in upon you, I told her that I could safely establish my innocence at any time. Naturally, she pressed me to do so at once, particularly as your father, although he believes in me himself, will not consent to our marriage until all fear of my danger is at an end; and then I had to tell her that, for the sake of this man's relatives, I was bound to keep silence. She did not see it——"

"Ah, girls are so beastly selfish," Tommy broke in. "It's the way they're brought up."

"Perhaps so," said Jim, drily. "However, she did not see it, and even went so far as to say that she should tell your father, and get the mystery cleared up somehow; and then I had to say that I would not have your father know it for any consideration, and she guessed."

There was a long and death-like silence; but at last Tommy looked up. "And what is she going to do?" he asked.

"Nothing!" returned Jim. "She is going to wait. But she charged me to tell you that she forbears only for your father's sake; that she has neither pity nor mercy for you; that, but for him, she would willingly deliver you up to justice to-morrow. And she says that, just so far as is necessary to blind your father, she will be to you as she was before, but no further—that if you at any time do the smallest thing that she disapproves, she will go to your father at once and tell him every-thing; and she told me to remind you that *she* is bound by no promise to shield you, and has no reason for concealment."

For some time Tommy sat staring into the fire-place blankly, trying hard to recover from the blow which Beautiful Jim's words had dealt him ; but at last he looked up.

"Am I to spend the rest of my life in purgatory under Nancy's thumb ?" he asked, hoarsely.

"I'm afraid that's about it," returned Jim, stolidly.

"But I tell you it was an accident, a pure accident," he persisted, miserably.

"Oh! yes of course; most murders are," replied Jim, quietly. "It couldn't be *your* fault for pitching a seven-pound dumb-bell at Owen when his back was turned, but poor dear Owen's fault for getting in the way of it. I believe that's generally the way with murders ; but, unfortunately, jurymen are such infernal blockheads that they can't often be got to look at the matter in the right light. It's a devil of a nuisance, of course, but there the juries are, and their decision is law."

"Life won't be worth having," Tommy groaned, abjectly.

"Neither would it at Portland, even if you got let off so easily as that," returned Jim, with what Tommy designated in his own mind as unfeeling brutality. "And you should have thought of that, you know, before you took to shying dumb-bells about."

And then all at once, and without warning, Tommy burst out crying and sobbed convulsively for some minutes. "It's too hard," he burst out, "that my whole life should be ruined like this. I tell you I'd no idea, no notion, not the smallest, of killing the fellow. He always was a contrary, cross-grained brute——"

"Take care, take care," muttered Jim, between his teeth.

"He was—perhaps not to you, but to me from the very first and always," Tommy cried passionately. "And that day, after spying and busying himself about my private affairs, which had and could have had nothing to do with him, he goaded me almost —*almost*," fiercely—"nay, altogether to madness by his cold, icy, supercilious, damnable airs. I was mad when I did that, but mad as I was, I had never a thought of killing him, I swear I never had."

"At the same time," said Jim frigidly, "you would find it uncommonly difficult to persuade a jury to look at it in that light."

"I know it," Tommy rejoined wretchedly, "but do you think I ever forgot it? Night and day alike I have that horrible *thud* in my ears, and Owen's dead face as I saw it in the morning before my eyes—good heavens, man, don't you think that I have suffered a very hell of regret, and that I don't suffer it still every day, every hour, aye, every moment of my life?"

"No, I don't," returned Jim, no more moved by this outburst of passion against a self-wrought fate, than he would have been by a blue-bottle fly buzzing up and down a window-pane. "I saw you in the Winter Garden an hour ago and, 'pon my soul, even knowing you as well as I do, I was astounded at your powers of enjoyment—I was indeed."

" You told me yourself," cried Tommy, fiercely, "that I was to look as usual, that I was not to go about looking hang-dog and wretched."

" So I did; but I never expected to see you take up your little flirtations again with quite the zest you displayed this afternoon. However, it's no use going over the old ground again and again in this way. I have given you your sister's message and, for the present, you appear to be safe, though of course, one never can tell what may or may not turn up. I don't think you need imagine that she is going to make your life a burden to you, for really I don't believe she will ever want to see you or be in any way mixed up with you again. I think what she means by ' your doing anything that she disapproves ' is the chance that you might want to marry —the girl at the Duck's Tail, for instance."

" Oh, that is altogether out of the question," said Tommy, in a relieved tone and with a ' last-of-the-Earles ' air about him.

" Yes, I'm sure it is," said Jim, " for Miss Meeking simply would not look at you now. All the same, I don't think your sister would stand you marrying *any*body; she wouldn't think it right to let any lady go blindly into such a mine as a marriage with you would be. Least of all would she allow your marrying one of the Leslies, so you had better let your attentions cool off in that quarter."

" I can't see what difference——" Tommy began, when Jim cut him short.

" Do you think you are fit to marry any good

woman ? " he asked. "Why, you know as well as I do, that if any one of the Leslie family had the least idea of the truth, they would shun you as they would shun a leper. You know it; so be warned in time, and be sure that your sister would never allow a marriage with one of them to take place without fully acquainting Mr. Leslie of your past. I daresay it is hard on you—wickedness and crime do fall heavily on those who commit them, and very properly too. And I'll tell you, Earle, the very first thing you've got to do to make your life better than it is now and your mind easier—that is, get rid of the false idea you've cajoled yourself into believing of Owen's death being *an accident;* it was no more an accident than my asking your sister to marry me was an accident, so the sooner you acknowledge the truth to yourself and try to conquer that cowardly temper of yours, the better." And with these words Jim got up and unlocked the door, as an intimation to Tommy that the interview was at an end.

CHAPTER XXVIII.

THE LAST OF POLLY ANTROBUS.

BUT Beautiful Jim soon found that Tommy was incorrigible. True, warned by the threat conveyed in his sister's message, that young gentleman had almost entirely ceased his visits to the Leslies' house and his attentions to the blithe and bonny daughters thereof; but apparently his mind had quite (as a general rule, that is to say), thrown off the events of the past, and he was having just as good a time as he had ever had. Only he was careful, unless Beautiful Jim was safely out of the way, to confine his flirtations to the married women, to whose houses —being such a mere boy—he was always welcome

Just about this time Polly Antrobus's wedding came off, and she was, with much pomp and ceremony, transformed into Mrs. Mandarin, of Thelston House, Liverpool, and of—Shanghai.

It was a cruel sacrifice, and indeed everybody spoke of it as such, although everybody in Blankhampton flocked to witness it, and freely discussed the hideous proportions of the festive bridegroom, from the bald spot on the back of his large head to the squat flat feet on which his squat flat little body was supported.

And everybody discussed poor Polly—with her face of living agony, and her pretty, soft blue eyes staring out from the soft frame of her snowy veil, and full of a great speechless flood of pain and woe—more as if she had been some curious and unique specimen under a microscope than a living breathing woman of flesh and blood, who had been a child and had grown up to the full perfection of her beauty among them. Poor Polly, poor dear Polly; with that brave morning's fine array she passed away from the old city which had known her as a pretty child, as many and many a girl had done before her, to be henceforward little more to it than a name—to be " a personage" viewed by the general public through the somewhat uncertain sheen of her mother's oily descriptions. Poor Polly! She was not the first nor yet the last pretty girl that I have seen married in Blankhampton in the same way, and, alas, I fear there may be many another to come.

For the girls of the old city do not often marry with any prospect of remaining therein—for which small blame to them, for change is good for the soul. But, oh! some of the marriages that I have seen made up for the pretty Blankhampton girls—they make my heart ache to think of them.

They are so innocent and so pretty; their lives are a little hum-drum, perhaps, but so good and so refined. They go a great deal to the Parish, and are very devout indeed—they go to London once in a blue moon (I'm not quite sure what a blue moon is, but it means a long time), and to half-a-dozen balls in the course of a whole winter; and then they trot up and down the High Street a good deal, and have a bazaar now and again, or a garden-party at the Palace or Deanery, and sometimes an afternoon "hop" at the barracks. Dear little Cathedral maids! And then the town is convulsed by hearing that So-and-So is "engaged."

One pictures pretty So-and-So in all the pleasant flutter of love's young dream, and hopes she will be happy and draw a prize in the lottery; and then a whisper creeps out that her mother has been giving the latest details—and if you do not happen to have seen So-and-So at the Parish, or in the Winter Garden, or sauntering down the High Street with her new possession in tow, you may be pretty sure that the latest details prove to be that she is making " quite a marriage of prudence," or that it is a great match for Effie or Georgie, as the case may be.

And oh, the marriages of prudence and the great matches that I have seen consummated in Blankhampton! I can never make up my mind who arranges them—whether it is that the girls get tired of the somewhat uneventful round of life in the old city, or whether the mothers " hook " the eligible men and persuade or cajole the daughters into consenting to their fate. There is something very odd in seeing the girl whom you have known for years and years, whom you have seen advanced from the long black legs and sailor frocks, as you knew her first, to the dignity of her first ball-frock, suddenly—after a marriage of prudence—taking her place as the wife of a staid professional man thirty years older than herself, for whom she never could have felt any of that sweet romance which does so much to oil the wheels of the matrimonial chariot. It is so odd to see the little first wifely airs and graces of the young matron, who is perhaps starting her married life precisely where her mother left off—the half-unconscious display of a diamond ring, or the rustle of a richer gown than she has ever worn before; it is so interesting to see her in the different shops giving orders with an air, "Well, you may send me that," with ever so slight an emphasis on the "me" which marks her as different from the girl of a year ago, who used as often as not to do her mother's shopping for her; and it is most odd of all to see her making her first call at the Deanery, under the shadow of the elderly wing under which, from prudential motives, she has made up her mind to shelter herself henceforward—or to see her presiding over her first dinner party!

It is all very well for a few years: the elderly husband seems for a time to have renewed his youth, and the nursery fills at an alarming rate; and then, why then, this man dies suddenly or sinks into an old, old man, and in either case the wife is left with diminished income (or none), and youth gone for ever, to fight the world alone, to bring up the children, who ought to have their father's care, as best she can! Alas, I have seen it more times than one, and I always find myself wondering where the prudence of such marriages comes in.

But, of course, with Polly Antrobus the matter was rather different. Hers was not a marriage of prudence, but "such a good match, don't you know." Undoubtedly there was money and to spare, and Polly's settlements and so on were lavish enough to secure her from ever having to face the world with a diminished income, supposing that Mr. Mandarin should be at any time translated to a higher sphere. And if Polly's blue eyes were filled with a living agony, why nobody in all the crowded church on the morning of her marriage knew anything about her liking for Lord Charterhouse, or the bitter disappointment which his marriage had been to her.

But stay! Yes, there was one person in the crowd who knew—aye, and would have given the half of his fortune to have been able to forget the knowledge—that was Charterhouse himself. For he was there! Not willingly—in truth, most unwillingly—a spectator of the ceremony of sacrifice in which all Blankhampton was so keenly interested. No, it was not of his own free will at all, but because Nell—Lady Charterhouse, that is—had struck up a violent friendship with Mrs. Antrobus, and had accepted the invitation to the wedding for him, and had even promised that on no account should he fail to make his appearance.

Therefore, poor little Mr. Winks, with his aching heart and his breezy, buoyant, boisterous wife, was among the first to enter the sacred edifice where the rite which had so little that was sacred about it was to be performed. And, little more than bridegroom as he was, right wretched did he look and feel. Such a contrast he made to his dashing wife, who, in honour of the occasion, had come out in a white cloth Redfern gown, profusely and elaborately braided and broidered with gold, and looked as radiant as the brilliant summer sunshine which was streaming through the old stained windows and flooding the church with gay coloured light.   And a good many people were quick to note the contrast; and although nobody actually *knew* anything about it, yet more than one guessed that there was some truth in the report that he would have got off his marriage with the handsome girl standing near him in all the bravery of her white and gold, for the sake of the pretty blue-eyed bride of that morning; and they guessed, too, that this was the solution of the apparently inexplicable mystery of Polly Antrobus having the heart to give herself to the yellow-faced squat little gentleman then waiting, with all the assurance of unique ugliness, at the steps of the altar.   So I say again, poor, poor, pretty Polly!

It had just struck the quarter before twelve when she came, looking lovely it need hardly be said, dressed in white from head to foot, plain, simple, and severe, from the hem of her long gown to the snowy tulle which half hid her golden head, her only ornaments a cluster of orange blossoms near her throat and an enormous bouquet of delicate and rare white blossoms in her hand.

"And not a single one of the superb jewels we've heard so much about," whispered one in the crowd to her neighbour.

"Oh, I daresay they're like To-To's grand marriage, all imagination," was the reply.

But it was not so.   The jewels were in existence sure enough, but Polly had flatly refused to wear them on her wedding morning, although her mother

had coaxed and persuaded, and the bridegroom had
been evidently much disappointed that his bride's
world should not see in what honour he held her.
Still Polly was obdurate. Wear them she would
not, and did not—not even the beautiful string of
pearls, which, as Mrs. Antrobus plaintively said,
would just have made all the difference between her
wedding and all the other weddings that took place
in Blankhampton.

On this point To-To had stood her friend, and had
backed her up vigorously in her resolve not to appear
on her wedding morning blazing with jewels.

" You're perfectly right, Polly," she said with her
own delightful little matronly air. " I always think
it such execrable taste to wear jewels for a wedding,
simply execrable,"—and would you believe it, there
were people among the relatives and intimate
friends of the Antrobus family ill-natured enough
to say that the young Mrs. Herrick Brentham did
not wish the difference between her wedding-gifts
and her sister's to appear in too startling contrast ;
but, of course, that only shows how inordinately ill-
natured people can be in this world, and particularly
in Blankhampton.

Those same evil-disposed folk remarked that poor
little To-To had gone off in looks a good deal, and
that for the young wife of a fairly well-off husband
she was not as well dressed as she might have been
on a smart occasion like the wedding of a sister ;
but then they did not take certain circumstances
into due account—for instance, that although To-To

had been a very pretty girl, she was not a little woman who might be said to show off her clothes. But, of course, I do not pretend to know much of the cost and value of feminine garments, though I do know that I never saw that particular little person, either as To-To Antrobus or as Mrs. Herrick Brentham, look well dressed in my life ; and perhaps—judging from the gift with which this famous couple came around to do honour to Polly's marriage—the evil-disposed folk were not altogether out of it when they ascribed To-To's gone-off looks and unhandsome garb to a certain trait in the festive Herrick's character rather than to any short-comings in the little woman herself. What do you say, my dear madam who is now honouring this chronicle with your attention ? Oh, what was the present ? Well, it was a set of small Dresden salt cellars—a dozen of them—and they cost two guineas. But fie, fie, you should never look a gift-horse in the mouth, and Polly herself said that they were " quite lovely, dear To-To, quite lovely ; " so surely no one else had any " call," as they say in Blankshire, to cavil thereat. I am surprised at you, madam, I am indeed, fairly surprised.

CHAPTER XXIX.

NANCY AND ROSE MEET.

IT must not be supposed that during this time the police at Walmsbury were idle. On the contrary,

they were putting forth their best efforts to find out
something—or, for the matter of that, anything—
about the mysterious case, so as to prove themselves
better up in their work than the two Scotland Yard
men, who were employed in the interests of the
Owen family, and who, like their fellows at Walmsbury, seemed to be at a dead-lock.

But, puzzle their brains and poke and pry as they
would, it seemed impossible to find out anything
more than had been done already.

They had both abandoned that clue which seemed
to point to Mr. Beresford as the guilty person, and
towards young Earle the finger of suspicion had
never seemed to point at all.

A suggestion had been made that Rose Meeking
perhaps knew more than anyone else about the
matter ; but that astute young lady being. fore-
warned was thus forearmed and, in spite of the
many and extraordinary questions which were put
to her, contrived to throw them off the scent completely, showing plainly that she was neither to be
frightened nor trapped into admitting a single word
more, concerning the interview with Captain Owen
on the afternoon of the murder, than she had
admitted at the inquest.

In her way she had been true enough both to her
promise to the dead man and to young Tommy.
She still saw the force of all that Owen had urged
against a marriage between her and the last of the
Earles ; but, while she was filled with horror at the
way in which he had come by his death, and every

spark of admiration for her gentleman sweetheart had died out, she was yet determined not to betray him into the hands of justice. So out of Rose Meeking, neither the Scotland Yard detectives nor the Walmsbury police got any information whatever.

About this time the somewhat difficult meeting between her and Miss Earle was brought about.

Nancy had puzzled herself a good deal over it, as it was to her mind as difficult for Rose to come up to Town as it would be for her to go down to Walmsbury. But Jim, in obedience to his dear lover's wishes, found out that it was not so, and that Rose, in fact, was a London girl, whose parents were living at Notting Hill.

It was comparatively easy for him to run over to Walmsbury on the pretext of finding out what discoveries had been made, and to put up at the hotel which bore the sign of the Duck's Tail. And once in the house, it was easy enough to arrange with Rose that she should as soon as possible ask for a few days' holiday that she might go home and see her parents, and, while in London, take the opportunity of seeing Miss Earle.

A few days after Jim had returned to Blankhampton, Miss Meeking preferred her request to the landlord, Mr. Brown, who, being fully aware of her value as a barmaid, and also deeply impressed with a feeling that the girl had been shamefully and unreasonably worried about the death of Captain Owen, very readily gave permission; and accordingly a few days later she went off on her holiday.

And during this time, as had been arranged by Jim, she went to see Miss Earle, who received her in her own little morning-room, having carefully guarded herself against interruption of any kind.

It must be owned that Miss Meeking was profoundly impressed by the air of luxury and wealth at the house in Hans Place, and could not help giving a sigh to the memory of the fact that once she had been on the eve of being mistress of just such a house and establishment as this. Nor did Miss Earle herself tend in any way to lessen the feeling of regret. She was simply dressed in a fresh white gown, and rose to meet her visitor with a grace and kindness such as Tommy in his palmiest days had never possessed.

"I am very glad you have come to see me," she said, holding out her pretty slim hand in a very winning way, "because it was impossible for me to come and see you, and there is so much that I need to say to you."

"I was very glad to come, Miss Earle," said Rose Meeking, a little shyly.

There was a moment's silence, which Nancy broke.

"Mr. Beresford tells me," she began, with a painful effort, "that you know everything."

"Near about everything, Miss Earle," returned the barmaid simply.

"And so I wanted to see you," Nancy hurried on, "to—to—thank you and bless you for your goodness in keeping silence. Miss Meeking, my father is a very old man—he is so honourable and so good that

if all this came out it would be his death-blow, his
death-blow; and it is so merciful of you to help us,
that I could never, never thank you enough or do
enough to show you my great gratitude if I tried
for ever."

Rose Meeking looked decidedly embarrassed.

"Well, Miss Earle," she blurted out, "of course
I'm very sorry for you—it must be a dreadful thing
to have on your mind; at least, I know it is on
mine. And, of course I'm very sorry for the poor
old gentleman, though as he knows nothing about
it he perhaps don't need it. But I may as well be
honest first as last, and it's no use my pretending
I've held my tongue for the sake of the family, for
I've done nothing of the kind. I don't say, Miss
Earle, now that I've seen you, that I shouldn't do it
just for you alone—but that's a different thing altogether. Of course, I know that you and Mr. Earle
would have been dreadfully put out if I'd gone and
married Tom. I'm older than he is, and I'm not a
lady like you; but, all the same, I was real fond of
him, and if we'd been married I'd have done my
best to make him a good wife—that I would. But
it wasn't to be. Captain Owen found out what was
going on, poor fellow, and he convinced me that it
wouldn't do—that I hadn't a chance of making a
swell young fellow like Tom happy. So I made up
my mind to give him up, and I'm one of that sort,
when I make up my mind to do a thing, I do it, and
I don't argue about it. So I gave him up in spite
of everything he could say against it, though, of

course, I'd no thought of his going straight off and doing anything like—well, like he did."

" No, no, of course not," murmured Nancy, with momentarily increasing respect for this girl, and struck by the delicate way in which she fenced round the mention of Stuart's shameful act.

" Still, for all that, Miss Earle," Rose Meeking went on, " I haven't quite forgot the past. He was fair and honest enough with me ; he wanted to marry me and make a lady of me, and I'm not going to forget it. I wouldn't marry him *now*, not if he went on his bended knees every day for a year to ask it. I couldn't. I should never know a minute's peace night or day again ; but, at the same time, I was fond of him once, and I mean to stand by him so far, if only for that."

" You are a good woman," Nancy cried. " Oh ! you are good. I don't know how to thank you enough. Some day, perhaps, when you have got over it all and feel inclined to settle down with— with—a—a—better man, I may be able to help you in many ways. And you will let me do that, won't you ? " she ended imploringly.

" Well, Miss Earle," returned Miss Meeking bluntly, " I won't say no. It's not that I want to *sell* my silence, but I've been brought up to fight my own way, and a barmaid's life isn't the easiest one in the world, I can tell you. So I won't say if there was a chance of your being able to do me a good turn that I'd refuse it."

" I will make the chance," said Nancy, pressing

the other girl's hand. "And for to-day, I have got ready a little present, which I want you to accept from me as a token of my heartfelt gratitude and thanks."

She rose as she spoke and fetched from a side table a little, plain, but very handsome hand-bag, such as ladies in Town carry with them; it was of Russia-leather, with a plain silver clasp, and had a small monogram in silver on one side—R.M.

Nancy opened it. "You see it has a purse and everything that we women use—and as you probably know, it is *very* unlucky to give away an empty purse, so I have put enough in it to break the spell. You won't be offended, will you?"

"Miss Earle," said Rose Meeking earnestly, "I don't think *you* could offend me if you tried, and I'm sure——"

"I never shall try," ended Nancy laughing, though her eyes were tearful. "Never, my dear, never. I owe you far too much."

So the two women, so widely different in training and worldly standing, separated, the barmaid won over to Nancy Earle for ever, Nancy Earle full of a vain regret that the circumstances of this world were such that it was impossible for Stuart ever to marry this woman, for whose sake he had sinned so deeply.

"She is shrewd, sensible, honest and true," she said, "and if she had been *Lady* Rose she would have been that wretched boy's salvation."

So the bright summer days slipped over, and the

Earles, father and daughter, began to think about making a move to their country place, Earles Hope. And scarcely were they settled there before Beautiful Jim came—came without a word of warning—came only for a few hours—that he might take a passionate farewell of her whom he loved best in all the world, and three short words were enough of explanation, " Active service—Burmah."

CHAPTER XXX.

SECURITY.

THE Blankshire Regiment was off to the East so suddenly that but little leave, even of a few hours' length, could be granted to its officers for the purpose of making farewells. Beautiful Jim had been especially favoured by the Colonel, and had been granted permission to leave Blankhampton only from five o'clock in the afternoon until officers' call the following morning.

Naturally enough all the officers wished to have the same privilege, but young Earle was not amongst those who pressed for it, so, as he was anything but a favourite with his commanding officer, he was not one of those who were singled out to receive it.

In truth, the lad was anything but anxious to go to Earles Hope. If his father and sister had been in Town, it is probable that he would have begged hard for leave, and have made his farewell to them, and

other farewells at the same time. But being at
Earles Hope, and alone, Tommy had no heart for
begging a favour of his Colonel, whom he knew dis-
liked him, that he might go and face Nancy and all
the airs and graces she would give herself on account
of what she knew about him. No, and besides that,
the way out of the difficulty was so easy, leave was
so difficult to get, in fact next door to impossible,
and by not asking with much anxiety for it he got
passed over for those that did, so that it was an easy
matter to write home that he was grieved not to be
able to come and say good-bye, but that leave was an
impossible favour to obtain with so little service as
he had.

Unfortunately for the success of this wise calcu-
lation, Beautiful Jim spent his few hours of leave in
going to Earles Hope, arriving there late in the
evening and having but two hours to stay.

And, in answer to the old man's anxious enquiries,
he replied that he was afraid Earle had not the most
remote chance in the world of getting even six hours'
leave out of Blankhampton, while to Nancy he con-
fided the fact that her brother had not got leave because he had, to his knowledge, not asked for it.

"Did he tell you so?" she asked. "Did he give
any especial message to my father?"

"Not he, my dearest, he never speaks to me if he
can help it; and you can understand that I don't
exactly seek him out as my friend," Jim answered.
"No, the fact was, I thought, not being much of a
favourite with the chief, that he might have a good

deal of difficulty in getting that or any other privilege, so when I had got mine I put in a word for him. I thought your father would certainly be very anxious to see him. However, the Colonel cut my hint precious short. ‘ If Earle *wants* leave, Jim,’ he said, sharply, ‘ he can at least *ask* for it ; ’ and so, of course, I hadn’t any more to say, though I guessed from that that the young beggar wasn’t keen to come home at all.”

Nancy understood her brother’s feelings well enough ; she knew that he lacked courage after what had happened, to come home and face his gallant old father’s honest eyes ; she knew that he did not dare to face her at all.

It was, therefore, not a little to her dismay that, some ten minutes after she had said good-bye to her Jim, Mr. Earle came to her and told her that he had given her maid and his man orders to be ready to start for Blankhampton by the earliest train in the morning, “ which passes Marchton (their nearest railway station) at twenty minutes past six,” he ended, briskly.

Nancy stared at him for a moment, simply speechless with surprise. “ But, Father, my dear,” she exclaimed, “ it will knock you up altogether, you are not fit for it—you———”

“ Nonsense—nonsense. My only son does not go off to active service every day,” he answered brusquely ; “ and time is precious, they leave Blankhampton on Thursday morning at ten o’clock.”

It was close upon the midnight of Tuesday, so

that, as Mr. Earle very truly said, time was precious. Nancy knew, from the experience of her whole life, that it would be but lost labour to try to persuade him to give up the journey to Blankhampton at this point, and moreover a wild joy shot through her heart that after all she had not seen the last of her Beautiful Jim; and so, as women do at such times, she dried away the tears with which her cheeks were still wet, and went off to her own room as gaily as any lark, to tell her maid exactly what gowns to take, and then sought her bed for the few hours of sleep which were possible to her before morning light should break, and straightway sank into a serene slumber as though meeting instead of parting lay before her.

So to Beautiful Jim's unspeakable delight and to Tommy's unutterable disgust, on the following morning, before any one of the Blankshire Regiment had so much as had time to think about anything so comfortable as luncheon, Mr. and Miss Earle arrived at the Infantry Barracks in an hotel carriage.

And Tommy looked as he felt—*done!* However, he had no excuse but to go through the day as best he could, although he wished himself already in Burmah over and over again, and fairly hated Nancy for the part which she played, giving him a limp hand for an instant without a shake in it, looking right over his head when she spoke to him, giving him the edge of her jaw to kiss if he wished to do so. Only once indeed did she look at or speak to him fair or straight.

"Stuart," she said sharply, when they were just going back to the town again, "the Colonel says you will be free at three o'clock to come and see us. I want to see you *alone*. Do you understand?"

"Can you arrange it?" he asked sulkily, not daring to refuse.

"Yes. Mr. Beresford is coming at that time also, and I will take you into my bedroom while I say what I want to say to you. It will not take me more than ten minutes."

"Very well," said he curtly.

Miss Earle looked at him—and she knew him pretty well, so was able to read what was passing through his mind as easily as if he had been a book.

"And don't attempt to shirk it," she said sharply, "because I've got something to say to you and I mean to say it before you go. Do you understand?"

"Oh, perfectly," returned Tommy with a sneer. The sneer roused every feeling of evil that had any foothold in Nancy's gentle heart; they were not many, but they were enough to make Tommy thoroughly uncomfortable for the rest of that day.

"If you fail to keep your tryst," she said coldly, "our father knows *every* thing before seven o'clock to-night," and then she turned from him without another word and rejoined the others, who were walking towards the carriage.

So almost before the clock a little way up the High Street had struck the hour, young Tommy made his appearance in the sitting-room which was for the time being that of his father and sister, and a few minutes later was followed by his comrade, Beautiful Jim.

Then was Nancy's opportunity, nor did she neglect to take advantage of it. "Oh ! Stuart," she said, in a tone so admirably easy and like her own that Beautiful Jim was fairly startled and looked up quickly, fully convinced that in the pain of parting his gentle sweetheart had forgotten all the past, "I have something to show you—come into my room for a minute. Jim, you will talk to my father till we come back, won't you ?"

Jim bowed and made some polite rejoinder, and Nancy went briskly out of the room, followed by Tommy.

They found her maid busily arranging her gown for the evening. "You can go down for half-an-hour, Susan," said Nancy, and, as the maid obeyed, closed the door behind her and turned the key in the lock. Then she went across the room to Tommy's side—and surely if Beautiful Jim could have seen her at that moment, he would not have found much forgetfulness of the past in the sternly compressed lips and the shining scornful eyes.

"I have not asked you to come here to reproach you, Stuart," she began, looking straight at him with her clear, grey, shining, honest eyes.

Young Tommy shifted irresolutely from one foot to the other. "I should think," he blurted out, "that you could hardly be so mean as that when

I'm just off to active service, and may never come home again."

"A very good thing if you never do," she responded coldly, "but all the same it is just because you are going to the front, and perhaps never may come home again, that I asked you to come up here. I want to know if you have considered that in the event of such happening, it is possible, even probable, that your guilt may fall on the shoulders of another who is perfectly innocent?"

Tommy looked at her blankly. "What do you mean?" he asked.

"I mean," said Nancy, steadily, "that, supposing you happen to be killed out there or to die, and Mr. Beresford gets home safely, the charge against him might be raked up again, and he might find it difficult or even impossible to clear himself."

"I never thought of it," said Tommy with evident sincerity.

"I don't suppose you did—you don't think very much of anyone but yourself, you know," said Nancy, very scornfully. "I have thought of it, however, and I mean you to secure him from any such risk."

"How?"

"By leaving a written account behind you of Captain Owen's death."

"I shall do nothing of the kind! Do you think I'm going to incriminate myself in that way? No. I'll be shot if I do," he cried, indignantly.

Nancy eyed him coolly. "Hanged, you mean," she said, with extreme quietness.

Tommy made a great start. "Nancy," he said, hoarsely, "are you trying how far you can go ?"

"No," she replied steadily, "for I have no need. *I know* exactly how far I can go, and you also. You will sign that paper before you leave this room," she added, "or I go straight to my father with the whole story. If you were a man," with great scorn, "you would be only too glad to save one who had borne so much for you, from such a risk ; but you are the same Stuart you have been all along, bad, selfish and reckless to the lowest depths of your wicked heart."

"Beresford has not kept silence for *me*," muttered Tommy, sullenly.

"No, but he has done so for me," she rejoined ; "and therefore I am going to secure him from running any further risk through your sin than he had done before."

"*You* are going to do this and that ; *you* won't have the other," Tommy cried furiously. "'Pon my soul, Madam Nancy, you will carry things too far, if you don't mind. I shall not stand very much more of your high hand, I assure you. By Jove, Madam," he blurted out in a vain attempt to bounce Nancy out of her stronghold, "you forget yourself. Do you know who I am ?"

Nancy looked at him for full a minute before she spoke. "Yes," she said, slowly ; "I am sorry to say I do know exactly *what* you are. *You are Captain Owen's murderer.*"

All Tommy's artificial indignation died out instantly. "No, I'm not that—it was an accident," he stammered.

Nancy smiled. "It is not worth while to mince matters between you and me," she answered. "It does not signify what you call it, you killed him; that is enough for me. Now, we have no more time to waste over this kind of argument; sit down there and write out what I wish."

Tommy sat down and rested his head dejectedly on his hand. "I—I don't know what you want," he said, forlornly.

"I knew you would not," said Nancy, taking her keys out of her pocket, and unlocking her desk. "I have put down exactly what I want you to copy and sign—here it is."

She handed a sheet of note-paper to the wretched boy, on which was written the following :—

"I, Stuart Earle, lieutenant in the Blankshire Regiment, being on the eve of departure for active service in Burmah, do testify that on the —th of May, 188—, I caused the death of my brother officer, Captain Richard Owen, by throwing a dumb-bell at him. I swear that no other person was in any way involved in his death, or knew anything whatever about it."

"I tell you it was an accident," said Tommy, fiercely.

"Then you can add it, if you choose," said she.

So Tommy seized a pen and passionately copied out the few words, adding at the end that the entire

17

affair was an accident; that although he had thrown
the dumb-bell at Owen in a passion, he had never
had the smallest intention of killing him, or even of
doing him any injury whatever. "And how do I
know you won't let this get out of your hands?" he
asked, raising a haggard and wretched face to look
at her.

"You may trust me," she said quietly. "Under
no other circumstances than the imminent danger
to an innocent person would I disclose the truth;
not on account of our family honour—which must be
poor indeed since it has not had a better influence
on you—but solely because of the blow it would be
to my father."

"And you won't use it to work in influence
against me with my father?" he asked. "To get
me cut out of my inheritance, for instance?"

Nancy looked at him in disgusted scorn. "Am
I *you*?" she asked contemptuously; and so, stung
to the depths of his ignoble soul, young Tommy
seized the pen once more, dipped it into the ink,
and signed his name at the foot of the page—
"Stuart Earle, Lieutenant, Blankshire Regiment."
"There, will that satisfy you?" he asked savagely.

Nancy took it up and read it carefully through,
then with the same deliberation put her own name
at the bottom. "Yes, that is all I wanted," she
said quietly, and folding up the paper, placed it in
an envelope and tied it carefully round with string.
Then she lighted a taper and sealed it in several
places, finally taking a pen and writing on the

back—"Private memorandum relating to Stuart Earle, The Golden Swan, Blankhampton."

"There, that is safe, I think. I don't want to keep you any longer," and with a little wave of her hand she dismissed him.

It would be hard to say how bitter were young Tommy's thoughts as he made his way back to the sitting-room, there to take up the weary burden of society with his old father.

Not that he went straightway there. Oh, no; he passed the door when he came to it, and took his way down to the bar, where he called for a strong brandy and soda, and then finding that it did not have the restorative effect that he desired, asked for green Chartreuse, and drank three or four glasses of that before he felt himself his own man again. And with each one he drank to his sister Nancy's eternal confusion and tribulation, with never a sense of thankfulness for the mercy that from one cause or other had been shown him.

Well, well, Lord Chesterfield is looked upon as an old-fashioned dowdy now, but all the same he knew a thing or two, and human nature was very much in his time what it is now; and he said, "The heart never grows better by age; I fear rather worse; always harder. A young knave will only grow a greater knave as he grows older."

CHAPTER XXXI.

OFF TO THE WARS.

QUITE a crowd was gathered at the station the following morning to see the gallant Blankshire Regiment go off to the wars. There was Mrs. Barnes with all her children ; and little Mrs. Seton, as brisk and as bright as a bee, laughing as loudly as if parting with her Major was one of the best jokes in the world, though to more than one who knew her best the laughter had an uncommonly suspicious ring about it and had a quiver through its rippling thrill which told of tears not very far away. And there were the Charterhouses and the Stauntons and the Marcus Orfords, all come to do the last honours to their friends, husbands and wives alike profoundly thankful that the fortune of war had not called upon them to leave home and all they loved behind and go out to fight for Queen and country in the tropics. And there was the handsome Dean, cheery and full of good wishes, and lovely Aileen, holding fast by Nancy Earle's hand as if she was afraid she should break down if she did not hold it tight enough.

Nancy understood so well what the pressure meant and once or twice turned her sweet dove's eyes upon her friend, just to show her that there were no tears there, and that she need have no fears for her composure. And last of all there was Mr Earle, tall and straight, and commanding in presence, with his handsome old face set like a mask and his white hair as well brushed and spruce as ever. Ah! but it was a terrible wrench for him, parting with his only son on such an errand, and almost at the same moment a thought flashed into the minds of Nancy and Beautiful Jim alike, a thought which said " Alas ! he is so old, so frail, and his belief in his only son is so great. I am so glad that we kept silence for—though it is a pang for us—knowledge would have held the bitterness of death for him."

Almost unconsciously Nancy slipped her hand within his arm and clung to it; but the old man mistook her meaning. " Don't give way, my dear," he whispered, " let them see the Earles can give up their best for Queen and country—even the heir."

He had forgotten her interest in Beautiful Jim ; he only remembered that his boy, his heir, the last of his name, was off to the wars, and might never come back.

Nancy dropped the arm. She forgot nothing !

Not that the old man noticed anything. He was intently watching for the last glimpse of the handsome young face of his only son, and as the train moved slowly out of the station, amid cheers and the frantic waving of handkerchiefs, to the gay and jolly strains of " The girl I leave behind me," he gave a great gasping sigh, which melted Nancy's momentary anger and made her clasp his arm tighter than ever.

And then little Mrs. Seton, who had joked and

laughed and cheered and waved with the best as long as her faithful Major's head was thrust out of the carriage window, suddenly created a *divertissement* by breaking down altogether into such a passionate torrent of tears, that even the dullest of those who had wondered at what they called her " spirits " but a few moments before wondered no longer, but said among themselves, as they wiped their own eyes, what a brave little woman she was, and what a treasure the big Major possessed in her.

" Oh, I'm going out at once," the little woman was saying brokenly at that moment to the sympathetic woman on whose breast she had poured out all her long pent-up feelings. " He said I wasn't to, but I shall.   Why, he might be wounded out there, or ill, and who would nurse him, I wonder?   He never can bear anyone but me about him, if he's only got a headache. But, all the same, when you've never done anything for yourself in all your life, and never even gone a long journey alone, it's no joke to face going out to India, or still worse to Burmah, without a soul to help you to do a thing."

Nancy Earle, who was standing by, took her hand. " My dear," she whispered, " believe me, it's far harder when you are so placed that you *cannot* go out whatever happens, when you know that even if you hear the worst and you feel you are wanted ever so badly, you are bound at home by ties and restrictions which you cannot break. Oh! It is nothing to let one's *husband* go, compared with the one who is everything and yet nothing to you."

Mrs. Seton dried her eyes and looked up. " Yes, he told me a good deal about it, dear," she said kindly, and with scarcely more than a faint sob catching her breath, " and be sure if he is in need of my help he will have it. I'd do anything for him for his own sake, but I'll do it for yours as well now, I promise you."

" How good you are," Nancy whispered fervently, " small wonder he is so fond of you, Mrs. Seton. Some day, perhaps, I shall be able to do something for you, and if I ever can—oh, how I shall jump at the chance of being able to do it."

By this time the people were gradually clearing out of the station, and as the handsome Dean had given his sturdy arm to Mr. Earle, Nancy and Aileen followed in their wake with Mrs. Seton.

The Dean was trying hard to persuade the old man to abandon his idea of returning home that day, and to change his quarters from the Golden Swan to the more luxurious ease and quietude of the Deanery, for, as he said, " It will be a change for you, and if you go home at once you will mope and get thinking of danger to the boy, when as yet no danger exists ; and besides, you do not know Blankhampton at all, though there is a good deal that is well worth seeing here, and there must be a great many people in the neighbourhood whom you know more or less well."

But Mr. Earle was obdurate ! He had no intention whatever of going out to please the Blankhampton neighbourhood, boring himself with interminable country dinner parties, where the usual September style of conversation would be in full swing and he would not be able to get a decent game of whist for love or money; still less had he a mind to let the dear, handsome Dean run him round his beloved "Parish," pointing out the respective merits of oak and old stained glass; drawing him up a corkscrew stair to study the internal economy of the finest organ in the world next to Haarlem and Utrecht, and one or two others which, from a long and varied experience of deans, Mr. Earle knew this particular one would forget the names of; to be then dragged up a tower nearly five hundred feet high to see a peal of bells which, in spite of their value and beauty *as bells*, Mr. Earle considered a disgrace to any enlightened and Christian age; then into Bishop Somebody's chapel ·to view vestments and other church furniture, together with divers relics which, bigoted old Tory that he was, he would like to have consigned to the Pro-Cathedral down the street; then into a dark and dreary crypt, to be made to think far more forcibly than he cared or desired of his own latter end. No, no—the dear and hospitable Dean might persuade as sweetly as he chose, and Mrs. Trafford might smile and put on her prettiest airs (which she did), but they and everyone else found that the head of the Earle family had a very, very strong will of his own, and that when he had once made up his mind to pursue a certain course, he pursued that one course and no other.

In this instance he had made up his mind not to return to Earles Hope, or, at least not to remain there longer than a week at the outside, and then to fly off to his beloved London, his comfortable home in Hans Place, and his ever-blessed haven of retreat—the club. Left to himself he would have gone straightway there; but, as Nancy reminded him, the servants were just then in the very middle of house-cleaning, and the cook was gone off on a holiday, so that to put in a week at Earles Hope, or elsewhere, was neither more nor less than an imperative necessity. All the same, convinced of this as he undoubtedly was, nothing would induce him to put in that week as a guest at Blankhampton Deanery, and the chief reason for his decision was the fear of being escorted in solemn state over the grand old pile of Gothic architecture which Blankhampton folk familiarly call "the Parish."

One more night, however, he did consent to remain at the Golden Swan, and he also promised to dine at Mrs. Trafford's to meet a select but hurriedly-gathered-together company; and as soon as he and Nancy had finished their somewhat early lunch, he told her that he was going to keep himself very quiet until dinner-time, and that he did not wish to be disturbed.

Nancy, therefore, put on her hat and went to see her friend, Aileen, who was tired too with the exertions of the morning; so the two girls dawdled away the lovely September afternoon on the terrace of the Deanery, in company, after an hour or so, with the girls from the Residence and one or two men from the Cavalry Barracks, who had found their way thither I don't quite know how.

Then came the evening, spent as brightly and gaily—for little Mrs. Trafford knew how to make her parties go off well and her guests enjoy themselves, none better — as if the scene at the station. that morning had been the beginning of a bridal tour for some especially fortunate young couple, rather than a setting out of some of their nearest and dearest to undergo the horrors of war. And to more than one it was a welcome relief from the dreary process of sitting down to think.

———

CHAPTER XXXII.

NEWS AT LAST.

" IF Nancy likes to come back to see you all when I am comfortably settled in Town," Mr. Earle said to Lady Margaret and her daughter during the course of the evening of Mrs. Trafford's little impromptu dinner, " I shall be very glad to spare her. Not that I do not miss her when she is away from me, mind, but I get very well looked after in Town, and can exist without her; and I do not forget," with a sigh, "that she is young, and that the tastes of May are different to the tastes of December."

" Oh, let us say October," put in Lady Margaret pleasantly.

But the old man shook his head very decidedly.

"Nay, my dear lady, not only December, but getting very near Christmas-time," he said gently.

"Then I hope Nancy will come back to us again," said Lady Margaret, ignoring the remark, with which, by-the-bye, she altogether agreed, "and stay a long time."

But Nancy had no notion of planting herself for an unlimited visit at a country town, where news would be a day old and letters several posts in reaching her, and she shook her head as firmly as ever her old father could have done.

"Dear Lady Margaret," she said, "I could come for a week or so, but not longer. He," laying her hand on her father's arm, "misses me far more than he will own ; he is afraid of making me conceited, I fancy. And besides that, I never feel easy in my mind when I am away from him. But why could not Aileen come up and stay with me for a few weeks ?"

"Well, I really do not see that there is any reason," said Lady Margaret with a laugh.

So they settled it, and the following morning the Earles left Blankhampton and returned to Earles Hope. While there, Nancy had letters from her Beautiful Jim, written, or rather posted, from Liverpool and Queenstown.

He said that they were all well and fairly cheerful ; that Tommy had been abjectly sea-sick up to that time, and had not turned out of his berth at all ; and then followed a good deal highly interesting to Nancy herself, but not bearing much on the points of this story.

They remained about ten days at Earles Hope, not from choice, but simply because the house in Hans Place could not by hook or by crook be got ready to receive them any earlier; and, on the whole, it must be owned that Nancy had rather a trying time of it, for the old man was a regular town bird, and loathed the country cordially. And, unfortunately, it was a wet September, when the floods literally descended and the rains poured, and all the green lawns and woods around his ancestral home became greener and greener as they got soaked and sodden with the wealth of waters, until he fairly longed for London mud and the luxury of his beloved club.

" Lawns getting a pretty colour," he said crossly one day when Nancy had meekly suggested that the rain was restoring the lawns to quite a spring-like verdure. " Ugh! as if one could live on colour. Give me a bit of decent London mud instead of this wilderness."

" But, dearest, we can't go back to London white-wash," Nancy protested.

" Of course not; I know we can't. But why you need have had a perfectly clean house upset in this fashion, at this time of year, simply passes my comprehension to understand," he growled; " particularly when we were on that abominable Riviera all the winter, when you could have had the place rebuilt if you'd chosen, without half this annoyance and inconvenience."

Nancy said nothing. If she had been an ordinary woman, with the customary length of tongue, she might have reminded him that certain necessary repairs were greatly wanted in the house in Hans Place, and that more than once he had bidden her write home from the sunny shores of the Mediterranean to the faithful old housekeeper left in charge, and say that under pain of incurring his most intense displeasure, nothing in his especial rooms must be touched; that no alterations or unusual house-cleanings were to be attempted; and that they might be expected to return home at any time, and without any notice whatever.

She might have reminded him of these trifling facts, and also that he had given special permission to have any such work done during their autumn sojourn at Earles Hope, adding, as an additional reason for choosing that part of the year for it, that it was real selfishness to invariably have such work done in the spring-time, leaving nothing for "the poor devils of workpeople" to do all the autumn and winter, when they wanted the money most.

But Nancy said nothing. She had been brought up an Earle, you see, and the Earles had always been accustomed to consider patience and forbearance the most delightful virtues for their womenfolk to cultivate. Moreover, even for an Earle (who didn't count), Nancy had great tact, and so she suffered the unreasonable old man's unreasonable reproaches in silence. Wise Nancy!

At last, however, the welcome news came from

Town to say that the house was ready, and Mr. Earle became a different being all at once.

"First train in the morning, my dear," he said, joyfully. "The very first train in the morning."

"Oh! Father, dear!" Nancy cried in dismay. "*Not* the five o'clock train!"

"Oh, well, no; not the five o'clock train. I didn't quite mean *that*," he admitted.

Nancy did not hesitate, but struck while the iron was hot. "And the one at eight is very slow, dear," she said mildly. "We tried it once, if you remember, and you sw—— you found fault all the way to St. Pancras. *Don't* you think we had better say the express at eleven-fifteen? It's such a comfortable train, you know, dear."

"Yes, of course—of course," exclaimed the old man testily. "How dull you are getting, Nancy. That was the train I meant, of course."

"How stupid of me," murmured Nancy in her gentlest tones.

She had her reward; they reached London in time for her father to have lunch and then go off to his beloved club, whence he came back to dinner —not because he would not rather have dined there, but simply from a sense of duty to his daughter— in the best possible spirits.

"'Pon my word," he chuckled, "I heard one of the best stories I ever heard in my life to-day. Maturin told me. It seems before he became a Harley Street big-wig he had a country practice near Stroud; and not long before he made a move the Squire was taken ill—ve-ry ill, poor old chap, of the complaint that eventually carried him off. Well, one day, the Squire, having been docked off one little luxury after another until life was hardly worth living, said to Maturin—'Look here, Doctor, don't you think I might have a glass or two of Madeira? Do you think it would hurt me?'

"'Well, Squire,' said Maturin, who thought his case so hopeless that nothing would make much difference to it, 'I really don't think it would. At all events, try a couple of glasses to your lunch and we'll see what effect it has on you.'

"Well, after a little chat he left him and went home; and on the way he met the parson, a jolly rich old chap, one of the best judges of wine in the country, and owning about the best cellar of wine. 'Well, Doctor,' said he, pulling up his horse, have you been to see the Squire? And how is the dear old fellow to-day?'

"Maturin shook his head. 'H'm—very so-so. However, he's asked leave to have a glass of Madeira, and I've told him to try, and we shall see the effect it has on him. Between ourselves, Rector, I don't think it will make much difference, and if it doesn't do him any good it can hardly do him any harm.'

"'Well, now Doctor,' said the Rector, 'I'm real glad you told me this. I see my way to doing a kind Christian neighbourly action, for our dear old friend up yonder'—jerking his thumb towards the Hall—'though he's got a decent cellar of wine, he doesn't happen to have a drop of good Madeira in it. I'll send him up a couple of bottles of my best at once. Good-bye, Doctor, good-bye.'

"Well, Maturin went up to the Hall the next day and found that the old Squire had just finished his lunch.

"'And did you have the Madeira?' he asked. He noticed a couple of bottles on the sideboard.

"'Oh, yes. And I feel wonderfully better for it,' the Squire answered, 'quite comfortable and like myself again.'

"'And what's the second bottle?' asked Maturin.

"'Why,' returned the Squire, with a laugh, 'like the dear good fellow he is, the Rector sent me down a couple of bottles of his best, as you had told him I might try a glass or so of Madeira. Dear old chap he is. But there, what's the use of it—I can't drink it. Why, the dear old fellow hasn't got a decent bottle of Madeira in his whole cellar'"—and then Mr. Earle laughed long and heartily at the story, and Nancy joined him.

She knew from that that he was better—that the great wrench of parting with Stuart had passed over, so she was much more easy in her mind about him, although she did not think it advisable to pay the promised visit to Blankhampton.

Instead, however, her friend Aileen came to stay with her, and the two girls spent a very pleasant time together. There was not much doing, and the town was still rather empty, but at its worst it was a lively change from Blankhampton.

So the greater part of November slipped away, and Aileen returned home, leaving Nancy to her lonely life, for Mr. Earle, being almost all day at his club, could scarce be counted as having much to do with it.

The dreary winter days passed by; Christmas came and went—to the household in Hans Place a festive season without any festivity about it—then the old year died out and the New Year dawned.

And all this time there was no especial news from the Blankshire Regiment. In every letter they were longing for fighting, to get to the front, for anything decisive which would bring the miserable campaign to an end. And at last there came an evening when Nancy opened the *Evening Standard* to read: " Great engagement in Burmah," and to see standing out as in letters of fire two names, " *Lieutenants James Beresford and Stuart Earle.*"

CHAPTER XXXIII.

SUSPENSE KILLS.

WHEN the words " *Great Engagement in Burmah* " caught Nancy Earle's eyes, and immediately afterwards the names of *James Beresford* and *Stuart Earle,* she was for a minute or two too terrified to look at the paragraph again. Then she summoned up all her courage and prepared herself to face the worst.

The announcement was a usual one of its kind. It said that a party of the Blankshire Regiment had been out on the search for Dacoits and had been surprised by an unusually large band of these native robbers, with the result of complete victory to the English troops. Unfortunately, however, the loss on our side had been five killed, and eight men of the Blankshire Regiment had been more or less severely wounded, one of whom had died on the way back to camp. Besides these, two officers of the same regiment had been very severely wounded —Lieutenants James Beresford and Stuart Earle.

It was, of course, utterly absurd of the correspondent out at the scene of action to have sent home such a heading to such a paragraph as "Great Engagement in Burmah"—or if he had not been responsible for it, for the person who had done so— but Nancy, poor girl, did not stay to think of that. To her, it was the most important battle that had ever been fought in the world's history—for were not the two soldiers in whom she took more interest than in all the rest of the army put together lying at that moment grievously wounded, if not already dead ?   In the shock of that moment, her bitterness against her brother all died out, but it must be owned she thought of her Beautiful Jim the most. She felt Jim's wound racking her own delicate body ; she felt every jolt of his litter or inequality of his rough bed ; she thought of the heat and the flies and the absence of proper attention; and she thought but little of Stuart one way or the other.

She was already dressed for dinner, very simply and plainly, in a dark velvet gown, with her pretty slender throat just showing from out of its soft lace ruffles; and as she sat by the fire-side, her little tender hand somehow got stealing up and down the soft velvet of her gown, until all at once the luxury of her surroundings struck her with a sense of wrong, as if by living among them she was doing a positive injury to him who needed them so much more than she did, and to whom, at that moment, they were an impossibility, far out of reach.

Not that she could help herself—her duty tied her hard and fast in her father's house, just as fate had sent him to meet what had already perhaps proved his death—her father was so old and——and then, oh! she suddenly remembered him in the midst of her own trouble, remembered that he would see the evening papers at his club, and would look eagerly for news from the front, and so would receive the intelligence of his son's danger without in any way having it broken to him.

Quickly, almost as the thought struck her, she jumped up and ran down into the hall, where the fire was blazing away cheerily and casting pretty gleams of light up the tall quaint screen which formed a sort of chimney corner to it. There was nobody there, so without waiting to summon a servant to enquire if he had returned home, Nancy turned and

18—2

ran up the staircase again, going this time to his dressing-room.

He was not there either, but as Nancy pushed open the door after knocking twice, his man Darby came out of the bedroom with a can of water in his hand.

"Has Mr. Earle returned yet, Darby?" Nancy asked breathlessly.

"Not yet, Miss Earle," he answered, with a glance at the little horse-shoe clock on the chimney-shelf; "and it is twenty minutes to eight, rather less, for that clock is a minute or two slow."

"There is awful news from Burmah, Darby," said Nancy, trembling. "There has been a great engagement—and Mr. Stuart is wounded, severely wounded."

"You don't say so, ma'am," exclaimed Darby, who, in common with all the servants both in Hans Place and Earles Hope, detested the heir to the old name. The tone was not very sympathetic; in fact, it expressed the well-bred surprise of a good servant rather than sympathy at all—but he was sorry for Nancy, and his thoughts went straight to the effect the news might have upon his master. "I hope the master will not see the papers at the club, Miss Earle," he said anxiously.

Nancy was about to speak, when a furious peal at the bell of the outer door sounded through the house.

"There he is," she said, and ran out of the room and down the stairs just as the servant, who had come up from below, opened the door.

But it was not her father, and instead of his tall and striking figure appearing out of the gloom of the winter's evening, a short, stout, and roseate gentleman walked into the house.

"Oh! Sir George," Nancy cried, recognising one of her father's most intimate friends.

"My dear young lady," said Sir George St. Leger, kindly, "I am sorry—but there is sad news!"

"I have seen the papers—I know," Nancy answered quickly. "And my father?"

By this time he had drawn her to the fireside, and was holding her hands in his.

"I am very sorry, my dear, that your poor father has seen them too," said he very kindly, "and the shock—it's no use my trying to spin it out; I told them at the club that I was the wrong man to send on an errand of this kind," he broke off.

"Oh! go on. Don't keep me waiting," Nancy said imploringly. "Tell me the worst at once. Is he dead?"

"Oh! no—no—*no*, my dear child," cried the little old gentleman eagerly, "certainly not—nothing of the kind. But it was a very great shock, of course, to our dear old friend, and he had a kind of seizure —a faintness, or something of that sort—and they are bringing him home, some of the others, in his own carriage, so I took a cab and hurried on to say it would be safer to get the doctor here as quickly as possible. Just a precaution you know, my dear," pressing her hands ere he set them free.

Nancy put the hand which was nearest to him back into his.

"How good you are," she said, turning round at the same time. "Jones, will you send out at once for Dr. Davies? Don't let them lose a moment. Darby, you have everything ready for my father, have you not?"

"Everything, ma'am," said Darby, who had been prepared for trouble of this kind from the moment the young mistress had told him the last news of the young master.

"You would like me to stay until they come, or is there anything that I can do, my dear?" asked Sir George, kindly.

"Oh! no. There is so little that any of us can do," she answered hopelessly; "but do stay, please."

So Sir George drew her down on to the cosy couch sheltered by the tall Chinese screen, and together they waited during the few minutes, that seemed so interminably long, before the sound of the carriage was heard without.

Naturally enough, Darby was the first to approach the carriage, and as soon as his eyes fell upon the helpless and motionless figure of his master, he looked over his shoulder at the butler and said imperatively, "Get Miss Earle out of sight—it's paralysis."

Thus bidden, Jones did his best, but Nancy was close behind him. "I am quite prepared for anything, Jones," she said, with intense calmless. "Don't waste time trying to persuade me to go away—they need your help."

She was not unreasonable in the least, although she would not be put away from her father's side when she felt that he needed her the most; but she stood aside to let them carry him into the house and up the wide stairs to his own room.

"He will recover from this a good deal after an hour or so, my dear," said Sir George with a kindly attempt at consolation, as they watched the sad procession pass out of sight.

Nancy turned her soft dove's eyes upon him with an incredulous look and shook her head.

"No, Sir George, he will never be any better," she said mournfully. "He has not strength enough to bear up against a shock like that—he is so old and so frail—so frail."

Even Sir George could not think of anything to say—and, in his heart of hearts, he confidently believed that his old friend was dead already. There was the sound of a hansom dashing up to the door, and then the Doctor came hurrying in.

"Yes—I've heard all about it," he said, as Nancy met him. "A pity—a pity. A shock like that is a nasty thing to fight against at Mr. Earle's age; however, I'll go straight up, if you please, Miss Earle. Well, yes—I think you had better let me go first. I won't keep you in suspense or away from him a moment longer than is absolutely necessary." Then he, too, disappeared up the stairs, and Nancy sat down on the sofa again to wait for news with the best patience she might.

"You want to be going—your dinner," she said wearily to Sir George.

"No—no—I am dining at the club—any time will do. I could not leave without hearing what the Doctor says, in any case," he replied hastily; and so they sat on side by side while the clock in the corner ticked steadily on, not speaking much, rather, indeed, holding their breath to listen for the first sound that should come to them from the hushed and quiet chamber above. Dr. Davies did not keep them waiting very long, for in about twenty minutes he came down again, treading quietly, as medical men do. Nancy rose and went to meet him.

"We can do nothing at present," he said gently, "for an hour or so your father must be kept perfectly quiet; but I have given Darby complete instructions what to do until the nurse comes. I will send one in at once, unless you like to wire to St. John's House for one—use my name, and ask for Nurse Provis if she is there. I will come back again in an hour."

"I may go up to him?" Nancy asked.

"Oh! yes; but have you dined? No? Then get a glass of wine and some strong soup, or something of that kind before you do so; and do not touch him or disturb him in any way, even if he seems uneasy and restless. He knows nothing, and, at present, suffers nothing whatever."

"Very well," said Nancy obediently.

Sir George St. Leger bade her good-bye then.

saying that he would look in on his way home later
in the evening and ask after his old friend. "And if
there is anything that I can do, you will command
me ?" he added.

"Oh! yes, Sir George, I will indeed, and thank
you so much," returned Nancy gratefully.

And at last she was free to go upstairs into her
father's room, to go and sit beside him, to watch
him as he lay helpless and unconscious upon his
bed, with Darby, his faithful man, at hand to do
all that medical skill could devise, until the nurse
should come. And after a while she came—a
small, slight, brown-haired woman, with a fair
pleasant face, and good, bright, hazel eyes. She
came in as if she had lived in the room all her life,
her footsteps making no sound, her light gown no
rustle, and she stood beside the bed and looked
down upon her new patient while Darby repeated
in a whisper the instructions which the Doctor had
given him.

And then Darby went down to get his supper,
and Nancy crept round to her side.

"Do you think he will die, nurse ?" she asked,
with a world of entreaty in her looks and tones.

The nurse turned her bright eyes upon her.

"I think that he is very ill," she said guardedly.

"But do you think he will die ?" Nancy persisted.

"With great care he might pull round again,"
returned the nurse, unwilling to commit herself
one way or the other.

So Nancy went back to her place again, and took up her occupation of watching the set grey face on which the darker shadows were fast stealing. She knew only too well what the nurse's unwillingness to speak conveyed, that there was no hope, no hope!

Oh! what sad, sad hours they were, with the old man who had been so much to her dying before her, and in her mind the continual thought of that other one stricken down in the full measure of his youth and strength, and lying—if it were not all over before this—in discomfort and misery, without one loving hand to help him. And then she thought of the unhappy, headstrong, passionate boy, who was not twenty years old yet, but who had wrecked her life and had sent her brave and gallant lover to his death—for had there not risen up that obstacle to their marriage, Jim Beresford would have left the service or have exchanged into a home regiment many months ago.

Darby crept into the room again after a while, and the nurse put up a warning finger that he might make no noise.

"Is he worse?" the man asked in an awed whisper, but the nurse only closed her lips a shade tighter, and kept her eyes fixed on the sunk and haggard face.

Dr. Davies came very soon, having no need to ask questions or make examination, only, indeed, raising his eye-brows a little as he cast a glance at the unconscious figure.

But he did not go away. He stood at the foot of the bed and waited. But not for long! The minutes passed slowly by. The little clock on the dressing-table ticked steadily on, and the hands pointed hard on the hour of midnight; no one moved or stirred. Nancy sat just where she had sat for several hours, her hands pressed hard together, but no sound escaped her lips or any tears falling from her eyes. And then the little clock began to chime the midnight hour, and ere the twelfth tiny stroke had rent the air, the last of the Earles had passed away, killed by the news of harm to the son who had never been but a shame to him, and without word or look for the daughter who was only a girl, who was born an Earle, yet an Earle that did not count.

CHAPTER XXXIV.

WAITING.

EARLY the following morning, Sir George St. Leger came to ask for Nancy and to find out if there was anything he could do to serve her, or in any way lighten the duties which lay immediately before her.

"There is something that you could do for me, Sir George," she said, when she had answered his greeting, "and it is to telegraph out to Burmah for me, to get the last news. The servants are very good and anxious to do all that they can, but none of them know whom to send to or where to send, and I cannot tell them. But I thought you would be sure to know or be able to find out."

" To be sure, to be sure," Sir George made haste to reply. " I will do it at once."

" I can give you the last address I had, if that would be any use."

" Oh ! no. I'll go down to the War Office and get the latest information as to route and so on."

" And, Sir George, it would be best, I think, *not* to send my brother any news from here," Nancy said hesitatingly. " You see it might be told to him suddenly and just turn the scale with him, if he is very badly wounded, as they say."

" I will be sure to word the message very carefully," said little Sir George, feeling a very suspicious lump rising in his throat at the thought of the double sorrow which had come upon this fragile girl with the golden head and dove's eyes.

There was a moment's silence.

" And—and would you also enquire especially after Mr. Beresford ? " she said, flushing a lovely shell-like pink over her sweet face.

" Mr. Beresford—that was the other man who was wounded," Sir George exclaimed. " Is he a friend of yours, my dear ? Did you know him ? "

" I am going to marry him some day," she said, then she at once began to sob piteously, " if—if— "

" No—no—let us hope for the best. Don't think of that," the little man cried, almost beside himself with distress. " While there's life there's hope, you know, my dear, and they are both young and strong — not like our dear old friend who went away from us yesterday, but young men in the very flower of their strength. The chances are a thousand to one in their favour; but I'll go along at once, my dear, and then your mind will be more at rest about them," and off the good-hearted little man went, and Nancy was once more left alone.

There was a great deal for her to do naturally, but it was really only in the way of giving orders. The family solicitor came as soon as he received the news of Mr. Earle's death, and all the weight of arranging for the funeral and the other business fell upon him.

The day wore slowly away, but Sir George did not return with news from Burmah. Then Darby brought in the evening papers, and Nancy saw from the expression of his face that the worst had happened to one or both out at the front.

" Which is it, Darby ? " she asked faintly, feeling a deadly numbness stealing over her.

" Miss Earle," he said very gently, " you are the last of the name now. Mr. Stuart only lived a few hours after they got him into camp."

" And Mr.—Beresford ? " Nancy whispered.

" No mention of him, ma'am," the servant answered, " so he is alive at all events," and then he put the paper into her hand and pointed to the place where she would find what she wished to see.

It was so short, cruelly short, as war-dispatches always seem to those who are the most keenly interested, just saying that Lieutenant Stuart Earle and one private of the Blankshire Regiment had died, shortly after reaching camp, of wounds received in an engagement with Dacoits on the —th.

And there was not a single word about the condition or fate of Lieutenant James Beresford! However, in a certain sense, there was relief in the very fact—at all events he was not dead, so that there was a chance for him yet!

She had to wait a long time—or what seemed so to her, poor girl—before she got any definite news about him, for although the papers contained various shoit dispatches he was not mentioned in any of them.

Still no news was good news, and at last Sir George St. Leger came to her in triumph, with a telegram which had come by various stages right from the fountain head.

"Major Seton to Sir George St. Leger. Earle died almost immediately after reaching camp. Beresford badly wounded in head and arm, but is going on very well. If no fever every chance of his getting through it. Will wire to you if there is any important change."

And after this Nancy had no choice but to sit down and wait. Still she was not and could not be idle, for there was much to be done. The putting of a large household into mourning—the hearing and approving of arrangements for a funeral which was almost a public one—the melancholy journey down to Earles Hope—the ordering of baked meats and so on for the tenantry who would attend—the answering of letters—the receiving and arranging of the dozens of wreaths and flowers and other remembrances which came from far and near to show the affection and respect in which the old man had been held—all these offices fell upon her.

Then the day before that of the funeral came, and early in the afternoon they went down to Earles Hope, and the last of the Earles was carried into the house of his fore-elders for the last time. Yes, the last of the Earles after all, for young Stuart had been dead already some hours when the news of the engagement in which he had been wounded reached his father and sister. So the long sad evening wore away, and the following day, amid blinding snow, the lengthy procession passed from hall to grave-yard, and Nancy, the one who had never been of any count before, was the only Earle left of all the proud old race who had ruled at Earles Hope for many and many a year.

She was the last of them all, the owner of all that wide estate, of all their great rent-roll; she was the sole mistress of everything around, free and unencumbered to do exactly as she chose—to come and go as she liked, to remain an Earle to the end of her days, or to wed with whom she pleased.

And Jim Beresford, the man she loved most in all the wide world, was lying at that moment hovering between life and death, on the other side of the globe, lying in discomfort and misery, to endure the cruel torture of ghastly wounds inflicted by the weapons of Burmese Dacoits—a striking instance of the irony of fate.

It was several days after Nancy had returned to Town that Sir George came to her in something like triumph with a dispatch, or more correctly a telegram, from Major Seton.

"Great news, my dear, great news!" he said.

And so it was. For it told that, after a sharp attack of fever, Beresford had taken a decided turn for the better, and if he went on as he gave every promise at that time of doing, he would be moved homewards in about a fortnight or so. By homewards he meant to say that they would get him down to Calcutta, where he would be able to have more comforts and a better chance of recovery.

"Sir George," said Nancy suddenly, "I am going out to Calcutta by the next steamer!"

"Alone, my dear?" asked the little man, somewhat in dismay.

"Oh! no. I shall take servants with me, but I shall go," she answered.

"And you will be married out there?"

"It is very likely."

"But you cannot go alone."

"Oh, yes. Mrs. Seton is there; I shall go to her. If not, there are plenty of other people who will be friendly to me. Anyway, he is ill, and must want me—and I am going."

CHAPTER XXXV.

TOGETHER.

FOR perhaps the first time in all the twenty-two years of her life, there was apparent in Nancy Earle's behaviour a spice of that dare-devil, headstrong self-will which had sent her young brother to his ruin. And having made up her mind to go out to Calcutta, and yet further, to reach her Beautiful Jim's side, if he didn't happen to be there, she did not let the grass grow under her feet, but set about making her preparations at once for the journey.

In vain did Sir George St. Leger represent to her that for a young unmarried lady of great personal attractions to undertake so long and so formidable a journey was a very serious matter—that the world would look upon such a proceeding as altogether out of the common, and——"

"But it *is* out of the common," said Nancy looking straight at him with her wonderful clear dove's eyes. " I am going to be married to Mr. Beresford very soon, and he has been very severely wounded. He must have the most dire need of me ! "

" But people will think is altogether so odd," the little man persisted.

" The Earles have never troubled themselves much about what people might think," said Nancy a little proudly; then all at once remembered that there had been *one Earle* who had not given much care to the traditions of his house, though it would

have been better for them all had he done so.
The remembrance was enough to send the hot blood
flying to her cheeks, and she turned to her old friend
with a softer manner and a gentler tone.

"Dear Sir George," she said, "you are very very
kind to take so much interest in me, and I daresay
you think I am a very foolish and headstrong young
woman, who ought to be locked up until she has
learnt what is good for her. But, indeed, I am not
acting so foolishly as may seem to you. I have
thought it all out, and I believe if my poor dear old
father were here and knew everything, he would
approve *every* thing that I am doing. As to my
going out there, I *know* he would approve of that;
and, besides, you know I am not going out to
strangers. Mrs. Seton is in Calcutta, and I am
going straight to her."

"But supposing she has left it when you get
there?"

"I shall telegraph to her at once. If she has to
leave before I get there, she will have made the
way smooth for me, never fear."

Thus Sir George gave up the conflict, seeing that
Nancy was proving herself to be a real chip of the
old Earle block, and that he was but wasting his
breath in arguing with her.

And then the old family solicitor had an attempt
to dissuade her from a course which he considered—
to put it much more mildly than he did—Quixotic.

"My dear lady," he said in his most legal tones,
"it would not become me to say a word as to the
propriety of your scheme, and, moreover, I am convinced that your father's daughter could in no way
compromise the honour of the family. But there

is one fact which you evidently overlook. It is that you are now a very rich heiress, the sole representative of a very old and honourable name, and that you run a great risk of extinguishing the family altogether by exposing yourself to the perils of a long and dangerous journey."

I am bound to confess that, full of trouble and grief and anxiety as she was, Nancy, at this point, burst out laughing, the first time that she had laughed for many and many a day.

"I *might* be walking down the street," she cried, "and a chimney-pot *might* fall on my head and crack it; or I *might* miss my footing at the top of the stairs and tumble down and break my neck; or I might," with a sudden change of tone, "I *might* stop here and eat my heart out, and he might die without seeing me—and oh! Mr. Moore, don't try to keep me; I should go right out of my mind if anything like that were to happen."

So she won the day and carried her point, and the preparations for the journey went briskly on. She decided to take her maid, who had been with her three years and was a very steady reliable kind of woman, well accustomed to travelling, and also to keep Darby, who had been her father's valet for something like four times that period. With her own woman and with Darby, she would, she knew, be more safe and also travel in greater comfort than with half-a-dozen fine society ladies to do chaperon. And, moreover, she gave a thought to the journey back and to the comfort and help that Darby would be to her Beautiful Jim on the voyage home. And with such indomitable energy did she work that by the time the very next P. and O. steamer went out to the shining East, she was on board, feeling, it is true, a little more lonely than she would for all the world have admitted to the group of friends who had gone to see her off—waving a rather tearful farewell to them and her native shores.

But that was a feeling which very soon passed off. The novelty of her surroundings was good for such sad thoughts as hers necessarily were, and though in a general way an unusually good sailor, she began, after a few hours, to feel certain very uncomfortable sort of qualms, which sent her off to her berth without any desire to spend more time gazing at the fast receding shores of her own country. And after that, she lived the ordinary life on ship-board, coming in for a large share of admiration and attention in spite of the fact, which soon became known among the passengers, that she was engaged to be married to a man in the Blankshire Regiment, who had been badly wounded in an affair with Dacoits in Burmah, and that she was going to Calcutta, and possibly even further, to nurse him.

They knew, too, that her brother had been killed in the same affair, and that her father had died about the same time—that she was a great heiress and the last of her name. And they all said, men and women alike, that the fellow in the Blankshire Regiment was just the very luckiest man who had ever been born, if indeed he had not been so unfortunate as to die of his wound.

There was quite a wave of excitement on board when, at Suez, a telegram from Calcutta was brought on for Miss Earle, who, poor girl, had hardly courage enough to open it. It was short—but inexpressibly sweet.

"Jim much better—on his way here.   Seton."

Nancy tried hard to laugh over the good news, and very nearly succeeded in breaking down into a storm of tears, the relief was so great.   Then some one called out "Three cheers for Jim—long life to him!" and straightway three rousing shouts went up for the hero they had never seen; and his lovely sweetheart, in spite of a certain dewiness about her dove's eyes, managed to turn the threatened outburst into smiles after all!

Strangely enough, the journey did not seem particularly long to her, nor the time half so wearisome as sitting at home waiting for Jim's return would have done.   There was a sense of doing something for him in every turn of the screw, in every movement of the ship, in every order that she heard given and saw carried out.   And the long voyage agreed with her well; and, as they drew near to their destination, she bloomed out like a rose in June, and the wistful look of sadness in her soft eyes all died out.

At last it was all over, the suspense, the waiting, the putting on of the time, and she found herself tight clasped in Mrs. Seton's arms and her feet trod Indian soil.

"He is well?" she asked breathlessly.   "He is with you?"

"Dear child, yes; where should he be?" the little woman cried.   "Not exactly *well*, you know, but getting—getting on.   Not well enough to come to meet you, but so awfully impatient for you.   I only told him yesterday.   I thought he would worry himself to a shadow if he knew that you were on your way.   *Now*, I wish I had told him a few days earlier.   And about your baggage?   Oh! you have a man and maid! Then give up your keys and come along at once. They will manage it all far better without you. Why, child, how you are trembling! Ah! I know—I know—you have gone through so much since we parted," and then she drew Nancy into the carriage which was awaiting her, and bade the coachman drive straight back to the hotel.

Poor Nancy could hardly breathe for the excitement, and although she knew so little and wanted to know so much, not a question came into her mind or rose to her lips. She only kept one hand in Mrs. Seton's and pressed the other hard upon her breast, trying to still the mad beating of her heart.

But happily it was not for long. They drew up before a large hotel, and the little woman by her side said, in a tone of intense relief, " Here we are," and went before her into the house. " You will not expect to see him looking very robust, will you, dear child?" she said by way of preparation.

"Oh! no—no," Nancy answered.

" And if it is rather too much for him, if the meeting upsets him a little, you won't be frightened?" anxiously.

"I will be very good every way," said Nancy, trying to smile.

By this time they had reached the door of Jim's room, and Mrs. Seton opened it.

" Here she is," she announced, and gently pushed the girl in and then closed it behind her, with an imperative sign to the native in attendance to betake himself out of the way.

And Nancy went in to find a ghost!—or what seemed so to her in the first shock of surprise —a gaunt skeleton lying helplessly back on a couch, with a punkah waving to and fro over his head. And then this gaunt skeleton stretched out a skinny hand to her, and she realized that it was her love—her Jim—whom she had come so far to help; and then there was a rush, a scuffle, and the next moment she was down upon her knees beside him, holding his head upon her breast, and it was all right!

Somehow, now that I have got to this point, I cannot tell more about that meeting; it is too sacred a theme for me to write or you to read—it belongs to themselves alone, and you and I are in reality only outsiders, though I have loved Beautiful Jim dearly, very dearly, and I hope that you have loved him too.

But I can and will tell you just what happened afterwards—how the happy days slipped by, and with each one Jim got a little stronger and shook off more and more of the weakness and lassitude which he had brought as his portion out of Burmah. How he began, after a while, to totter about in an uncertain baby sort of fashion on his very own feet, with only the slight support of Nancy's slim young arm to help him—how they began to take lovely drives in the early mornings and in the cool of the evening, and best of all, how one day she said, quite simply and unconcernedly, " If you go on improving like this, dear, we shall be able to be married ever so much sooner than I thought."

And then poor Jim blurted out the last faint shadow of his doubts and the sorrows of their past.

" My darling," he said, trembling in spite of himself, " do you think I am quite free to take advantage of—of—circumstances ? "

Nancy looked, as she felt, startled.

"Why not, Jim?" she asked, her thoughts flying wildly to some obstacle of which she was in ignorance.

"Of course we can please ourselves ; but your father's objection was possible danger and trouble to you in the future," Jim answered. "And, of course, young Tommy is dead now, poor chap, and I don't want to say or feel anything against him ; but supposing poor Owen's death was brought up again and they fixed upon me? I might find it very awkward and——" but Nancy had risen and gone out of the room, and while Jim was still wondering at the suddenness of her movement, she came back with a sealed packet in her hand.

"I foresaw something of this," she said quietly, as she broke the seals, "and that last day at Blankhampton I made Stuart leave your safety in my hands," and then she gave him the paper, and he read the poor dead lad's passionate confession.

A few days later the heiress of the Earles and Beautiful Jim of the Blankshire Regiment were wed, very quietly and simply, with only Mrs. Seton and a man who had been very very good to him in the first days of his long illness, to witness it ; so it was over—

> "All was ended now, the hope and the fear and the sorrow,
> All the aching of heart, the restless, unsatisfied longing,
> All the dull, deep pain, and constant anguish of patience."

THE END.

LIST of WORKS by JOHN STRANGE WINTER

"The author to whom we owe the most finished and faithful rendering ever yet given of the character of the British soldier.'
—MR. RUSKIN in the *Daily Telegraph, January 17th*, 1888.

CAVALRY LIFE.
REGIMENTAL LEGENDS.
BOOTLES' BABY.
HOUP-LA!
IN QUARTERS.
ON MARCH.
PLUCK.
ARMY SOCIETY.
GARRISON GOSSIP.
MIGNON'S SECRET.
THAT IMP!
MIGNON'S HUSBAND.
A SIEGE BABY.
CONFESSIONS OF A PUBLISHER.
BOOTLES' CHILDREN.
BEAUTIFUL JIM.
MY POOR DICK.
HARVEST.
A LITTLE FOOL.
BUTTONS.
MRS. BOB.
DINNA FORGET.
FERRERS COURT.
HE WENT FOR A SOLDIER.
THE OTHER MAN'S WIFE.

WORKS BY JOHN STRANGE WINTER.

Small Crown 8vo., Paper Covers, 1s. each ; Cloth, 1s. 6d. each.

IN QUARTERS.

" ' In Quarters ' is one of those rattling tales of soldiers' life which the public have learned to thoroughly appreciate."
—The Graphic, December 12th, 1885.

" Will be received with pleasure by the entire English-speaking public. 'In Quarters' is simply a mighty shilling's worth of amusement."—*Sunday Times, December 6th, 1885.*

ON MARCH.

" This short story is characterised by Mr. Winter's customary truth in detail, humour, and pathos."—*Academy, April 17th, 1886.*

" By publishing 'On March,' Mr. J. S. Winter has added another little gem to his well-known store of regimental sketches. The story is written with humour and a deal of feeling."
—Army and Navy Gazette, March 13th, 1886.

MIGNON'S SECRET.

" In ' Mignon's Secret ' Mr. Winter has supplied a continuation to the never-to-be-forgotten 'Bootles' Baby.' . . The story is gracefully and touchingly told."—*John Bull, December 11th, 1886.*

" ' Mignon's Secret ' deals with children's character and their influence on men of the world in a manner which cannot be too highly spoken of."—*Sheffield Telegraph, November 17th, 1886.*

THAT IMP!

" This charming little book is bright and breezy, and has the ring of supreme truth about it."—*Vanity Fair, May 21st, 1887.*

MIGNON'S HUSBAND.

" To say that the little story abounds in brightness and humour, accompanied by an undertone of genuine feeling, is another way of saying that it is written by 'John Strange Winter.' "—*County Gentleman, November 12th, 1887.*

The dialogue is brisk and clever ; and the characterisation is as crisp as when ' Bootles' Baby ' first took the reading public by storm."—*Bristol Observer, October 29th, 1887.*

BOOTLES' CHILDREN.

" Clean, healthy, and pure, without being the least bit tiresome or mawkish."—*The Star, July 10th, 1888.*

" Pearl and Maud are two of the most delightful girls in fiction—next to Mignon . In fact, the whole book is charming, and one wonders how so much that is delightful can be compressed into such small space."—*Glasgow Herald, August 18th, 1888.*

F. V WHITE & CO., 31, Southampton Street, Strand.

Pears'
SOAP.

DR. J. COLLIS BROWNE'S CHLORODYNE

ORIGINAL AND ONLY GENUINE

Coughs   Colds   Asthma   Bronchitis   Toothache   Neuralgia

Diarrhœa   Cholera   Dysentery   Fevers   Ague   Spasms   Etc.

TRADE MARK
Price of this Bottle 1s. 1½d.
DR. J. COLLIS BROWNE'S CHLORODYNE
SOLE MANUFACTURER J. T. DAVENPORT

IS THE GREAT SPECIFIC FOR CHOLERA,

COUGHS, COLDS, ASTHMA, BRONCHITIS.

DR. J. COLLIS BROWNE'S CHLORODYNE. — Dr. J. C. BROWNE (late Army Medical Staff) DISCOVERED a REMEDY to denote which he coined the word CHLORODYNE. Dr. Browne is the SOLE INVENTOR, and, as the composition of Chlorodyne cannot possibly be discovered by Analysis (organic substances defying elimination), and since the formula has neverbeen published, it is evident that any statement to the effect that a compound is identical with Dr. Browne's Chlorodyne *must be false.*

This Caution is necessary, as many persons deceive purchasers by false representations.

DR. J. COLLIS BROWNE'S CHLORODYNE. — Vice Chancellor Sir W. PAGE WOOD stated publicly in Court that Dr. J. COLLIS BROWNE was UNDOUBTEDLY the INVENTOR of CHLORODYNE, that the whole story of the defendant Freeman was deliberately untrue, and he regretted to say it had been sworn to. — See *The Times,* July 13th, 1864.

DIARRHŒA, DYSENTERY. GENERAL BOARD of HEALTH, London, REPORT that it ACTS as a CHARM, one dose generally sufficient. Dr. GIBBON, Army Medical Staff, Calcutta, states: "2 DOSES COMPLETELY CURED ME of DIARRHŒA."

From SYMES & Co., *Pharmaceutical Chemists, Simla. Jan.* 5, 1880. *To* J. T. DAVENPORT, London.

DEAR SIR, — We congratulate you upon the widespread reputation this justly-esteemed medicine has earned for itself all over the East. As a remedy of general utility, we much question whether a better is imported, and we shall be glad to hear of its finding a place in every Anglo-Indian home. The other brands, we are happy to say, are now relegated to the native bazaars, and, judging from their sale, we fancy their sojourn there will be but evanescent. We could multiply instances *ad infinitum* of the extraordinary efficacy of DR. COLLIS BROWNE'S CHLORODYNE in Diarrhœa and Dysentery, Spasms, Cramps, Neuralgia the Vomiting of Pregnancy, and as a general sedative, that have occurred under our personal observation during many years. In Choleraic Diarrhœa, and even in the more terrible forms of Cholera itself, we have witnessed its surprisingly controlling power.

We have never used any other form of this medicine than Collis Browne's, from a firm conviction that it is decidedly the best, and also from a sense of duty we owe to the profession and the public, as we are of opinion that the substitution of any other than Collis Browne's is a deliberate breach of faith on the part of the chemist to prescriber and patient alike. — We are, Sir, faithfully yours, SYMES & CO., *Members of the Pharm. Society of Great Britain, His Excellency the Viceroy's Chemists.*

DR. J. COLLIS BROWNE'S CHLORODYNE is the TRUE PALLIATIVE in NEURALGIA, GOUT, CANCER, TOOTHACHE, RHEUMATISM.

DR. J. COLLIS BROWNE'S CHLORODYNE is a liquid medicine which assuages PAIN of EVERY KIND, affords a calm, refreshing sleep WITHOUT HEADACHE, and INVIGORATES the nervous system when exhausted.

DR. J. COLLIS BROWNE'S CHLORODYNE rapidly cuts short all attacks of EPILEPSY, SPASMS, COLIC, PALPITATION, HYSTERIA.

IMPORTANT CAUTION. — The IMMENSE SALE of this REMEDY has given rise to many UNSCRUPULOUS IMITATIONS. Be careful to observe Trade Mark. Of all Chemists. 1s. 1½d., 2s. 9d. and 4s. 6d!

SOLE MANUFACTURER J. T. DAVENPORT, 33 Gt. Russell St. W.C.

A WONDERFUL MEDICINE

BEECHAM'S PILLS

BEECHAM'S PILLS
BEECHAM'S PILLS
BEECHAM'S PILLS
BEECHAM'S PILLS
BEECHAM'S PILLS
BEECHAM'S PILLS
BEECHAM'S PILLS
BEECHAM'S PILLS
BEECHAM'S PILLS
BEECHAM'S PILLS
BEECHAM'S PILLS
BEECHAM'S PILLS
BEECHAM'S PILLS

Are universally admitted to be worth a Guinea a Box for Bilious and Nervous Disorders, such as wind and pain in the Stomach, Sick Headache, Giddiness, Fulness and Swelling after Meals, Dizziness and Drowsiness, Cold Chills, Flushings of Heat, Loss of Appetite, Shortness of Breath, Costiveness, Scurvy, Blotches on the Skin, Disturbed Sleep, Frightful Dreams, and all Nervous and Trembling Sensations, &c. The First Dose will Give Relief in Twenty Minutes. This is no fiction, for they have done it in countless cases. Every sufferer is earnestly invited to try one Box of these Pills, and they will be acknowledged to be

Worth a GUINEA a Box.

For Females of all ages these Pills are invaluable, as a few doses of them carry off all humours, *open* all obstructions, and bring about all that is required. No female should be without them. There is no medicine to be found to equal BEECHAM'S PILLS for removing any obstruction or irregularity of the system. If taken according to the directions given with each Box, they will soon restore females of all ages to sound and robust health. This has been proved by thousands who have tried them and found the benefits which are ensured by their use.

For a Weak Stomach, Impaired Digestion, and all disorders of the liver, they act like magic, and a few doses will be found to work wonders upon the most important organs in the human machine. They strengthen the whole muscular system, restore the long lost complexion, bring back the keen edge of appetite, and arouse into action, with the rosebud of health, the whole physical energy of the human frame. These are facts testified continually by members of all classes of society; and one of the best guarantees to the nervous and debilitated is BEECHAM'S PILLS have the largest sale of any patent medicine in the world.

FULL DIRECTIONS ARE GIVEN WITH EACH BOX.

Sold by all Druggists and Patent Medicine Dealers everywhere, in Boxes at 9½d., 1s. 1½d. and 2s. 9d.